T0279222

DRAW
DOWN
THE
MOON

ALSO BY
P. C. CAST &
KRISTIN CAST

Sisters of Salem

Spells Trouble

Omens Bite

Hex You

The Dysasters

The Dysasters: The Graphic Novel

House of Night

Marked	*Hidden*
Betrayed	*Revealed*
Chosen	*Redeemed*
Untamed	*The Fledgling Handbook 101*
Hunted	*Dragon's Oath*
Tempted	*Lenobia's Vow*
Burned	*Neferet's Curse*
Awakened	*Kalona's Fall*
Destined	

DRAW DOWN THE MOON

P. C. CAST & KRISTIN CAST

WEDNESDAY BOOKS
NEW YORK

First published in the United States by Wednesday Books, an imprint of St. Martin's Publishing Group

DRAW DOWN THE MOON. Copyright © 2024 by P. C. Cast and Kristin Cast. All rights reserved. Printed in the United States of America. For information, address St. Martin's Publishing Group, 120 Broadway, New York, NY 10271.

www.wednesdaybooks.com

Designed by Jonathan Bennett

Library of Congress Cataloging-in-Publication Data

Names: Cast, P. C., author. | Cast, Kristin, author.
Title: Draw down the moon / P. C. Cast & Kristin Cast.
Description: First edition. | New York : Wednesday Books, 2024.
    Audience: Ages 12–18.
Identifiers: LCCN 2023051633 | ISBN 9781250865168 (hardcover)
    ISBN 9781250354600 (international, sold outside the U.S., subject to
    rights availability) | ISBN 9781250865175 (ebook)
Subjects: CYAC: Fantasy. | Magic—Fiction. | Schools—Fiction.
    Interpersonal relations—Fiction. | LCGFT: Fantasy fiction. | Novels.
Classification: LCC PZ7.C2685827 Dr 2024 | DDC [Fic]—dc23
LC record available at https://lccn.loc.gov/2023051633

Our books may be purchased in bulk for promotional, educational, or business use. Please contact your local bookseller or the Macmillan Corporate and Premium Sales Department at 1-800-221-7945, extension 5442, or by email at MacmillanSpecialMarkets@macmillan.com.

First Edition: 2024

10 9 8 7 6 5 4 3 2 1

For Emily

DRAW
DOWN
THE
MOON

ONE

Wren

I'm pretty sure that, at any moment, blue and red lights will flash and the local sheriff will tear down the street and stop me. Again.

"Wren! Hurry up!" Lee whisper-shouts at me from the shadows.

With the hand not squeezing an entire bottle of Seventh Generation Powered by Plants dishwashing liquid into the fountain, I make what I hope is a calming gesture. "It's fine. It's natural. Won't hurt the ecosystem at all. Plus, it's not like we can actually go to prison for this."

"Well, *you* can't, but . . ."

I brush a hunk of white-blond hair out of my face and glance over my shoulder as Lee makes a motion that takes in his long, leanly muscled body, his deep brown skin, and his neatly braided cornrows. *How did he get so grown-up looking? He's only been gone two years? He was shorter when he moved away—short in height, short hair, short on muscles—just a kid. My prank partner. My buddy. I mean, I've seen him since he moved away. We've FaceTimed a million times and practically stalk each other's Insta and TikTok. Rationally, I know he's older. I'm older, too! But actually putting eyes on him in real life is something else. Something different. Something new . . .* I feel my cheeks flush hot and know my blush is as glowing pink against my porcelain skin as the fuchsia dyed ends of my hair.

"I'll hurry." I quickly unscrew the cap and the rest of the dishwashing liquid glugs into the fountain. Balancing with my arms spread out, I tightrope walk around the lip of the basin that holds the three-tiered stone water feature situated in the middle of the quaint little courtyard in the heart of downtown Fern Valley. As I reach Lee, my Vans slip on the water-splashed stone, and I start to fall.

Lee's strong hands catch me before I splat against the pavement. I look up and grin at him as I catch my balance and plant my feet firmly on the ground again. Yeah, he's older, bigger, stronger. But he's still my prank partner. My best friend who always has my back.

"You almost fell into . . ." Lee's words trail off and I watch his eyes widen at something behind me.

I turn and do a little celebratory dance. "Yes! This is even better than I thought it was going to be, and I knew it was going to be epic."

Lee's head shakes back and forth, back and forth. "For

the record, when I agreed to sneak out tonight, I did *not* know this was what you had in mind."

"You didn't *really* agree; I peer pressured you into it."

"I think you mean *coerced*," says Lee.

I grin, but not up at him. I'm too busy taking in the glorious sight of bubbles billowing from the fountain's basin up, up, and up. The opalescent suds lift into the night sky like the sea-foam on our rough Oregon coast. "Admit it. This is magnificent."

"It's vandalism."

Sure, he said the *v* word, but I could hear the familiar smile in his voice.

"It's the perfect birthday present," I say. What I don't say out loud is that what actually makes my birthday perfect is the fact that he's home. It's so great to see Lee that not even knowing he's leaving again tomorrow night can ruin my happiness. (I won't let it ruin my happiness.)

"It's not officially your birthday"—he takes his phone from his pocket and glances at it—"for fifteen more minutes. And I did not get you felony behavior as a gift."

"This is a misdemeanor at best," I correct him, and link my arm through his. "And I didn't mean it's my present from you. It's my selfie birthday gift. You know, like last year my selfie gift was—"

"A wren. Tattooed on your lower back. How could I forget? I was on the phone with you for the whole thing." Lee speaks a lot more quietly than me as he guides us into the concealing shadows the full moon casts under the pines circling the courtyard. "I also remember how you lied about your age to the sketchy tattoo artist. I'll bet your uncles do, too."

I don't want to think about the semi-hysterical apoplectic

meltdown Uncle Joel had last summer when he'd noticed the wren's wingtip poking above the waistband of my shorts, so I quickly turn and face Lee as I change the subject. "But speaking of birthday gifts . . ." I waggle my eyebrows at him, cup my hands together, and hold them up expectantly.

"You can't wait fifteen more minutes until it's your *actual* birthday?"

"I'm sure it's more like thirteen and a half minutes by now, but no. No, I cannot." I give him the *smile*. I know it's going to work on Lee. He can't help it. Just like I can't help the fact that he's my person and has been since I moved to Fern Valley five years ago, newly orphaned, broken and lost, and not wanting to ever care about anyone again. Lee has been there for me since day one of eighth grade, and that has never changed—even when his mom got such a big promotion that their family had to relocate all the way across the country to Brooklyn. Lee and I stayed close, no matter the distance between us.

"Okay, turn around."

I frown. "How am I going to get my present with my back turned?"

He takes my shoulders in his big hands and spins my body around so that I'm facing the fountain. For a moment I forget that he's birthday gifting me, because the bubbles have spilled from the basin and are tumbling across the well-tended grass like they're pouring from a dishwasher someone (perhaps me) accidentally put dish *soap* instead of dishwashing *detergent* into. *Who knew that could make such a massive mess?*

Then I feel something settle around my neck. I look down. The watery moonlight, speckled by the concealing boughs of the pines, catches the silver chain. I lift it and see the beautiful full moon made of a blue stone I recognize immediately. Aquamarine—the exact color of my eyes—glitters with a magick that I know I will never feel.

I turn and look up at Lee as I swallow several times and blink a lot, trying not to burst into tears. "I love it," I finally manage to whisper.

His smile looks sad. "Mom and Dad put a little moon magick in it. It won't last because you're . . ." His words trailed off.

"Because I'm a Mundane," I finish for him. "Lee, for the zillionth time. It's okay. I don't mind not having any magick, and this necklace is beautiful with or without any help from the moon. . . ." I pause, flash him my most mischievous smile, and add, "My sparkling personality is magickal enough all on its own."

Lee's Moonstruck. Like the rest of his family, he's filled with the magick of the full moon he was born under. My mom and dad were Moonstruck, too. But not me. I wasn't born under the right moon sign and the moon definitely hadn't been full. So I'm just . . . me. And that's okay. I made peace with being a Mundane when I was a kid. Wishing for something I could never have is a ridiculous waste of time, plus I like me just as I am.

Lee blows out a long breath and, as always, gives me a look that says he cannot understand why I'm fine with having no magick. "Well, I'm glad you like it. I wanted you to have something that you could wear so you don't forget about me this summer."

I press my hands against my ears like we're kids again and he's trying to tell me one of his scary stories. "No no no, it's my birthday. I'm not listening. No sad talk tonight."

"Wren, it's Saturday. Almost Sunday. I leave Sunday

evening for Moon Isle. I really wish we had more time to hang out, but we don't. I'm going to be gone. Tomorrow. And you know they confiscate our phones and computers. I'm not going to be able to talk to you for *months* and then—"

"No! We're not talking about that!" The words shoot out of me louder than I expect. I don't want to talk about the *thing* that seems to be lurking, big and sad and permanent between us. We are different. Not because I identify as a girl and him a guy. Not because I'm white and he's Black. We are different because Lee is Moonstruck and, even though I shouldn't be, I'm a Mundane. This difference between us never bothered me before now because turning eighteen and graduating had always seemed a million years away. Now that those million years have passed, I realize that it does bother me. But not because of the magick, or my lack thereof. It bothers me because I just got him back—for what seems like a split second (well, twenty-four hours, but it feels like a split second)—and now he's going to leave and go to a magickal isle full of other Moonstruck where he'll learn all about how to use his magick and head into an amazing future. A future without me. Will we still be best friends afterward? Will he think I'm too boring? Too ordinary?

I don't want to think about it. I don't want to talk about it. Not in the sliver of time we have left together, and it's my birthday, so I don't have to. "Check the time. I'll bet it's my actual birthday now. Hey!" I go on before he can stop me. "Take a pic of me in front of the fountain!"

Lee sighs but takes his phone out of his pocket again. "Five minutes until midnight."

"Yeah! Come on! I'll be really fast—and stealthy." I sprint

toward the fountain, now a giant, sudsy mound. Bubbles are everywhere and I dash into them giggling as they lift around me. I turn to face Lee and hold up the delicate necklace so that the full moon sways gently as it glitters like the bubbles that surround me in the silver light. "Lactose intolerance!" I grin at the words he and I have been substituting for *cheese* since our disastrous eighth-grade school photos.

Lee laughs softly and takes the picture. Before he can put his phone away I say, "Wait! How long until midnight now?"

He glances at the screen. "Two minutes."

"Perfect. Let's take another pic at exactly midnight and send it to Sam. It'll be like she's here with us." Samantha Hopp is my other best friend and the only other Moonstruck kid I know. Sam and I have been inseparable since we met in Mrs. Johnson's first-grade class at Arrow Springs Elementary School. She was the smartest one in our class, which got her bullied. Way back then, I was the tallest kid in our class (I'm five feet nothing; I swear I quit growing in elementary school), which meant I backed every one of those bullies down. Moving two hours away from her the year I turned thirteen was the second most awful thing that had ever happened to me until Lee also moved away. Sometimes it seems like everyone I care about leaves me.

"Okay, I'm counting down," called Lee. "Ten . . . nine . . . eight . . ."

I mentally shake myself and quickly step a little to the side and pose with a hip cock and a knowing look at the fountain that will tell Sam, *I'm responsible for the tidal wave of bubbles,* though I'm 100 percent sure she will already guess that.

"... five ... four ... three ... two ... one!"

I grin and take a breath to shout *Lactose intolerance!* again, but the words never leave my mouth.

A spear of moonlight, silver and impossibly bright, strikes me. It invades me, and heat shivers through my body as my skin prickles with gooseflesh. My teeth chatter, though I'm filled with warmth, and my heartbeat gallops so hard and fast I might pass out.

For the first time in my life, I feel it, moon magick, and it isn't like anything I imagined when I was a kid watching my parents wield Her lustrous power. It also has no similarity to the spark of energy Lee and Sam have described to me as their powers began to mature. It's raw and overwhelming.

My head tilts back, and I feel my hair lifting around me like I've been electrocuted. But I have no time to think. My focus is pulled one place—up. My gaze locks on the full moon that dominates the sky above me. I can feel Her. She sees me. I know She does. I'm filled with warmth, and for the span of one gulping breath, in and out, I am Moonstruck and it is glorious.

The sound of a police siren shatters my focus and I collapse against the soapy ground with a loud "*oof.*"

Lee's there, bending over me, his dark eyes wide with worry. "Wren! Wren! Say something! Can you hear me? Are you okay?"

I look up and can barely see him through the bright spots of light messing up my vision. I try to stand, but my legs feel rubbery, like I just hiked up Saddle Mountain. I try to tell Lee that I can't make my legs work, but my voice won't obey me, either. My breath comes out in panicked gasps, and I wrap my arms around myself as another siren splits the quiet night. "Cops," I manage to gasp through chattering teeth. "We gotta get outta here."

"It's okay. I got you." Lee doesn't wait for me to calm down. He lifts me, and cradles me close to his chest as he sprints from the courtyard and into the dark alley that connects the stores lining Main Street.

My head is too heavy to hold up, and I rest it against Lee's shoulder. The red and blue lights of a Fern Valley sheriff's cruiser make kaleidoscopic shapes on the brick buildings lining the alley, but only for a moment. Lee's moving fast. I know he's spent a lot of time in the gym over the past two years, but I'm amazed at how effortlessly he carries me. Buildings blur as he runs through our little town. Lee cuts through alleys, sprints from shadow to shadow, and races across streets. For once, I'm glad of the sleepiness of our small town. It makes it easier for Lee to avoid being seen. His speed and smarts do the rest.

I feel strange. My mind is hyper-focused. I know exactly where Lee is headed—to our place, an apple orchard that frames the west side of town. My body is empty, exhausted, numb. My hands and feet are cold, but everything else is flushed and hot. I can't figure out whether my clothes are wet from the suds I fell into or from sweat. And time is . . . *off*. It seems like it's only been seconds since the fountain, but Lee stops, and this time it's not because he's slipping from shadow to shadow. I lift my head from his shoulder and look around.

"Granny's Place. Our orchard." My voice works, but it's scratchy and weak.

"Can you stand?" Lee asks.

I clear my throat before I answer. "I think I should sit first."

He nods and carries me far enough into the orchard

that there is no chance of us being seen by cars driving by. Lee places me gently down under a gnarled old tree. I lean against the rough but familiar bark. Remnants of apple blossoms perfume the night air with sweetness. Unlike the larger farms surrounding Fern Valley, Granny's Place is a small, old-timey orchard. The ground between the mature apple trees is carpeted by thick grass and wilted blossoms. The rows aren't industrially spaced. The trees dot the field like they are old friends instead of soldiers lined up for inspection. There is one light at the irrigation outbuilding near the road. It and the full moon illuminate the orchard just enough for me to see Lee's brow furrow as he crouches beside me, staring into my face.

I meet his gaze. "What. The. Hell. Was. That?" I enunciate each word carefully because my teeth would still like to chatter.

"You have magick!" he blurts.

I shake my head. "No. How? No. *How?*" Then I realize I sound like a caffeinated parrot and press my lips closed.

He sits in the grass across from me. "Don't know how, but there is absolutely no doubt about it. Wren, you're Moonstruck."

Dizziness washes over me as I begin to realize the extent of what that means. I'm not supposed to have magick! Ever! I've figured out my life as a Mundane and been totally cool with it, but now? Who am I now? If I really do have magick, all my plans will be void. I won't attend the local community college to take the business classes I need so I can manage Pages, my uncles' awesome little bookstore.

I will have to leave this place where I'm safe. This home where I survived losing my parents and reinvented myself.

Where I found the happiness I thought I'd lost forever.

My hand trembles as I brush hair back from my face. "This isn't like anything that happened to you or Sam," I say in a last effort to keep change at bay.

"No, it isn't. What just happened to you is *more*."

"But Lee," I whisper. "I'm not a Moonstruck. I'm just me—non-magical me." My chin quivers and the warmth of tears dampens my already-heated cheeks. "I want to stay home. I *need* to stay home. Maybe it's all just some kind of weird mistake." A sudden thought hits me, and I struggle to sit up straighter. "What if breathing in the bubbles did something to us? Like, I don't know, a mutual hallucination or something?"

Slowly, Lee takes his phone out of his pocket. He touches the screen and its bluish light illuminates his face. He taps it, stares at it for several breaths, and then turns it to face me.

In the picture I'm awash with silver light—like it's coming out of me. My head is tilted back and my hair, which has always been so light it's almost white, is spread around me haloing my body. As I stare at this unfamiliar version of myself, all I can think is that the bright pink ends of my hair look like neon blood in the moonlight. I pull my gaze away and my trembling hand covers the screen. Lee puts the phone back in his pocket, and I can't control the sobs any longer.

"I'm s-scared." Tears break my voice.

Lee scoots beside me and puts his arm around me, squeezing my shoulder gently. "It's going to be okay. There's nothing to be scared of. Wren, I'll be with you for the whole thing."

And it hits me—Lee's going away again, but this time I'm going, too! My voice is a tremulous whisper as I try to swallow down my fear. "B-but we won't be home."

"Home is in here." Lee takes my fisted hand and holds it against his heart. "Inside us. We'll take it with us."

I open my fist and let my palm rest on his chest. His steadily beating heart calms me. Exhaustion crashes over me and my vision gets all weird and blurry again, and I realize I'm still crying. I force myself to stop, hiccupping a little.

"Here." Lee takes the end of his T-shirt and wipes at my cheeks and nose.

I look down at the wet blotches on his shirt. "I think I just got snot on you."

His chest rumbles with a chuckle. "I know you did."

"Were you exhausted after this happened to you?" My voice is soft, unsure.

"No. The opposite. And my hair didn't lift up, either. But you've never done things the normal way." His attempt at a joke falls flat and he hurries on. "When it happened to me, I only felt it for an hour or so afterward. Close your eyes and rest. I'll walk you home in a little while. We've got plenty of time. It's Sunday. Your uncles don't get up until it's time for brunch."

I almost remind Lee that it's my birthday, which means my uncles will be up early. There's not much Uncle Joel likes more than gift giving and celebrations. But I don't want to think about my birthday anymore. I don't want to think about anything anymore. I just want to close my eyes and feel Lee's steady heartbeat under my palm.

TWO

Lee

Something tickles my cheek. I swat at it and roll over. I'm having a great dream, and I don't want to wake up. I keep my eyes closed and try to recapture the images, but they're melting as fast as ice in the hot Oregon summer. Even though it's pooling against my mind, absorbed into the memories that I can only reach while sleeping, the ghost of dreamland Wren is still vivid.

I press my lids more tightly together to hold on to her a little longer. And it works. If anything, she's becoming more alive, because I swear I can smell her. The breeze brings with it a lungful of Wren's sugar cookie scent, and I let it wash down into my toes. I'm only mildly aware of the fact that my room isn't usually so windy, and my bed not so hard.

My eyelids fly open, and I jerk awake as reality booms like a gong inside my chest.

This isn't a dream. I'm back in Fern Valley, and *we never went home*.

The morning sun bleeds like a stuck yolk across the sky as I gently place my hand on Wren's shoulder. I could write a whole poem about this moment, about finally being back, and as much as I want to remain here and let her sleep after her exciting and terrifying Moonstruck experience, it wouldn't be right. It was hard enough for me to go against my better judgment and sneak out. Well, maybe not too hard. When it comes to Wren, I'm not good at saying no.

"Hey!" I squeeze her shoulder and slide my hand up to her cheek, brushing back the fuchsia-tipped strands of blond that fell across her face in the night.

"No, it's too early. I can tell." She keeps her eyes closed and stretches her arms overhead, unflinching when her fingers scrape the earth. "What time is it?"

I pull my phone from my pocket and grimace as I tap the screen. If there's a limit to how many missed calls one person can get, my mom most likely reached it hours ago. Luckily, my phone is dead, and I don't have to deal with the feeling in my chest I get when I let my parents down. They've been through enough.

I tuck my phone back into my shorts and hold my hand up to the horizon. "The sun's about a fist high, so . . ." I shrug. "Yeah, I have no idea how to tell time that way."

Her eyelids flutter open with a laugh and, not for the first time, I wish I could capture it and set it as my alarm tone. What a perfect sound to wake up to.

"My uncles are going to kill me." She sits up and surveys the apple trees surrounding us. "If this is going to be my last morning on earth, we might as well go get breakfast."

"Not happening." I shake my head. I want to stay on Bradley and Joel's good side. Adding another infraction to the list will only make it that much more difficult for me to dig myself out of the hole I'm in.

"You've turned into such a rule follower."

I stand up and brush the dirt from my shorts. "Thank you."

"That's not a compliment."

"Only because you don't appreciate rules." I bend over and offer her my arm in the same way the nineteenth-century noblemen do in all the Regency-era shows and movies she's made me watch, because, again, I can't say no to the girl I just spent the night next to. "My lady."

"My lord." She takes my arm and rises as gracefully as a queen. *My* queen. If I could only get up the nerve to make a move. I *am* leaving soon, so maybe today is the day.

My heart skips a beat. *Wren's coming, too.*

I open my mouth to blurt that she's Moonstruck. That she's coming with me. That we'll be together all summer, no uncles, no parents, no job or school or Mundanes to worry about. But she's looking at me in a way that makes my mouth too dry to speak.

She stands in front of me, her cloudless blue gaze on mine. "Lee . . ."

Words clog my throat as she shifts onto her tiptoes and reaches up toward my face. She is rising like she's coming up for air, her pink lips parted, her smooth, white skin golden in the early morning light cascading through the trees, and for a wild second, I feel like I'm back in one of my dreams.

Her fingers brush my temple, and my heart starts to beat in my stomach.

"You have tree trash in your hair." She waves a twig in the air before dropping it and turning in the direction of Main Street obscured by the gnarled boughs of old apple trees.

"Oh." I manage to get out around the rush of air fleeing my lungs like a stuck balloon.

Wren and I have been friends since she moved from Portland to Fern Valley five years ago. We were drawn together. At least, that's how I describe it in poems. In reality, lunar magick connects us. Our parents were in the same class on Moon Isle. They weren't close, but when tragedy strikes one of us, it strikes all.

I clear my throat and with it the swell of emotion that squeezes my lungs. My family had its own tragedy, but I don't want to think about that.

Regardless, no matter my connection with Wren, magickal or otherwise, every day that goes by cements me more firmly in the friend zone. And my two years in Brooklyn didn't help.

"So, what happens now?" Wren interrupts my current internal struggle as we make our way around the trees and toward the two-lane road leading into town.

I pat the back of my head, feeling for any more tree trash. My cornrows are a mess, so even if I can sneak back into my house without my parents noticing, I'm still going to have something to answer for.

"Your uncles won't really kill you, and Joel never sticks with any of the punishments he and Bradley give. You'll probably serve a few hours before you're out on good behavior and back to breaking the law." I duck under a branch heavy with pink-and-white blossoms and hold it up, clearing the way for Wren.

"*Not with my uncles,*" she sighs, and hunches over even though she doesn't need to. She hoped it would, but her height hasn't changed since I left. It's a part of her pre-served in amber while other parts became edgier, more completely Wren. I let go of the branch after she's clear and petals drift to the ground. I want to take a moment and stand there a little longer, thinking of ways to describe them, but Wren is pushing forward, an arrow through the trees.

"With, you know, the whole *magick* thing." She whis-pers the word as if there's anyone else out here but us.

Honestly, I'm glad she brought it up, because, after my initial jolt of energy, I'm not sure how to. She was set on being a Mundane and fitting in with the majority of society unaware that real magick exists. Now she knows she's spe-cial. There's proof of it. Although I never doubted.

"Guess you're coming with me." I sling my arm over her shoulder, and she groans. I don't take it personally as I slow my stride, aware of how much shorter her legs are than mine. The perturbed sigh wasn't because of me. It was because of Moon Isle.

We break away from the apple trees and stride through the crimson clover that skirts the two-lane road leading into town. We walk like that for a while, comfortable enough with each other that the silence has become just another part of us.

This is a good time to say it. Say, Wren, I like you. I have a whole journal of poems about you.

Maybe not that last part.

My mouth is dry, my tongue like tacky paint against the roof.

But now we have the summer together. There's no real rush.

Yeah . . . I'm not scared; I'm just letting things flow.

"I don't feel anything."

I frown and drop my arm from her shoulders. Can she hear my thoughts?

"Sam says she feels *things*," Wren continues. "Moon magick things. But I don't feel anything."

"Uh . . ." It takes my brain a minute to switch from hopeless romantic to guy who can do more than grunt. "Yeah, I mean, I feel moon magick things, too. Even when the sun is up, the moon is always there. She never leaves us. Neither does our magick."

I smooth my palm across my chest and over the comforting warmth that's rested beneath my heart for as long as I can remember. A constant reminder of the moon and my connection to Her.

"Then I'm free and clear," Wren chimes. "It was a fluke. I had a one-night stand with the moon, and it'll never happen again."

"I'm pretty sure that's not how it works."

"But you're not one hundred percent. Plus, I wasn't even born under a magick moon sign." She stops, fastens her hands to her hips, and looks up at me with that gleam in her eye that says she's ready to argue, but this isn't something she can talk me out of.

"Your parents were Moonstruck, and you're *you*. It doesn't matter when you were born. You were never going to be like Bradley and Joel. You were never going to be a Mundane."

Her gaze falls to the street, and she resumes walking. More slowly this time, like voicing the truth has taken away a part of her. But that part was always missing.

"Wren . . ." I catch her hand in mine and turn her to face me. "After this summer, we'll have a way of living, access to things that Mundanes can only dream of. Moon Isle will change our lives."

"That's what I'm afraid of." She pulls her hand from mine and continues her trek toward the row of brick buildings that line Main Street.

I don't know what to say, so I follow her, not saying anything. For as long as I can remember, I've been waiting for my life to change. My parents have drilled into me success and our family's legacy, and now it is completely up to me.

"What do I tell my uncles? Bradley and I have never said anything to Joel about magick, so how do I tell him—" Her voice breaks, and she speeds up, but I close the distance between us with two steps. "Tell him that I've suddenly changed my mind? That I want to leave them and the store and Grace Kelly and everything I love?"

Her voice trembles, and I know she's crying. My hands tingle to reach out to her and hug her against my chest, comb my fingers through her hair and tell her that it will all be okay. But I don't. This is Wren. Last night was the first time I've seen her cry, and she won't make that mistake again.

"We'll think of something. We always do."

"Whatever I say will be a lie. At least to Joel. I want to tell him the truth. I *should* tell him the truth." She sniffs and swipes her cheeks. "I'm *going to* tell him." She looks at me, her expression stormy, her blue eyes dark with challenge.

"It's forbidden." There's an edge to my voice that I haven't used with her before, and she stiffens. "Wren, this is one rule you cannot break."

Behind us, asphalt crunches and the growl of an engine vibrates against my back, cutting the tension between us and replacing it with something new. A black SUV slows down behind us, and we move to the side of the road to let it pass. It doesn't. Instead, it creeps at our backs like a shadow.

I stop, guiding Wren farther into the crimson clover in bloodred bloom along the side of the street.

The SUV stops, too.

I squint at the windshield, trying to see through the streaks of sunlight camouflaging the driver.

In true Wren Nightingale form, she steps back onto the road and glares at the vehicle. I follow suit, every muscle in my body tensing, making myself as huge as possible, which isn't difficult ever since I spent every afternoon in Brooklyn in the gym instead of home.

"What are you doing?" she shouts, throwing her hands into the air. "Go around!"

The hairs on the back of my neck rise along with my untamed magickal abilities. They're stronger now, burning in my chest like a piece of the sun. Healers are good in a fight if only because we won't stay down long.

"Go! Around!" Wren repeats the order as I stare at the light-glazed windshield.

My hands tighten into fists, and I'm about to tell Wren to run back to the orchard when the SUV's wheels turn and it rolls past us into town.

"What the hell was that about?" she says, stuffing her

hands into her pockets as we watch the black vehicle drive along Main Street and disappear around a turn.

We resume our walk home, and I exhale a stored breath and shake my head. "Townies," I say, although the adrenaline surging through my veins tells me otherwise.

"So annoying," she grunts.

I relax my jaw and clear my throat, trying to calm the humming in my chest.

Wren and I are close enough that I hear her phone vibrate. It's the distraction I need, and my magick quiets as she takes her phone out of her pocket and answers.

"I'm alive," she says before it's pressed to her ear.

Bradley's low, grumbling voice booms, but I can't make out what he's saying. Whatever it is, it has Wren shrinking in on herself and her cheeks ablaze.

By the time her uncle finishes his tirade, we've reached Pages, the small bookstore on the south end of Main Street that Bradley and Joel own and Wren has managed for the past year. The side of the building is covered in a mural painted by the high school art club of 1986. It's faded now and pockmarked with missing chunks of crumbled cement, but the high school mascot, an enormous black-and-gold hornet, is still visible.

"No, it's not like that, Uncle Brad." Wren tucks her pink-tipped hair behind her ear. "It's just Lee."

Just Lee? Damn.

This is what does poets in—unrequited love.

I ignore the part of my brain that reminds me that my love can't be unrequited if Wren is oblivious and turn my attention to the stores waking up around us. A few doors down, Alton emerges from the barbershop with a sandwich board advertising a sale on summer cuts. I lift my chin in a silent greeting to the man whose chair I grew up in. He stops mid–chin tilt, the lines etched into his dark skin deepening as he stares at me.

I remember the state of my braids, and now my posture matches Wren's. I grab her hand and lead her across the street and away from Alton, but the damage is already done.

"I have a spot at three! I'm puttin' your name down!" he yells. "Can't have you walkin' all over town with that mess on your head. Is that what they think looks good over in New York?"

"Thanks, Alton." I wave to him and hope he doesn't text my parents.

"Thanks? Boy, I should charge you twice." He adjusts his denim apron around his thick middle and heads inside the brick-walled shop.

Wren mumbles a few final words and ends her call, linking her arm through mine. I swear a jolt of electricity crackles in my bones. If she's not magickal, I don't know who is.

"Your uncles freaking out?" I ask as we pass Beans & Breads Coffeehouse and Bakery.

"That's putting it mildly. Joel was literally shouting in the background. *Shouting*. I've never heard him raise his voice."

"What about that time you—" I cut myself off when the black SUV speeds past. I try to get a look at the driver, but they're speeding through our small town.

"Hopefully, they're going back to Portland." Wren's grumble ends just as the vehicle's tires squeal, and it makes a U-turn.

"They're not . . ."

She doesn't need to finish her sentence. I know what she's thinking, and the answer is yes. The SUV is heading right toward us.

I hug Wren to my side and take the shortcut into the alley between Beans & Breads and Dr. Vought's Optometry. Unless it's a delivery truck, there's no reason for a car to come this way. We're safe.

This isn't about you, I remind my coiled muscles and the magick sizzling beneath my skin. Nevertheless, Wren and I are silent, and she's nearly running to keep up with me.

Gravel crunches as the SUV pulls into the alley. I don't wait for another sign. This one's big enough.

I grab Wren's hand and sprint toward the back road at the end of the alley that bisects Main Street from the houses beyond, pulling her behind me like a flag. We reach a privacy fence, and I give Wren a boost before climbing over. I land on my feet and wince as the thorns of Mrs. Culley's prized rosebushes spear my calves.

"Keep going," I grunt as we extract ourselves from the trampled bushes Mrs. Culley will chastise us until the end of time about ruining. "Get to your house."

I see the gleaming black SUV's roof rails over the fence and don't give Wren a chance to respond before I nearly drag her across the lawn and through the gate. We emerge on Walnut Lane and don't slow down, zigzagging our way through the neighborhood that I'd spent my whole life in up until two years ago. We turn onto Pecan Avenue, Wren's street and my favorite pie, and my blood runs cold.

The SUV is in Wren's driveway.

THREE

Wren

There's no one inside the SUV. Breathing hard, Lee and I skirt around it and head to the porch.

"What is going on?" I whisper frantically to Lee.

"I don't know, but I don't like it," he says.

I fist my hands at my sides to keep them from shaking as we climb up the stairs to the wide front porch Uncle Joel is so proud of. My heart is like a jackhammer in my chest. This is too much. Too much unknowing. Too much change. Too much fear. *Did my uncles freak out about me being gone all night and call in some kind of private investigator to find me? Why? It doesn't make any sense. None of this makes any sense.*

Lee puts a warm hand on my shoulder and squeezes. "Take some deep breaths."

I nod and try to breathe calm into my body. I hear Uncle Brad's deep rumbling voice. I can't tell what he's saying, but I can hear his tone.

"He's pissed," I whisper to Lee with my hand on the door. "You don't have to come in. This isn't going to be fun, even before *that*"—I jerk my chin at the strange SUV—"whatever *that* is showed up."

"I'm not leaving you." Lee touches my shoulder, and I turn my head to meet his gaze. The door swings open to reveal Uncle Joel.

"Oh, do come in." His voice is laced with sarcasm and he makes a sweeping gesture to the inside of the neat, artistically decorated house that has become my home.

"Hi." I grin cheekily at my uncle's husband. "Happy birthday to me!"

When he doesn't even crack a smile I know I'm seriously in trouble, so I try something else.

"Uncle Joel." I drop my voice and step close to him. "Why is the creeper SUV in our driveway?"

"Why is it a creeper SUV?" Uncle Joel counters. The more upset he gets the more often he answers questions with questions.

"Because it was following us," says Lee.

"Well, hello, Mr. Young." Uncle Joel's sharp gaze travels from Lee's shoes to his grass-stained clothes and his messed-up braids, and I realize he still has a piece of tree trash in them. "You are looking uncharacteristically disheveled. I suppose that is a byproduct of keeping our Wren out *all night*."

"Uncle Joel," I explain, "Lee didn't keep me out. I kept him out. He was helping me celebrate my birthday and—"

"Wren Bliss Nightingale, get in here. Now." Uncle Brad's voice booms from the living room.

And, yes, that is my real name. My parents claimed that they weren't smoking weed when they decided on it. No one has ever believed them.

"Crap!" I say under my breath because Uncle Brad sounds even more pissed than Joel.

Lee steps up beside me and squeezes my hand. "They're going to understand," he says softly.

I start to walk forward, but Uncle Joel blocks my way. His gaze has changed from irritated to concerned. "Wait. Has something happened? Are you okay?"

Lee and I share a quick look and he nods encouragement. "Yes," I say. "And yes, I think so, but it's complicated."

Uncle Joel touches my cheek. "Well, we'll figure it out whatever it is. Together. And happy birthday, my little Wreny."

I have to blink several times as my eyes fill. I want to throw myself into Uncle Joel's arms and tell him everything, but from the living room I hear the rumble of a strange male voice and remember the SUV. I tiptoe and kiss Joel on his cheek. "Thank you." Then with Lee beside me, we walk through the foyer and into the living room.

The living room is lovingly decorated in amethyst and teal velvet, with highlights of cream. The sofa and two wide chairs are modern, but comfortable. Fresh lilies in two large vases shaped like naked male torsos fragrance the room. A stone fireplace is the focal point, but what everyone notices first are the floor-to-ceiling bookshelves filled with beautiful hardbacks and abstract statuettes that Uncle Joel insists are objets d'art.

Today all I notice is the man sitting in the teal velvet chair. He's older, probably fifty or so, but looks like he's still in decent shape. His suit is expensive. I know because Uncle Brad has made me an expert on expensive suits. The old guy has a gray goatee. I've never liked goatees. His eyes are a striking hazel that seem to skewer me. I pull my gaze from him and face Uncle Brad.

"I'm really sorry I worried you," I say quickly.

"*We're* really sorry, sir," Lee says from beside me. "Something happened. . . ." He pauses as his gaze goes to the stranger in the room and I feel the jolt that goes through Lee's body and he says nothing else. He just stands there staring at the stranger.

I glance up at Lee, but before I can whisper anything like *WTF is wrong*, Uncle Brad begins speaking. "We will talk about that later," says my uncle firmly. He's sitting on the couch. There are two cups of coffee in front of him, and as Joel takes his seat beside his husband, Brad sips from his mug. He's trying to calm his temper. Uncle Brad isn't really scary. Sure, he's big—like six two or so—and looks like a well-dressed lumberjack, but his insides are as kind and squishy as Joel's. He just hides it better. But he can't hide it from me. He's too much like my mom. He has her eyes, her mouth, her cheekbones, and even more important, he loves me probably as much as Mom did. "Wren, this is Quincy Rottingham, dean of the Academia de la Luna, and a member of something called a Lunar Council."

Uncle Brad doesn't notice that Lee appears to be frozen as he stares at the dean, and keeps talking. "Dean Rottingham, this is my niece, Wren Nightingale, and her friend Lee Young."

Dean Rottingham smiles at me. "I'm glad to meet you, Wren." Then his brownish-green gaze locks on my best friend. "And Lee, it's good to see you again under more pleasant circumstances. I still think of your sister often. She was the best intern I ever had. Her loss is a terrible tragedy to our community. I have been looking forward to welcoming you to Moon Isle tonight."

Uncle Joel makes a little sputtering sound. "Lee, I thought you were going to Europe with a backpacking group this summer."

"No," Dean Rottingham says. "That's just what you were told because you're Mundanes. The truth is a bit more complicated."

Uncle Joel's gaze finds me. "*Complicated.* That's the same word Wren used to describe last night. Isn't that interesting?" Then he faces Dean Rottingham. "And I thought you were here to meet with Wren about a scholarship. What is going on?"

"I apologize for the slight subterfuge," the dean says. "But Wren is here now, so I can make everything clear."

"But no, you can't—" Lee begins, and then he cuts himself off mid-sentence. I glance up at him again and his expression is as rigid as his body. His cheeks are ashen with shock.

"Lee, I understand what you're feeling. The secret I'm sharing is one you've been taught your whole life to keep. And I agree with our ancient rule of hiding our powers from Mundanes, but in extraordinary circumstances we must reveal ourselves for the good of one who is Moonstruck." Rottingham nods as if Lee has agreed with him instead of remaining completely silent. "What is our alternative? Steal Wren away and cause her and her uncles pain and suffering? No, that won't do at all." He returns his attention to my uncles as he continues in a very matter-of-fact voice. "You see, Mr. Lionas and Mr. Glencoe, your niece—and her friends Lee Young and Samantha Hopp—are Magicks, which means they and their parents before them, and those before them for generation after generation, have been Moonstruck. Born during a full moon in Aquarius, Taurus, Leo, or Scorpio to magickal parents, they have each been gifted with special abilities. Aquarius moons are healers. Taurus moons have unusual memory gifts and are able to search through an internet-like database and recall almost any and all information available, think Google personified. Leo moons can manipulate group emotions and behaviors, and Scorpio moons are gifted with high-octane physical intensity. . . ." He pauses and nods as if my uncles are agreeing with him instead of staring at him like he's a science experiment gone wrong.

"When a Magick turns eighteen, their moon powers awaken, though the young adult has been feeling the stirring of powers since they were a child. Isn't that right, Lee? I believe you are an Aquarius moon, a healer, correct?"

"Y-yes," Lee stammers.

The dean nods again. "I remember because I, too, am an Aquarius moon. And Wren's other magickal friend, Samantha, is a Taurus moon. No surprise that she is valedictorian of her class."

Joel's gaze shoots to me. I just told him a couple of nights before that Sam made valedictorian.

"But I digress. The summer a Magick turns eighteen, they are required to attend one of our schools, an Academia de la Luna, where they will learn how to control and use their burgeoning powers. From there, we assist them with choosing the correct path for their adult lives. Lee and Samantha will be attending our academy here in the Pacific Northwest on Moon Isle, where their parents also attended. They are fortunate to do so. Our Moon Isle is the site of the very first Academia de la Luna. It is a very special place."

"I've never heard of an island off the Pacific Northwest coast called Moon," says Uncle Joel. I notice that Uncle Brad has gone absolutely still.

"Of course you haven't. You're a Mundane, and under normal circumstances you would live your entire life not knowing there are Magicks among you. We have learned from centuries of tragedy that we must hold the secret of our magick close. Moon Isle exists, but it is cloaked. Tonight, when the other Magicks her age leave for our schools, Wren, Lee, and Samantha will join them on Moon Isle."

Uncle Joel surges to his feet and begins to pace in front of the fireplace. "This is completely unbelievable. I think you should leave. Now."

"He cannot." Uncle Brad's deep voice takes on the architect-in-charge tone he uses when he explains to corporate executives why they can't use cheap supplies for the buildings he designs. He goes to Joel, who has stopped pacing and is standing in front of the fireplace, staring at his husband. "He cannot leave because Dean Rottingham is telling the truth. There are Magicks and Mundanes in our world. Christine and Roy were Moonstruck." His eyes find me. "And until today I believed like my sister did— that Wren, who like me was not born under one of the magick moon signs, has no magick."

Shock courses through me and I stare at my uncle as if I've never seen him before. "You knew?"

Uncle Brad runs a hand through his thick salt-and-pepper hair. "Yes."

Beside me Lee gasps.

"How long have you known your sister and brother-in-law were Moonstruck?" asks Dean Rottingham softly.

"I've known about Magicks since I was a kid," he tells Rottingham, and then Uncle Brad turns to me. "Wren, I was raised in a Moonstruck family—just like you were. My parents were Magicks. My sister was Magick. My grandparents were Magick. I was the odd man out."

"Which actually doesn't happen very often," adds Dean Rottingham. "It is rare that a Mundane is born into a Magick family."

Uncle Brad nods and continues. "Can you imagine your mom and dad trying to keep their magick from you?"

I manage to shake my head and say a soft "No."

"Right. Impossible. So I've known about Moonstruck for as long as I can remember. And all that time I've also known how important it is to keep that knowledge a secret." He sighs. "Your parents updated their will a few months after you were born. Before they did so they asked me if I would raise you, be your parent, if anything happened to them. When I said yes, they made me swear to continue to keep their secret—to not discuss magick with anyone. And because you were not born under one of the magick moon signs I wasn't to speak of it even to you, Wren." His gaze finds Rottingham again. "I haven't spoken about moon magick since that night. Christine and Roy and I never talked about it again." Brad takes Uncle

Joel's hand. "Forgive me for not sharing the secret with you, but it wasn't mine to tell."

"Magick is real?" Uncle Joel whispers.

"It is," says Uncle Brad.

Uncle Joel's face flushes and he fans himself with the hand Brad isn't holding. "I may need a moment. It's just all so unbelievable."

"I understand why it seems so to you, but I assure you moon magick is as real as electricity or radio waves." The dean's gaze shifts from my uncle to me. "Your power awakened last night, didn't it?"

It feels like my throat is filled with dust, and I have to swallow several times before I can speak. "Yes, but it wasn't normal. Not like what happened to Lee or Sam. And before then I've never felt even a tiny bit of magick—nothing like Mom and Dad."

Uncle Joel starts pacing again. "I'm sorry, but this is a lot for me to take in." He looks at me. "Your mom and dad, Christine and Roy Nightingale, were magickal beings."

I give him a shaky smile. "Well, yeah. Mom was a healer, an Aquarius moon like Lee, and the reason Dad was such an awesome coach is because he was a Scorpio moon."

Uncle Brad runs a hand through his hair again. "It's more than just that, Joel. Moon magick runs in family lines."

"Do you mean it's *normal* in some families to be—what's the word again?" Joel asks.

"Moonstruck," I say.

"Yes, Moonstruck," Uncle Joel says. "Like it's normal for some families to have blue eyes?"

Dean Rottingham clears his throat, pulling my uncle's attention back to him. "That is correct. Wren and your husband are the anomalies within a powerful line of Moon-struck descendants. Mary and Jamison Lionas are as magickal as Janet and Charles Nightingale." His gaze returned to Uncle Brad. "I'm assuming Wren's parents asked you to raise her instead of either set of her grandparents because you and Wren are the only Mundanes in your family."

Uncle Brad nods. "Yes. That and the fact that they live in British Columbia and Christine and Roy didn't want Wren uprooted and moved to a different country."

"Understandable. Very understandable." The dean glances down at the cup of untouched coffee in his hands before he adds, "We Magicks are few compared to Mundanes. We guard our families and our secrets as if our lives depend upon it because *our lives depend upon it.*"

I watch the dean closely, and when he speaks those last words his face shifts from that of a concerned college professor to something else. Something . . . dangerous?

"So you're saying our Wren is supposed to leave her home today and go to some make-believe island all summer to, what, dance under the full moon?" Uncle Joel flicks the spinner ring on his right thumb—a sure sign that he is massively stressed.

"It's real." Lee speaks quietly as everyone turns to stare at him. "They're all telling you the truth."

"No." Uncle Joel shakes his head as he frowns at Dean Rottingham. "If you think that we're just going to let our Wren walk out of our lives, think again."

"She has to go." Uncle Brad doesn't raise his voice, but it seems to slice through the air in the living room.

"I said no!" Uncle Joel shouts.

Before Rottingham can respond, a terrible sound like

a small child scream-crying erupts from the little storage closet under the stairs.

Uncle Joel gasps dramatically. "Now you've done it. Grace Kelly's awake and death yodeling." He hurries across the living room to the ajar door to the closet, opens it, leans down, and when he straightens he's holding a fawn-colored French bulldog in his arms. Her front right paw is bandaged, and she's panting in pain.

I rush across the room to join them. "Isn't she better?"

"I don't think so, Wreny. Last night she wouldn't even walk on that paw. Brad and I decided to take her to the emergency vet today, but—" He glares from Brad to Dean Rottingham before looking back at the Frenchie who wriggles to get closer to me.

I hold out my arms and Joel gives Grace Kelly to me. I nuzzle her as she snortles and licks my face.

"Your dog is injured?" Rottingham asks.

Uncle Joel and I turn to look at him. "Yeah," I say. "She did something to her paw. There's no cut on it, but she's not getting better."

"If you allow it, I believe I can help your Grace Kelly and give your uncle a demonstration that will alleviate his doubts."

When I don't speak, the dean looks from me to Uncle Brad. "As I said earlier I, too, am an Aquarius moon."

My uncle speaks up right away. "Let him help Grace." He meets Uncle Joel's conflicted gaze. "I understand this is difficult for you. I grew up knowing about Magicks, but it's been so long since I've had anything to do with it that it's shaken me, too."

"I have a feeling day drinking would help," quips Uncle

Joel as he turns to face Rottingham. "But as this coffee isn't spiked, what do you propose?"

"Oh, nothing too dramatic. Just bring Grace Kelly to me."

I know Rottingham can heal Gracie. Mom had been a pediatrician, and in the privacy of our home, she and Dad had talked often about how fulfilling it was for her to use moon magick to help her patients. But I wait for Uncle Joel to nod permission. This isn't just difficult for him. It's hard for me, too. I love Uncle Joel. What if he hates me for keeping this secret from him? What if this causes Uncle Joel to question whether he should trust Uncle Brad? It doesn't matter that Brad and I didn't think I had any magick—that I *still* don't truly believe I have any magick. This is a big secret.

Please don't let Uncle Joel hate us. I couldn't bear it if he hated us.

"Go ahead, Wren," Uncle Joel finally capitulates.

I bite my lip and carry Grace to the dean. He holds out his hand and speaks softly to her so she can get used to him, but little Grace Kelly, like most Frenchies, is full of joy and loves attention and meeting new people. She happily goes to him when he opens his arms to her. Gently, he peels off the tape and then unwraps the gauze that makes her paw look mummified. Under it her slim doggy ankle is puffy and her paw is red.

Dean Rottingham places his right hand on Gracie's hurt paw. He lifts his other hand, folds his pinky and thumb so that they touch, leaving his three middle fingers extended. He closes his eyes, draws in a deep breath, and as he exhales he passes his hand down Grace's body, beginning at her stubby tail and ending over her hurt paw. I recognize the hand gesture as vaguely similar to the one my mom used whenever I'd scraped my knee or cut myself, but I do not recognize the power that suddenly sizzles within me.

It's not like Lee described—like static electricity zapping along his skin. That doesn't come close. It's not something happening outside of me. *It's under my skin, beneath my ribs,* a flush of heat that reminds me of last night and a new pulling sensation as if something is tugging on my soul. I bite my lip to keep from gasping and fist my hands. And then the feeling is gone. When Dean Rottingham opens his eyes, he stares directly at me with an expression so intense that it makes me shiver.

But no one notices because Gracie is snorting and wriggling happily and trying to climb up Rottingham's chest to lick his face. The dean looks away from me, chuckles, and rubs behind Gracie's ears. Then he smiles up at Uncle Joel. "You won't have to take her to the emergency vet. She bruised her paw and sprained her ankle. Did she jump off someplace high?"

"She did. On our walk two days ago she suddenly got the ridiculous idea that she could jump off a culvert at the edge of the park. She yelped in pain and has been limping since." Uncle Joel scoops Grace from the dean's lap and begins inspecting her paw. Joel's gaze finds Brad. "He healed her."

"I hope someday I can do the same thing," Lee says. "But first I have to go to Moon Isle and the Academia de la Luna to learn how to control my power. And so does Wren."

"But I've never felt any power! Well, not until midnight last night," I blurt, not wanting to mention what just happened. Increasingly panicked, I continue to babble. "And even then it wasn't like Lee's power."

"Explain please," says the dean.

"I, um . . ." I suddenly know what I have to do, and I feel super foolish that I haven't thought of it before now, though I am glad Gracie was healed. I look up at Lee. "Show them."

Lee blinks in surprise, and I realize he, too, forgot about the picture. He takes his phone from his pocket, taps it, and then turns it to face my uncles and Dean Rottingham.

Rottingham leans forward. He seems mesmerized by the picture. He doesn't speak.

"Oh! Ohmygod!" Uncle Joel gasps and covers his mouth with one hand.

"This isn't some AI image or something you've photoshopped." Uncle Brad doesn't frame it like a question, but I answer him anyway.

"No, it's not, but I swear I didn't think I was Moonstruck before last night and since then I've felt totally normal." I tell the white lie as I look from Brad to the dean. "I don't understand any of this. Lee has felt magick as long as he can remember, and so has Sam. They were born under magick moons to Magicks. My parents were Magicks, but I wasn't born under any of the magick moons. It should've skipped me like it did Uncle Brad."

The dean nods. "Yes, that is usually the case, but once every several generations a special child is born from Magicks *not* under one of our moons, though on her eighteenth birthday that child suddenly exhibits extreme magickal symptoms. After training on Moon Isle, this special Moonstruck young person either discovers which of the moon gifts she has been given, or never again feels the magick and returns to life as a Mundane, though of course that person must swear to never reveal any knowledge about Magicks. . . ." The dean pauses and his dark gaze meets mine.

The intensity I see in his eyes sends a shiver of fear through my body that lifts the little hairs on my forearms. Do they really just let a Mundane return from the Academia de la Luna to live a normal life? I've never heard of that, but then again, I've also never heard of anyone like me suddenly becoming Moonstruck. My stomach clenches and my teeth worry my bottom lip. I'm so distracted that the dean's voice, now filled with warmth, makes me jump.

"Wren Nightingale, I am excited to welcome you to our Academia de la Luna." He smiles at me and then shifts his focus to my uncles, huddled together holding hands in front of the fireplace. Uncle Joel blinks quickly. His nose is reddening and his eyes look suspiciously bright. Uncle Brad just looks sad. "I am sorry for the suddenness of this. I know it is a shock. I am also sorry that you only have a few hours to prepare, but I promise both of you that I will look after Wren as she discovers who she really is this summer."

I go to my uncles and hold out my hands to them, which they instantly take. I can see the hurt in Uncle Joel's eyes and the fear in Uncle Brad's. I understand what they're going through because I feel it, too—this loss of what we've planned, what we've counted on to fill our future. I stare up into their kind, familiar faces. "I'll be back. I promise. Moonstruck or not, Magick or not, I will come home. I will not let this control my life. I will not let this separate us. Ever."

Lee steps up beside me. "And I'll be with her all summer. It's going to be okay. Promise."

"Oh, Wreny, we love you so much!" Uncle Joel sniffles.

Uncle Brad meets my gaze. "Your mother would be so proud." He attempts and almost succeeds at smiling through his tears. "Well, my girl, it seems we have some packing to do."

FOUR

Lee

I've only seen Moon Isle in my dreams. The Lunar Council has more than succeeded in its efforts to keep the schools sprinkled across the earth like stars hidden from even the most dedicated conspiracy theorist. Plus, no tech is allowed. They confiscated my phone as Wren and I boarded the ferry that takes us from the Port of Portland to the island. The only photos we can take will be stored within the folds of our memory.

That's why we're all silent. The thirty or so of us are huddled together and pressed to the boat's guardrail as it cuts through the fog. Every single one of us has magick, but none of us knows what to expect from Moon Isle.

"*Ohmygod,*" comes a groan from behind me. "I'm going to explode out of my skin if they don't uncloak the island soon."

Magick sizzles with the statement, and the hairs on the back of my neck rise. The spark of uncontrolled power isn't enough to cause harm. None of us are that strong. Not yet.

My fingers drum against the ferry's guardrail, hours of magickal hand gesture drills itching to be unleashed. I hear my father's commanding voice between my ears so clearly it's like I'm back in Brooklyn, back in his study practicing until sunlight leaks from the sky and my fingers ache.

Calm and collected, Leland. We do not use our magick unless we're calm and collected. It should be like breathing—natural, and most efficient when we're composed.

Ocean spray dots my knuckles as I cling to the cold metal railing and ride the waves that swell through the Pacific. Wren is right next to me, pressed against my side like a frightened kitten, and this is the only time in our entire friendship that I haven't put her needs above my own. I'm caught in a space between this moment and visions of two years ago when Dean Rottingham showed up on our doorstep.

Your sister . . . she's not coming home. . . .

I shake off the memory but can't pull my gaze from the water reaching up the side of the ferry. It came for Maya and now it's coming for me.

"You okay?" Wren asks, burrowing closer, the sleeves of her oversized tee flapping in the wind.

I'm thankful she's here. More thankful than she knows or than I could ever convey. I don't know what I would do without her beside me, making sure the waves don't pull me under.

"Maya was in this same spot two years ago—" Words clog my throat as I stare at the sea, and I can't tell if shuttered grief has filled my eyes with tears, or if it's the wind.

"I get it." She rubs my back, blankly staring ahead, her own eyes glossed with tears, and I know she understands. She understands better than anyone.

My hand is numb from squeezing the guardrail so tight. I relax my grip and glance around to make sure no one else has witnessed my moment of weakness.

You're a Young, and Young means power. Another lesson from my father. This one tenses my shoulders and lifts my chin high. I am a Young, next in line to a major pharmaceutical company that's donated more to super PACs than nonprofits.

Now that Maya's gone, I have to step up and be who my family needs. To do that, I can't get triggered by the water.

We pass a buoy. On it, a red-rimmed sign is emblazoned with WARNING! JAGGED ROCKS in all caps. Below the words are circled images with a line marking through each—one of a boat and one of a swimmer.

A lighthouse emerges in the distance, sweeping a halo of light against the fog and growing out of the jagged rocks like a fang. We drift closer to it and to the rocks emerging from the water wet and dark and deadly. I stiffen, my chest turning to steel as we slip along the surface feet from the gaping maw of stone we've been warned away from.

Nervous gasps bubble up around me, and Wren tightens her grip on my arm as we barrel into the rocks. And then we're through, craggy black stones jutting out from all angles around us like a glitch in a game.

I lean over the guardrail and reach out, the last vestiges

of the impulsive, reckless guy I used to be clawing to the surface before I can stop them.

Wren scoots closer, the breeze whipping the pink ends of her hair against my chest. "Lee, don't—"

My fingers slide through, meeting mist and air. The reality beneath the magick.

I come up slowly. Stunned, not by the magick. It's not a kind I've ever experienced, but Moon Isle is there to teach me more. I'm stunned by my thoughtlessness and how easily I forgot who I am now and how much rests on my shoulders.

"Do you think Mundanes know?" Wren's question jars me from my pensiveness. "I mean, do you think it's the same for them? Can they get through the magick?" She lifts onto her tiptoes and starts to lean over the railing.

My hand is on her shoulder before I even realize I've moved, and I'm pulling her back, away from the railing. I yank my hand away and clear my throat, smoothing my fingers over my fresh braids. She can take care of herself. I know she can. But we all thought Maya could, too.

"It, uh, it can't be the same for them." I shake my head and tuck my hand into my pocket. "There's no way the island would still be a secret if it was."

"If it's real to them . . ."

There's an unspoken question on Wren's tongue that buzzes through my thoughts.

If it's real to them, can it wreck their boats? Can the magick kill them?

But I don't have to answer. I don't have to think about what the Lunar Council is willing to do to protect us, because the rest of her words are swept away by a cloud of smoke so thick my eyes burn. Magick crackles through the air, biting at the bare skin not covered by my thin jacket. Just when I think the smoke is too thick to draw another breath, it's swept away. Ahead, the lighthouse is shrouded in fog, but on the ferry deck, the air is clean and fresh and clear. I suck in a deep lungful and taste the earth after a rainstorm, rich and fertile and alive.

There's a sudden *boom* and a deep rumble that grabs my lungs and shakes. We all duck down, and I tuck Wren against my chest, my body shielding hers from whatever happens next.

In front of us, the air ripples like a bough in the breeze before the night sky cracks in two, split by invisible hands and peeled apart like an orange. Beneath the magickal skin imprinted with the fog and the lighthouse and the danger from the slabs of sharpened stone is a reality more enchanting than any spell.

The crescent moon–shaped cove has a well-maintained dock on one end and a beach that stretches to the other point of the crescent. In the distance, the main building sits in the middle of a copse of ancient pines like a brick and stone mountain, dominating the skyline. It shines from within, the light beaming through the enormous leaded windows like the beacon of the magickal lighthouse. Part castle and part country mansion, the main academy building looks like something out of those English dramas Wren's obsessed with, but this building has a powerful presence. It reaches for me, tugging at my heart from across the water.

Our ferry drifts closer, slowing down as it prepares to dock. Silver light dots the campus from streetlamps shaped like the full moon. The round orbs throw opalescent pools of light across cobblestone sidewalks and courtyards filled with clusters of ferns and flowers, and reflect off glistening fountains situated among the giant pines.

The ferry docks, and I take Wren's hand and a deep breath and join the crush of excited students reveling in the majesty of Moon Isle.

My gaze returns to the main building. It's two stories of arched windows, rounded doors, and graceful peaks and towers. Generations of Moonstruck have been through those doors and looked out those windows, pulled by the magick like I am now. They've become the most powerful people in the country—in the world—and I will, too.

"We made it." I squeeze Wren's hand as we head up the wide, steep stairway that will take us from the dock to campus, but she doesn't squeeze mine back. "We're here."

I stare up at the stream of moonlight filtering down through the clouds to bathe the academy. My throat constricts as my thoughts swim from my sister to Wren to what this summer holds. The one thing I know for sure—Moon Isle will change my life.

FIVE

Wren

I can't tell whether I'm terrified or intrigued by Moon Isle. Maybe I'm just excited. Maybe if I tell myself over and over, *I'm excited! I'm excited! I'm excited!* it'll be a self-fulfilling prophecy. Even though it's the first day of June, it's the Pacific Northwest, which means when the sun sets the temperature drops, and the Pacific Ocean is always as cold as it is turbulent. So the ocean spray and the chilly night are what I blame for the way my body trembles as the little ferry comes to a halt and ties up at the dock.

(*I'm excited! I'm excited! I'm excited!*)

There's so much to see that it's tough to focus, especially if I give too much thought to the sizzling-under-my-skin feeling the magick that keeps the isle hidden from Mundanes gave me as we seemed to crash into the barrier of rock and fog that shrouds this place.

Do Mundanes really crash into those "rocks"? That can't be right. Right?

I slip my hand into Lee's as the ferry captain tells us to disembark. There are a couple dozen other students with us on the boat and it looks like about the same amount on three other boats in line to dock after us. We're jostling one another as we make our way down the dock and head toward a big, serious-looking brick building that lurks above the crescent-shaped cove. There are a lot of stairs to climb up to that building and I hold tightly to Lee's hand as we move, wavelike, with the other kids.

I glance up at Lee. His face is expressionless, which tells me a lot about the feelings that have to be churning inside of him. I know this is hard on him—this reminder of the last part of his sister's life must make him feel raw. I get it. My parents have been on my mind a lot over the past twenty-four hours. I imagine how amazed they would be that I'm here. As Uncle Brad said, I think they'd be proud, too, and eager to see what comes of this Moon Isle summer. Like Lee, I feel cheated at my loss—their loss—*our* loss.

As a group, we pour up over the wide, multi-tiered stairs, and I bite my lip so I don't gasp. Close up, the main building that looked lurky and creepy from the shore is actually elegant and castle-like. It's three stories of red brick with lots of Gothic peaks and rounded turrets (which I'm quite familiar with from my extensive reading of Regency-era romances). Cream-colored stones frame the bottom-story windows and doors in graceful arches. Matching but smaller stone buildings stretch on either side of the central one. There are huge pines everywhere and lots of ferns. Everything is green, which makes me feel a little more relaxed because it's so typically Pacific Northwest. But the most amazing thing about the campus is the lights! Big black wrought-iron streetlamps hold aloft huge moon-shaped globes that cast the silver-white light of a full moon in halos over wide cobbled sidewalks and little courtyards.

"I didn't know it would be so pretty," I whisper to Lee.

He shakes himself and looks down at me, blinking like he's forgotten that he's holding my hand. "What?"

"I was just saying that it's really pretty. Are you okay?"

Lee nods and smiles, but it doesn't reach his eyes.

We're milling around in small groups on the big paved area in front of the main building. There's an empty podium bathed in light from two extra big moon streetlights. I let go of Lee's hand because mine is suddenly sweaty.

"Are *you* okay?" he asks, and I shrug and give him a sheepish smile as I wipe my palms on my favorite pair of pink overalls.

"Just excited." I repeat my internal mantra, still trying to make it so.

Lee and I stand just outside the pool of light cast on the podium. Trying not to be super obvious, I check out the other students as they climb up from the dock. There's a lot of talking going on, but it's pretty subdued. No bursts of laughter. No shouts. None of the backslapping, shoulder-bumping stuff guys tend to do when they hang out with other guys. Curious, I try to count the number of students, though that's hard to tell for sure because there's a lot of movement and more people keep coming up over the stairs to mill around. I'm relieved to see that no one looks terrified.

It's easy to tell who comes from big cities because they congregate in larger groups of four to ten, and only in big cities would that many Magicks grow up around one another. Most of us are coupled up, talking quietly, or standing awkwardly alone and silent. I wish whatever is going to happen would hurry up and happen, and I turn to Lee as another wave of students washes up over the stairs, and from the middle of the new group a very off-key, very familiar voice belts out the opening lyrics of Belle's first song in *Beauty and the Beast*.

"Little town. It's a quiet village. . . ."

I turn as the sea of kids parts to reveal my other best friend. As usual, Sam Hopp looks like she's so filled with joy that it beams from her. She has her arms spread, mimicking Belle frolicking through her village, and as she sings her long dark hair flies around her. Sam's smile blazes with the lyrics, and in the moon-colored lights she looks like a mischievous elf who does not have one shit to give about the fact that she's a completely, utterly, painfully terrible singer. Sam's a Taurus moon, which means she's genius-level smart and amazingly good at *almost* everything. And by *almost* I mean she's good at everything except singing or anything artistic—though not because she doesn't keep trying to succeed at both. She fails miserably but tries, tries again. Sam's told me many times, starting in first grade when we began singing Disney tunes together at recess, that she doesn't understand why I.Q. is not what decides whether she has the ability to carry a tune. That is just one of the things I love about Sam—her eternal optimism.

Giggles rustle through the crowd of spectators. I can't tell if they're laughing *at* Sam or *with* her, but I know one thing for sure—Sam doesn't care which it is. She's the most fearless person I know. Sam is always 100 percent *Sam*. She told me one time that being scared will never change anything, so let's be brave no matter what because courage feels better than fear. I love how comfortable she is with herself. The more she sings (badly) the more my nerves (*I'm excited!*) fade away as I grin and open my arms wide, ready to hug her.

Before I can, a guy steps from a group of students watching Sam, who has just spun around as she sings, "*Oh, isn't this amazing.*" She's belting out the next line and smiling, Belle-like, at me when he sticks out his foot, hooks her ankle, and trips her. Sam's song sputters to a stop as she goes down hard. She catches herself with her hands, but even from several yards away I see her grimace in pain.

"Oh, *sorry.*" The tall redheaded guy laughs down at her. "Guess I didn't see you there 'cause you were being so quiet." Beside him a few other guys join his laughter. I notice that there are some girls in the group, one of them another tall redhead, but they frown and walk away from him.

I start forward, hands fisted and anger bubbling hot in my chest. I feel Lee's absence, surprised he doesn't rush past me to protect Sam, but I'm too pissed to take time to look around for him. *He'd just been there by my side, hadn't he?* Right before I reach Sam, a petite girl strides across the sidewalk and straight to the redhead. She stops less than a hand's length in front of the guy, who is at least a head taller than her, plants her fists on her slim waist, and looks steadily up at him. In a voice like ice she commands, "Do not *ever* do that again." And with one fast, fluid movement she pushes him—hard. He's lifted off his feet and flies back into the group of snickering jerks. They stagger under his weight and two of them fall to the ground with him.

In the next second I'm helping Sam up and she winces when I touch her bloody hand. The girl who'd pushed the jerk takes her elbow and guides Sam to her feet with me.

And then the redhead is there again. His hair is all messed up, his T-shirt is ripped, and his face is blotchy red with rage.

The petite girl who'd tossed him into his group of friends drops Sam's elbow, strides straight into his personal space, and puts her hands up like she's going to shove him again. "Oh, good." Her voice is deadpan, but her eyes blaze. "I enjoy teaching bullies lessons their parents failed to teach them. You want more?"

The guy hesitates and another beside him tugs on his sleeve. "Let's go, Luke. She's gotta be a Scorpio moon."

"I'll be seeing you later." Luke sneers at the girl as he lets his friend pull him away.

"I look forward to it," says our hero.

"Are you okay?" I take one of Sam's hands and turn it over. It's scraped and bloody.

"An Aquarius moon can help with that," says the petite girl.

"Oh, I'm fine." Sam's grin is back. She turns it on me first and gives me a fast, fierce hug. "Wreny! I can't believe we're here together!"

Before I can say anything, Sam lets go of me and smiles at the girl. "Hi, I'm Sam Hopp and this is Wren Nightingale. Yes, she has a double bird name. Thanks for being my hero."

The girl's lips barely tilt up, but there's a real smile in her expressive brown eyes. Her straight black hair is cut short, at the line of her strong jaw. Her skin is smooth and flawless, and this close to her I see that it covers lean muscle. "No problem. I hate bullies. *Konbanwa,* I'm Ruby Nakamura." She bows slightly to us and even that small movement is made with the lithe strength and grace of an athlete.

"Konbanwa." Sam mimics her bow. "You *are* a Scorpio moon, right?"

"Correct," says Ruby.

"Konbanwa?" I ask when they look at me.

Ruby glances from me to Sam and lifts one slim, dark eyebrow.

Quickly, Sam explains, "It's a Japanese greeting. Means 'hi, good evening.'"

"I didn't know you speak Japanese." Though I guess I should have. Sam says she doesn't know everything, but I think that's debatable.

"Oh, I don't really. Well, maybe just a *sukoshi*—a little. Barely enough to get around." Her eyes glitter as she looks at Ruby again. "I've always wanted to go to Japan."

Ruby just tilts her head, a little birdlike, and says, "Of course."

"Hey, where's Lee?"

Sam's question has me looking around. *Where is Lee?* "He was here just a second ago." There aren't any more students coming up from the dock and there's easily one hundred of us. I tiptoe to try to peer around to find Lee, but the parting of the crowd that let Sam's Belle through has closed and is now a sea of people surrounding me. And I'm short. Really short. I can't see anything. A woman's voice rings like a clear, sweet bell over the loudspeaker system and everyone turns to the podium.

"Attention, please! Everyone come closer."

"Oooh, it's Celeste, the leader of the Lunar Council." Sam hooks her elbow through mine. "Come on. Let's get up front so we can see. You, too, Ruby!" She hooks her other elbow through that of Ruby, who blinks a few times in surprise but seems fine with being dragged along by Sam's enthusiasm.

"'Scuse me. Coming through. Sorry." Sam keeps up polite apologies while she pulls us through the crowd until we stand front and center before the podium.

The woman behind the podium is gorgeous. She has amazing thick dark hair that cascades in perfect waves down to the middle of her back. It has one white stripe that starts at her right temple and goes the full length of her hair, which is cool, especially because even though she can't be, she looks young. I mean, *really* young. Like she could easily be mistaken for a student. Her skin is the color of sunlight through a jar of honey. She is dressed in a short black velvet dress. Held over her shoulders by a full moon brooch is the most beautiful cape I have ever seen. It's the same silver-white as the moon globes and the full moon above us that's only partially obscured by clouds. Every time the sky clears enough to allow Her to shine down, Celeste's cape glistens like there are slim strips of diamonds sewn into it. I squint and study the cloak closer as the crowd pushes around us and finally begins to quiet, and I realize it isn't diamonds that are sewn into the cloak but silver thread. It looks like mercury was somehow made solid and then used to embroider all the phases of the moon, over and over across the cloak.

"She's beautiful," Sam whispers to me.

"She's powerful," Ruby says, just loud enough for Sam and me to hear.

I stagger as a big body smushes between Ruby and me.

Lee's warm hand closes over mine. "Wren! There you are." He leans across me. "Hi, Sam."

"Lee! It's—" Sam begins, but Celeste's musical voice hushes her and everyone else.

"Hello, Moonstruck. I am Celeste, leader of the Lunar Council. Welcome to Moon Isle. Your lives are about to change forever."

SIX

Lee

A guy my parents told me I had to link up with as soon as I got to campus claps me on the shoulder, and I spin around. Apparently, he was given the same instructions.

"Leland, I knew you'd make it." The way the redhead says my name makes me feel like I'm already forty, already CEO of Titan Biomedical, like Maya's death was inevitable. "My mom was worried you wouldn't get back from New York in time, but I told her that the Youngs are nothing if not dependable."

I shake his outstretched hand like I've trained for interactions like this my whole life instead of being the one who was left at the banquet table with strict instructions not to do anything I would normally do. "And how is Senator Weatherford?"

Luke shrugs and rolls his eyes in a way that tells me he doesn't want to talk about his parents.

Good. I don't want to talk about mine, either.

"You're not a Leo, are you?" he asks, brushing his red curls from his forehead.

I shake my head. "Aquarius."

"Let's hope our dorms are close or there are golf carts or something. I don't want to hike for miles just to practice together."

"You want to practice magick . . . with me?" I jab my thumb into my chest to make sure he's clear on which me we're talking about.

"Dude, your family is known for two things." He holds up his hand, ticking the facts off on his fingers. "One, making or breaking someone's bid for president, and two, having massively great dexterity. You're like a bunch of octopuses. Octopi?" He shrugs. "Whatever you're doing—hand workouts, animal sacrifices—you have to let me in on it."

This is the exchange, the transition of power, the moment my father has drilled into my head as one of the most important in a relationship. Luke wants something from me: my tips and tricks, because finger dexterity is its own kind of strength within our magickal society. My family's ability to keep our hands down and weave our spells so subtly no Mundane would take a second look is a skill many covet but few have the dedication and will to achieve. If I share this with him, or at least let him think that I will, he'll be in my debt.

I clear my throat, suddenly feeling like a watered-down Patrick Bateman.

"Then bring a jacket," I say, lifting one brow and sliding my mouth into the same half smile my dad uses to break the ice with new clients. "Because those animal sacrifices get messy."

Luke's laugh is bigger than he is, and I can't help but join in.

"I had a feeling we'd get along." His attention drifts behind me, and he gives someone a nod. "Gotta make the rounds. You get it."

We shake again, closing the impromptu meeting.

"I'll catch you later, Leland."

"Lee!" I call after him as he jogs past.

"Way better!" He offers me a thumbs-up before disappearing into the crowd.

Only now do I realize how fast my heart is beating. That conversation gave me a rush. I don't know exactly what my parents have going on with the Weatherfords, but I know that I just did my part. Maya would be proud.

My throat tightens, and I look down at the cobbled path beneath my high-tops. "Maya would never believe it."

A sound like a dying cat grabs my attention, and I turn to ask Wren if she knows what's making that sound, but she's gone. I use my long legs to my advantage and stretch myself to my full six feet, four inches until I spot her signature pink ends.

I dip into the crowd, slipping between bouts of excited chatter and skirting the firepit as I make my way to her. I immediately recognize the brunette standing next to Wren. I've only seen Sam Hopp on video calls, but with her high-pitched laugh and eyes so round she looks almost animated, she's unmistakable.

I spot a space between Wren and a person in a bloodred

hoodie and squeeze in between the two. "Excuse me. Sorry about that," I say to the hoodie. Whoever's inside doesn't look up, only tightens the strings of their hood and grunts.

I grab Wren's hand and say hi to Sam before my attention is hooked by a voice so rich and sweet my teeth ache.

"Welcome to Moon Isle. Your lives are about to change forever."

It's like the leader of the Lunar Council is speaking to me and only me as she lowers her gaze, as dark as the new moon, to the crowd. She arches her thick black brows and raises her pointed chin, her sharp jawline cutting the air as she surveys us.

Even though she's been head of the Lunar Council for years, she doesn't look much older than we are. If she took her place when she was young, that means there's a chance for any of us.

"Each of you belongs to a moon sign. Together, you make a compass—Scorpio across from Taurus and Leo from Aquarius—all pointing our future in the right direction. Moonstruck are CEOs, politicians, Nobel Prize winners, your favorite celebrities, the best and brightest and most accomplished in the world not simply because we have magick, but because of what takes place here at the Academia de la Luna. The professors are here to offer guidance and specialized lectures to help you as you practice and train out in the open in a way you are unable to do in the Mundane world." She gestures to the row of teachers seated behind her, still as statues. "Throughout it all the council will be watching. *I* will be watching. . . ." She pauses, taking us in once again, and my chest swells. I want her to notice me, to log my face in her memory. Being on the Lunar Council would be better than CEO of

Titan Biomedical. It's what Maya would want if she were still here.

Why stop at CEO? she'd say. *Sure, I could be one of the richest Black women in the world and pretty much pick who runs for president, but who controls the president, Lee? Who controls the world?*

"I can feel your magick," Celeste continues. "And I know you are excited, but tonight you must focus on nourishment and rest. The Trials begin tomorrow along with the rest of your lives."

Her eyes meet mine and every muscle in my body tenses, my pulse quaking in my extremities.

"Lee!" Wren's hushed hiss pulls my attention, and I realize I've been holding my breath. "My hand." She shakes it free from my grasp and flexes her fingers. "It's not a stress ball."

Apparently, my breath wasn't the only thing I was holding too tight.

When I look back up to the podium, Celeste is gone, seated in her throne at the center of the platform.

Dean Rottingham has taken her place and nods his thanks before gripping the sides of the wooden dais. He seems older in the silvery glow of the streetlamps, his deep-set eyes and gray goatee pressed into his white skin like ink. He looks like a leader, decisive, like someone who would drive into town in a blacked-out SUV and reveal a secret as old as time itself. I understand why Maya was proud to work with him.

"Students, welcome. As our esteemed head of the Lunar Council mentioned, tonight is not for shows of jubilation. You will have one hour for dinner and another hour to settle in before lights out. Also, as I am sure you have noticed, this is a device-free campus. Along with that, Moon Isle does not have internet access. No Wi-Fi, no streaming, no social media."

There's a collective gasp as if he's just revealed we're to go without food for the entire summer. Getting straight to the point must be the dean's hallmark.

I stifle a cough and rub my chest, still uncomfortable with the fact that Mundanes know about our magick, even if they are Wren's uncles. But if Rottingham determined it to be necessary, who am I to object? He's a rule maker. Without him, without the council, our world would plunge into chaos.

He holds up his hands, quieting the crowd. "Yes, it will be an adjustment, but so, too, is learning to have dominion over your magick. Everything you need can be accessed by the librarian, a Capricorn moon, or found within the library's tomes, which are organized within the card catalog."

Instinctively, my fingers dip into my pocket before I remember that I don't have my phone and therefore can't look up the definition of *card catalog*.

The hairs on the back of my neck lift, and I swipe my palm against the tingling sensation. Uncontrolled and untamed magick stirs in the air around us as emotions ebb and flow. It's unlike anything I've experienced. Even at family functions when the two magickal limbs that make up my family tree are all present and accounted for, it doesn't feel like this. But they're mostly adults. They've all been through this summer and know they'll face the council's consequences if they operate outside our rules. Those of us who have yet to transition into our full power are few and far between. Nothing like the hundred or so gathered now.

A shiver curls around my spine, and this time I can't help but look over my shoulder. I scan the top of the crowd, only a few others as tall as I am, poking up from the throng like wildflowers, until my eyes find *her*. She's in the back, standing on a tree stump that's been carved into the shape of a crescent moon. She's feet above everyone, but it wouldn't matter if she weren't. With hair like fire, she's hard to overlook.

She looks just like her pictures. Her eyes stay locked on mine. I take a subconscious step closer to Wren.

"She's really pretty." Wren's voice makes me jump, breaking the spell cast by the redhead.

You're prettier. But, of course, I don't say that. Instead, I shrug and turn my attention back to Dean Rottingham.

"Quiet, quiet," he instructs, waving his arms like a music conductor. The crowd calms, though I'm sure the anxiety over being Wi-Fi-less is far from forgotten, and he continues his speech. "We are not the only inhabitants of this magickal island. Ancient beings, Elementals, call Moon Isle home. Outside the clearly marked borders of the Academia de la Luna, the Elementals should not be approached or antagonized. These great beings are to be respected. This land is not yours. It is not ours. It belongs to the Elemental factions: Aquarius Air, Taurus Earth, Scorpio Water, and Leo Fire."

As if summoned by the dean's speech, neon yellow flashes overhead, throwing out a gust of air so strong I shield my face. Another burst of electric light, this time as green as freshly cut grass, shoots out from the center of a tall pine. With it, the musty scent of tilled dirt. Out past the dock behind us, water splashes and a blue beam erupts from the black waves as a burst of neon red shoots from the firepit. We all scamper backward, knocking into one another like bowling pins as salt-tinged air fills my nose and the heat from the fire scrapes my skin.

The glowing blue and red forms glide toward us, inches above the ground. They're blurry at first, their outlines getting clearer, darker, more filled in with each second.

We part for the Scorpio Water and Leo Fire Elementals, their long black cloaks dusting the earth as they pass. They stare straight ahead, at the platform, at Celeste, as they approach the other two Elementals waiting on the ground beneath the dean's podium.

Their images are perfectly rendered now, but I'm only able to get glimpses of their neon bodies peeking out from their floating capes as they pass, eyes like Christmas lights pressed into the darkness beneath their heavy cowls.

The murmurs spreading through the crowd abruptly end when Celeste stands. Against me, Wren stiffens. She's tense, ready to run, but I have never been more transfixed. Dean Rottingham steps away from the dais, but Celeste doesn't stop moving forward. She passes him, passes the podium, and walks off the edge of the platform.

Sam gasps and claps both hands over her mouth, but the leader of the Lunar Council does not fall. The Aquarius Air Elemental lifts its arm, extending one brilliant yellow skeletal finger from its dark cloak. With it, the sound of rushing air—speeding along the freeway windows down—vibrates against my ears. Celeste's moon-white robe lifts around her calves, fluttering in an invisible cyclone beneath her feet.

"She's flying." The whisper comes from behind me, or maybe it comes from my own lips, because Celeste *is* flying.

The Air Elemental lowers its arm, instructing its element to gently place Celeste on the ground in front of us. Her robe stills, its silvery threads winking like stars in the lamplight. "As I call your moon sign, accompany your Elemental to your hall." She tucks her white strands of hair behind her ear and smiles. "Leo moons, your summer at Moon Isle has officially begun."

The Fire Elemental steps forward and neon-red flames magickally flash above the Leos' heads. The Elemental doesn't wait for the shock to wear off and its charges to line up and be escorted to one of the dorm buildings deeper on the island. This isn't that kind of school. Instead, the cloaked creature turns and glides away from the other three. Leos rush to not be left behind, ducklings unable to keep up with Mom.

Fiery auburn hair catches my attention, and I lock eyes with the mysterious redhead. As a Leo moon, she can manipulate group behavior. My stomach tightens. What would that power look like if it went unchecked?

"Scorpio moons," Celeste chimes.

Beside me, a neon-blue mist gleams above Red Hoodie's head. They march forward, the first to join the Water Elemental on its journey to Scorpio Hall.

Taurus moons are next. Verdant blades of grass sprout above Sam's head as she gives Wren a quick hug, whispering in her ear before waving to me.

Wren has curled in on herself, her teeth digging white lines against her bottom lip. I've been too busy, too distracted by the scope of magick around me to notice what it was doing to her. She tilts her head back, gaze fastened to the air above. She wasn't born under one of the four magick moons, and I hadn't stopped to think what that would mean for her or how nervous she would be as we break into our halls. I take her hand. The other elements haven't beamed over her, so she's with me. She's an Aquarius moon.

"Aquarius!" Celeste's voice is sharp, and I know she's saved the best for last.

A neon tornado glows above me, bathing my dark skin in yellow light as bright and happy as I am to be here, to be with Wren. I step forward toward the rest of the Aquariuses we'll be hallmates with for the summer, but Wren is rooted to the earth.

The tornado only lasts a moment and it's already gone when I turn to her, my brows lifted in a silent question. She continues her assault on her bottom lip, and her eyes plead for me not to leave.

The other Moonstruck are gone, trailing after the Air Elemental, casting quizzical glances over their shoulders, torn between keeping up with the magickal creature and staying behind to watch potential drama unfold.

Dean Rottingham's gleaming black shoes knock against the steps as he descends the platform and approaches Celeste. He tugs on his waistcoat and leans down to speak only to the leader of the Lunar Council. Celeste's jaw sets, her dark eyes narrowing on us while she listens.

I return her gaze. She may lead our magickal council, but I could, too, someday. We each have years ahead of us, and we *will* work together. I don't yet deserve it, but Celeste will eventually see me as her equal.

She approaches us, and I hold my breath, but she doesn't pause when she reaches me. She brushes past and stops directly in front of Wren, whose hands are climbing up my arm like I'm the rope to safety.

Celeste strokes Wren's hair, letting the magenta tips gloss her brown skin. "Your power is taking its time."

"I'm sure I can still catch the ferry and—"

Celeste holds up her hand, silencing Wren, and I'm surprised she complies. Celeste turns, pinning her dark, penetrating gaze to mine. "And you, why have you not joined the others in your hall?"

"I won't leave Wren," I say, giving her hand a squeeze. "We're friends."

"*Best* friends." Wren pulls me closer.

Celeste doesn't look at Wren. Instead, she cocks her head, and her white hair slips from her narrow shoulder. "And your friend's needs come before those of the Lunar Council?"

My mouth is dry, and my brain is a hamster wheel spinning, spinning, spinning, trying to come up with the right answer.

"We have rules for a reason, Lee."

My heart hangs unmoving in my chest. "You know my name."

"I know more than you could ever imagine." She blinks, her long lashes nearly touching her brows, and I want to ask more. I want to bring Wren along as we follow Celeste forever. She has all the answers. She is the reason we are safe, hidden from the Mundanes and united as a family of Moonstruck. I open my mouth to ask one of the million questions burning the tip of my tongue, but I'm already too late.

"Wren, you and your lagging Magick may choose whichever hall best aligns with—"

"I choose Aquarius." Wren doesn't wait for a response. She's no longer tense or nervous. She's strong and decisive and pulls me along behind her as she hurries after the Aquarius moons.

"Lee." Celeste's voice is so light that I could have dreamed it, but I look back anyway. Even if she hadn't spoken, she also hadn't finished. I can't leave like that. It's not the first impression I want to make.

"Next time . . ." Her lips barely move, her voice floating to me through the windless night. "Follow the rules and do as *I* say."

SEVEN

Wren

My mind wanted to explode when Celeste walked straight over to me. Okay, I know she's Queen of the Lunar Council or whatever and probably the most gorgeous woman I've ever seen in the real, but the closer she got to me the more I wanted to run. What is it about her eyes? Unlike the rest of her they look old, like a quarry filled with water. One of those that's so deep you can't see the bottom and you just know all sorts of stuff is hidden under the surface.

Pulling Lee along with me as we hurry to catch up with the other Aquarius moons trailing after the Air Elemental, I can still feel Celeste's eyes following me.

"Is she looking at me?" I whisper to Lee.

"Who? Celeste?"

"Yes, Celeste. The Queen of the Lunar Council." I peek over my shoulder at her and she *is* staring after me.

Lee snorts a laugh. "Wren, she's the *leader* of the Lunar Council. It's her job to be sure we're all settled in."

I mostly agree with Lee, but that doesn't mean I'm not getting some weird vibes from Queen Celeste. She petted my hair, which is so not cool. And come on. How old is she really? Before Sam went with the other Taurus kids she'd told me her dad's had a crush on Celeste since his summer here and that was around forty years ago. But Queen Celeste looks like she's in her twenties. What's up with that? One side-glance at Lee's face tells me this isn't the time to talk about her, though. We hurry and catch the others, rushing along a cobblestone sidewalk that winds through shadowy courtyards that look undersea and magickal in the puddles of light cast by the moon-colored globes.

Just as we reach our group they stop in front of a big brick building lit from within by warm golden light. It's built in the same castle-like Gothic style as the main campus building with elaborate stone arches decorating the windows and wide front door.

The Elemental pauses over—*yes, over*—the yellow-painted door of Aquarius Hall. The thing hovers above the entrance, bends, and touches it with a long, skeletal finger tipped with a neon-yellow claw. The door opens with the sound of a gust of wind. When no one moves, the Elemental floats down to stand (even though I can't make out feet or legs or really anything but yellow eyes inside the cowled hood) beside the door. The Elemental points inside the hall, and its black cloak parts to reveal a matte yellow body, churning like fog. We move together, all pushing forward, and enter the building almost as one.

I freeze inside the door and gasp aloud—like the full-out *gasp!* Elizabeth Bennet would give if Mr. Darcy showed up *unannounced* for afternoon tea. The foyer is amazing. The floor is cream marble veined with golden yellow. There are marble columns that separate big rooms on our left and right. One room is a mini library, and by *mini* I don't mean "little" unless you compare it to an actual city library. Gleaming wooden floor-to-ceiling bookshelves cover every inch of wall space that isn't taken up by windows. There are lots of comfortable chairs in the room—some solitary and others clustered around squatty tables.

The room on the left has several flat-screen TVs with big velvet sectionals grouped around them. The TVs are all sitting on entertainment centers that have DVD players tucked into them. *DVD players!*

"Did we get transported back to the 1990s?" I whisper to Lee.

Lee does not care about the time warp because he's focusing on brightly colored boxes that blaze names like SPACE INVADERS, MS. PAC-MAN, and DONKEY KONG. "Wren! They have vintage arcade games! And a foosball table! I'm so going to beat you."

"There's a big kitchen back here!" shouts a guy whose hair is cut into a mullet. Seriously. A mullet. (That can't really be coming back, can it?) "And it's filled with snacks and soda and stuff."

"Hey! Up here, everyone!" a girl calls from the top of the wide marble stairway that curves up to the second-story mezzanine. "The doors to the rooms have our names on them!"

My mouth feels dry because I know my name isn't going to be anywhere, but I remain attached to Lee's side and we head for the stairs.

There's a *whoosh* and my hair lifts around me. I smell Pacific Northwest fog—the kind that brings with it reminders of the forest and just a hint of the ocean—and the Air Elemental is circling Lee and me, cutting us off from the others who are already upstairs.

It keeps circling us, getting closer with each revolution, *and then it pauses right in front of me, bends its tall creepy body, and smells me!* Seriously. I can only see its neon-yellow eyes within the dark, cowl-like hood, but I can hear it sniffing.

"*Elegida!*" It hisses the word, circles us once more, and then flies right through the closed front door.

I look up at Lee. "What. The. Hell?"

His eyes are wide and he runs a hand over his face as if to wipe away his thoughts. "I have no idea. Did it speak Spanish? Was it sniffing us?"

"I don't know. I took French." I stare at the door the thing just flew through. *Me,* is what I want to say. *It was sniffing me.* But it all happened so fast that I can't be sure, though in a way it makes sense. The little yellow mini tornado hadn't appeared over my head like it had above all the other Aquarius moons. I don't belong. Maybe *elegida* means "fraud." *I need to ask Sam.*

"Hey." Lee pulls my attention back to him. "It's going to be okay. This is new for everyone. Come on. Let's find our rooms."

I walk beside Lee as he leads me to the left. The mezzanine is a big rectangle periodically dotted with tall wooden doors. A wide balcony with a waist-high marble railing frames the mezzanine. The flat top of the railing is deco-rated with long planters filled with vines that cascade over the edge. Sweet-smelling yellow flowers perfume the air with honeysuckle, making my nose itch. A huge chande-lier hangs from the center of the domed ceiling, dangling down to our eye level and casting spots of diamond light against the polished wood paneling.

For a moment I fantasize that I'm caught in one of the seasons of *Bridgerton* and am trying to figure out if that's a good or bad omen when Lee stops in front of a door so abruptly that I bump into him.

"Sorry," I mutter, and then look up to see him pointing to a wood plaque that has LELAND YOUNG written in glow-ing neon yellow.

"My room!" He grins down at me, sees my expression, then clears his throat. "Um, okay. Don't worry. We'll find your room, too."

We walk the length of the left side of the mezzanine and then retrace our path and head to the right side, dodging excited students squealing and opening doors. I stare at the doors as we pass and each name that isn't mine. We approach the last door. The plaque is empty. I turn my gaze to the floor as I fight the urge to either burst into tears or run down the wide, elegant stairs, rush out of the huge, stately hall, and flee back to the little ferry that brought us here when Lee laughs softly.

"Wren, look."

My gaze lifts in time to see the N of WREN appear as my name glows neon yellow. I raise my hand and hesitantly touch the newly formed letters that spell WREN NIGHTIN-GALE. They're cold under my fingers. "This is my room,"

I say softly. Then I draw in a big breath like I'm going to step into the always cold Pacific Ocean, take the crystal doorknob in my hand, and turn it.

The door opens silently into a pretty little room. I step in with Lee close behind me and stare at what will be my home for the next three months.

"Hey, this is way better than a normal dorm room," says Lee.

He is definitely right. I don't have lots of experience with college dorms, but my uncles did take me to tour a few university campuses before I decided to stay in Fern Valley, live at home, and take business classes at the local community college while continuing to run our bookstore. And this *suite* makes the dorms we toured look like prison cells in comparison.

There's a four-poster bed in the center of the room, a big wooden dresser, an armoire (*An armoire!* Be still, my Regency romance–loving heart), and a highly polished wood writing desk. A door opens to a modest bathroom with one of those clawfoot tubs that have a circular curtain so it can double as a shower.

"We don't have to share a big community bathroom?" I look at Lee. "You didn't tell me how fancy this place is."

"Wren, I had no clue until now, but it is definitely not going to be a hardship to stay in a place like this all summer—even without the internet."

I open my mouth to tell him he's blaspheming when a black speaker in the ceiling over the door crackles and Dean Rottingham's voice, sounding tinny, announces, "*All students to the dining room in Moon Hall, the main campus building, please. As I said in my introduction, you will have one hour for dinner and then another hour to settle in before lights out.*"

Doors open and close and we are an excited, whispering stream flowing down the marble stairway and out the front door where we pause, all with the same confusion stamped on our faces, until the Air Elemental returns, beckons with one cadaverous finger, and then leads us back through winding, moonlit sidewalks to the main campus building. We follow the crowd inside. There's little time to gawk, though I really want to. Moon Hall is all arched ceilings and carved wood and marble and chandeliers. I mean, it's *really nice*.

All four Elementals congregate just inside the building. Together they point brightly colored bony fingers straight down the wide front hall to open double wooden doors through which I glimpse a bunch of wooden tables, and then they whirl around us before they disappear. I swear the Air Elemental whirled extra close to me, causing me to freeze. I just stand there, hearing *elegida* echoing in my mind.

Lee doesn't pull on my hand or tell me to hurry up. He stands beside me like we have lots of time. That's one of the things I first loved about Lee—his calmness. I'll admit to sometimes having a penchant for drama. Lee gets it. He knows it's part of my dislike of change. When I run hot, like an almost-exploding star, Lee is the night sky—deep and soothing and always there. I mentally shake myself and look up at him.

"Thanks. We can go in now."

We're the last students to enter the dining room. Lee and I hesitate, and then Sam's flailing hand catches our attention and we make our way to her table. On it, like the rest of the tables, is a big platter of sandwiches, a bowl of salad, a bowl of chips, and a pitcher of ice water. Lee and I sit across from Sam.

"Hi, you two. Oh, hey, Ruby!" Sam waves her over and Ruby sits across from us, nodding hello.

"Okay, are the dorms cool or what?" Sam gushes as she scoops a couple of sandwich triangles and a pile of chips onto her plate. "I mean, my parents said the campus is nice, but we don't even have to share bathrooms! That's better than what I have at home."

Sam's enthusiasm instantly makes me feel better, and I grin at her. "I have an armoire. It makes me feel like a proper lady."

Ruby's hand stops mid–sandwich grab. "Do you want to be a proper lady?"

"No!" Lee and I say together, and then we laugh. I shake my head and continue. "No way. I just like pretending that being a Regency lady wasn't actually restrictive and repressive."

"She really just likes the clothes and the tea," Sam says around a mouthful of sandwich.

"And all the cookies that they call biscuits," I add.

"And the romance," Lee says, bumping my shoulder with his.

Ruby nods. "I get it. I like to pretend that I'm a Shogun for an ancient Japanese emperor, when the sad truth is because of my birth biology I wouldn't have been allowed to cut off anyone's head or even protect my emperor at all."

"Well, I think she'd be an excellent Shogun," says Sam. "Don't you, Wren?"

"*They,*" Ruby states. "I was born in this body, but that's not how I identify."

Sam stiffens. "I shouldn't have assumed."

"None of us should have," I say.

A burst of obnoxious laughter draws our attention to

a table closer to the center of the room. I look up in time to see a gangly guy slip on a sandwich and fall. I am not surprised to see the redhead who tripped Sam leading the laughter.

"What a douchebag," I mutter.

Across from me Ruby sighs and starts to stand, but before they can get to their feet another redhead pushes past the laughing table, helps the guy to his feet, and glares at the douchebag.

"Oh, chill," says the douche. "It's just a joke, big sis."

Big sis?

She shakes her head and turns her back on the table and as she does her eyes find us. I see her gaze go to Sam and immediately she starts toward us. We're staring at her, though not in a mean way, when she stops beside Sam. She's gorgeous—off the charts pretty. Her eyes are true green, like spring moss after the rain. Her hair is an amazing shade of red, light and long and wavy. Freckles dot the bridge of her nose and tops of her attractively flushed cheeks. The jeans and tight, cropped tee that proclaims WILD FEMINIST in black block letters show off her voluptuous curves.

She clears her throat. "Hi, um, I'm Lily Weatherford and that jerk"—without looking she points her thumb back over her shoulder at the table of obnoxious guys—"is my twin brother, Luke." Lily looks down and smiles hesitantly at Sam. "He won't apologize for tripping you earlier, so I will. I'm sorry my brother is an ass."

Sam's grin blazes. "I'm Sam and this is Ruby, Wren, and Lee." Sam points at each of us in turn. "Hey, you don't need to apologize. It's not your fault he's emotionally lacking."

Lily nods. "Emotionally lacking. That's a good way to

put it." Then she turns her attention to Ruby. "I saw you toss Luke onto his ass. Good job."

"Domo."

Lily's smooth forehead wrinkles. "Domo?"

"Means 'thanks' in Japanese," says Sam. "Want to sit with us? There's plenty of room." Sam shifts over so Lily can slide in between her and Ruby.

Then Lily turns those amazing green eyes on Lee. "Oh, hey! I saw you earlier."

"Yeah!" The word bursts from Lee. "I didn't realize who you were. I've only seen you in pictures. I, um, know your brother. Well, sort of," he adds hastily when I send him a shocked look. "My parents know his parents. Who are also your parents." Lee swallows and finishes, "I didn't know he had a twin sister, but that's cool." I watch his brown cheeks flush mauve. He grabs his glass of water and guzzles it like he's trying to put out the fire in his face, and my stomach tightens with something unfamiliar—something sticky and cloying and uncomfortable. *Jealousy? Seriously? He's my best friend (besides Sam). I'm not supposed to be jealous of other women, even if they are ridiculously beautiful.*

Lily smiles like Lee didn't just babble awkwardly. "Nice to meet you." As Lily's gaze meets mine I feel my cheeks flushing, too. "Hi, um, Wren, right?" she says.

"Yes." I nod and, using the social skills from my Regency repertoire, lift the plate of sandwiches and offer it to her. "Sandwich?"

"Oh, yeah, thanks. I'm starving." Lily snags three sandwich triangles and a big handful of chips. "So, I'm a Leo moon. What are you guys?" Before anyone can answer she grins at Ruby. "I already know you're a badass Scorpio."

Ruby's lips quirk up. "Indeed."

"I'm a Taurus," says Sam.

"I'm not surprised." Lily picks up a chip, pops it into her mouth, and looks expectantly at Lee and me.

"Aquarius." Lee pitches his voice so that it's deep and rich and I have to cross my legs to keep from kicking him.

"I'm with Lee in Aquarius Hall," is the only thing I can think to say, and I follow up quickly with, "So, is Leo Hall like a gorgeous manor house, too?"

"Well, it's not as amazing as Pemberley, but it's shockingly beautiful." She smiles at me and I can't help but be glad that there's a piece of lettuce stuck in between her front teeth because *of course she knows what Pemberley is— she's perfect.* Then her grin takes in the whole table. "Please tell me that I'm not the only one whose parents did not prepare her for all of this."

Ruby shrugs. "Mine just said *katsu.*"

"Ooh, wait, I think I know what that means. 'Win'?" Sam looks around Lily to Ruby, who gives her a small smile and nods once.

"Win what?" I ask.

"I don't mean this in any kind of a bitchy way, but I'm really glad your parents didn't fill you in, either," Lily tells me with another beautiful smile.

I feel my face getting hot. There's no protocol for how to tell new friends that I don't have parents because they're dead. It's been five years since the car accident, but it's not something that gets any easier. Thankfully, Sam saves me.

"My parents admitted they told me too much, but only because I bothered them incessantly about it." She leans in and drops her voice so we all have to lean forward and practically hold our breath to hear her. "I knew about how fancy everything is. My mom said it's because this place is so old and also the Lunar Council believes if they surround us with all this classy stuff we'll behave better." She takes a quick drink of her water. "Jury's still out on that, though. But they did tell me a bunch about the Trials."

"Trials?" I squeak. *Lee never said anything about us being on trial!*

"Don't worry." Sam pats my hand. "Trials as in tests, not as in evidence given before a judge."

"My dad only told me to come back like him. A winner," says Lee.

I look at Lee like he's from another planet.

Ruby speaks up. "Mine did tell me it is a competition that lasts all summer."

"Yeah," says Sam. "So, there are three Trials—one each month. They're difficult and dangerous, but important because they help us learn to control our powers."

"And because there will be a winner at the end of the summer," says Ruby.

"My parents said they expect us—Luke and me—to work as a team and do well." Lily snorts, which is a delicate sound. *How can a snort be delicate?* "But not hardly. I'm eighteen. So is Luke. I'm not his keeper anymore. I'm not working with that jerk. I'm competing against him."

I watch Lily's expression harden. She really doesn't like her brother. Not that I blame her. I get a sudden thought and ask, "Is there a prize?"

"Respect," says Ruby.

"My dad said the winner gets a prize, but no matter how much I bugged him he wouldn't tell me what it is," says Sam.

"The winner of the Trials gets the attention of the Lunar Council. They personally take an interest in the student and their future." Lee's voice takes on that new edge I think of as his *gotta excel at everything* tone. Lee is fun and funny, loves poetry, and I even suspect he likes my obsession with lords and ladies and such. But over the past two years, Lee has become highly driven to succeed. In everything. That's not a bad thing, but it's definitely a new Lee thing.

"When do the Trials start, and how do I—" I'm interrupted by the lights flashing on and off in the dining room. From a loudspeaker Dean Rottingham's tinny voice blares.

"Dinner has concluded. All students will now return to their halls. Your luggage has been delivered. You have an hour to settle in before lights out. Tomorrow breakfast is at oh seven hundred sharp with lectures and exercises beginning at oh eight hundred. Again, welcome to Moon Isle and the beginning of your future."

EIGHT

Wren

After Lee says good night and goes to his room, I unpack my bags and take a bath. I put on my favorite pj's (an oversized T-shirt that has a picture of a fat potato and a fat Frenchie on the front with an equal sign between the two of them) and curl up under the thick down comforter, close my eyes, and try to sleep.

The bed is soft. The sheets smell like lavender. The pillows are down filled and perfect. The dean said breakfast was at 0700 and that is less than—I glance at the alarm clock on the bedside table—seven hours away.

I yawn, squeeze my eyes closed again, and flop over on my side facing the big leaded window. The silver light of the almost-full moon paints mercury shadows against my closed eyelids. I can't believe I'm here. I'm on Moon Isle attending the Academia de la Luna. I'm Moonstruck!

Well, I was Moonstruck. Once.

What does that mean? Will it happen again? I did feel the brush of the magick as we crossed the strange barrier that cloaks Moon Isle, and until last night I'd never felt so much as even a tiny spark of magick. But does that mean I'll actually develop a magickal ability? It just seems so incredible, so outrageous. I've spent my entire life knowing, *knowing* I'm a Mundane in a world where there actually are Magicks, and I've been okay with that. Better than okay with it. I'd planned my life. I'd been content—even happy.

But what am I now? I'm happy that I'm here with Lee and Sam, but I can't say I'm content. There are too many unknowns. What kind of magick do I have? I was definitely Moonstruck last night. Lee has the picture that proves it. But what if my magick just fades away? Remembering the amazing power that I'd felt for that brief, shining moment sends a delicious shiver through my body and I allow my eyes to open a little. Just enough to see the slim line of moonlight that has escaped through the crack between the heavy drapes I thought I'd closed.

I shiver again.

I press my eyelids closed. *Go to sleep. Go to sleep. Go to sleep.* I try counting sheep, but they turn into wooly Grace Kellys, which just makes me miss home.

Home . . . And I realize that I haven't been this far from home without Uncle Brad or Uncle Joel with me since I came to live with them that terrible day five years ago. I'll bet they're awake, too. I'll bet they're missing me and worried and—

"No. That's not helping." I fling off the down comforter, stomp to the armoire, and pull on a pair of sweatpants before I slide on my shoes. "Chamomile tea. As Uncle Joel would say, a hot mug of herbal tea can help everything from a broken heart to a sleepless night," I mutter to myself before I open the heavy door to my room and peer down the hallway. I see no one. I step out into the hall and pause, listening intently, but I don't hear anything—not even muffled voices behind the closed doors.

As I head to the wide staircase I consider going to Lee's room to see if he wants to come with me to check out the kitchen, but I decide against it. What if Lee's asleep? It's already ridiculously late. I'll probably be a zombie tomorrow. No point in making Lee one, too.

I pad quickly down the stairs. The enormous chandelier has been dimmed, but that doesn't make it any less magnificent and I smile as Bridgerton comparisons fill my mind. I do love me some opulence. My feet seem lighter and I hop down the final stairs, but before I turn to head to the rear of Aquarius Hall and the kitchen, the glimmer of silver light catches my eyes. Its luminescence pulls me forward and I find myself walking through the library, for once ignoring the stacks filled with books as She draws me to the beveled glass. There are no other lights in the large room, and the silver turns the thick leaded windows to jewels.

I step within the beam of moonlight and feel Her touch. It's not like last night. There's no zap of heat and power. I don't levitate, but I do feel something. It's subtle, like silk slipping across naked skin. I've stood in the moonlight before. Lots of times. I've often appreciated the watery beauty of the moon. But I've never felt it. Never known Her touch until now. I lift my arms as if to cup the illusive white light, and for an instant I swear my skin glistens. Like the windows I, too, have been transformed.

I want this. The thought blazes through my mind with unexpected ferocity. *I want to be Moonstruck! I want to wield moon magick!*

I almost shout with astonishment and press my hand to my mouth. Is this really happening? Am I the same girl who has insisted for her entire life that she didn't need—didn't even want magick? I let my hand fall from my mouth. I turn it, my palm cupping the moonlight that glistens and winks enigmatically. No, I'm not the same girl. I'm not a Mundane anymore. I'm Moonstruck.

A shadow obscures the moonlight and I glance up, expecting to see cotton candy clouds floating across the night sky, but instead my breath leaves me in a rush as I stare into two glowing yellow orbs within a dark cowl. The Air Elemental hovers before me on the other side of the window. It's so close that if the glass didn't separate us I could reach out and touch it.

"*Elegida* . . ." The word shivers through the air between us, penetrating first the glass and then my soul.

My feet move without me telling them to. I lurch backward so quickly that I crash into one of the comfy chairs grouped throughout the large room. I glance away from the window long enough to navigate my way past it and when I look back again the Elemental is gone.

I definitely do not like the I'm-being-watched feeling that crawls up my spine as I hurry from the library and head to the rear of the hall toward the kitchen. What the hell is going on with that Elemental? I have got to remember to ask Sam what that word, *elegida,* means. Watch, it'll probably mean something like "*go to sleep.*"

The guy with the mullet had been right. The kitchen has lots of snacks and all kinds of drinks—everything from bottled water and cans of soda to a big pitcher of freshly squeezed lemonade. I shake off the creepy feeling the Elemental gave me and start opening cabinets as I look for tea and mugs, which are easy to find in the tidy kitchen. I even find a couple of different kinds of honey. The teapot is sitting on the stove, just like the pot we have at home—and this time remembering home makes me smile, though I do wish Grace Kelly were here. Her snores would definitely help me sleep, even though she's like a miniature furnace when she curls up against my back.

I do a little dance and softly sing what Uncle Joel and I call "The Grace Kelly Song" as I put a tea bag in a mug, add a big dollop of honey, and wait for the pot to boil (trying not to watch it because you know what they say about watched pots boiling). "Grace Kelly so smelly she has jelly in her belly—"

"And vermicelli from the deli, Grace Kelly sooooo smelly!"

Lee's deep voice has me whirling around with my fists raised (as if I've ever actually punched someone—which I have not). "Lee! You scared the crap out of me!"

Lee grins and makes a show of looking at the floor behind me. "Lies. I see no poo!"

I shake my head. "Gross. It's a figure of speech." Then I smile back at him. "I can't believe you remember 'The Grace Kelly Song.'"

Lee makes a *thwack!* sound and pretends to clutch an arrow shot into his heart. "You wound me, my lady. How could I forget The Duchess of Smoochington's song?"

My smile widens as I curtsey. "My lord! Never! Never

would I wound you. I might have the vapors just thinking of it!" Lee and I laugh together. One of the things I've always loved about him is how easily he and I can slip into our own world together. Most guys act like they're too cool to play—to pretend. Not Lee. Whether it's being the lord to my lady or singing songs to my dog, he does so with an open, unselfconscious joy that is as rare as it is wonderful. "Hey, why are you awake?" I ask.

"Why are you awake?" he counters.

The teapot whistles musically, telling me the water is ready. "Want some tea?" I ask as I pour the steaming water into my mug.

"Tea? As in caffeine? Like you'll ever sleep tonight?"

I look over my shoulder at him. "Not caffeine. Herbal. Chamomile." I say it in my fake British accent with a long *I*. "It'll make you sleepy."

"Oh. Then yeah. I'll have some. Maybe it'll help." Lee sits at the center island on one of the half dozen tall barstools.

I get a mug for Lee and fix his tea and then sit beside him. It's still a little weird that he's actually right next to me versus being on the other side of the country. He's changed, and not just physically. He seems older. Okay, yes, he is two years older, but that's not what I mean. Before, he was a boy. Pretty much carefree. And then Maya died. His family moved. So by *older* I guess I mean that there are more layers to him and some of those layers are heavy. We don't say anything at first. The spoons clink against our mugs as we swirl the honey and chamomile together. Finally Lee sighs and I look up at him. "Is it Maya?" I ask softly.

Lee's flinch at her name is so slight I almost don't notice it. Almost.

He sighs again. "Yes. No. It's a lot of things." His brown eyes meet mine. "What's keeping you up? Do you still want to leave? You can tell me. I won't say anything."

I blow across my tea and then sip it. I'm not sure why I'm stalling. I'm not sure why I don't want to tell Lee what I've realized tonight. I want to be Moonstruck. I want to feel that power again—to even excel at wielding it. Maybe I can't say it out loud yet because if I do and then I never manifest any more magick it will be too sad, too disappointing, too heartbreaking for me to bear.

"I'm okay with being here." I wave my hand dismissively. "I was just having a hard time shutting off my brain, that's all." I take another sip of tea. "Why can't you sleep?" Lee doesn't say anything for so long that I think maybe he won't tell me. Maybe we've been apart too long. Maybe he doesn't feel safe opening up to me anymore, and the thought of that makes me incredibly sad. I reach over and rest my hand on his arm. "It's me, Lee. You can tell me anything, remember?"

He'd been staring into his mug of sunshine-yellow tea, but his gaze lifts to mine. "Yeah, I think you're the only one." Lee draws a deep breath.

NINE

Lee

I stare back down at my tea, all too aware of Wren's palm on my arm. My hands engulf the warm mug, steam gently rising from the honey-scented liquid to dance in the moonlight like flames. For the past two years, she's been the only person I can be honest with. But I haven't been. I've been so busy trying to hold my family together and fill shoes that were never meant for me that I've buried who I am under a mound of responsibility. But there's something about the moonlight filtering in through the beveled windows and the way Wren is here right now even before I knew I needed her that has my heart aching to be free.

"When I was younger, my parents got me a fidget spinner," I say, slowly turning the mug between my hands. "I had really bad anxiety as a kid and used to get overwhelmed when we'd go places—events, the grocery store, anywhere, really. There was even this one time when Maya and I flew private to Manhattan to go shopping with our mother for some trip. . . ."

The memory comes to life behind my eyes, and I pause, savoring this remembered moment with my sister. She'd cut the crust off the PB&J the attendant had given me, made it into perfect triangles, and added fresh strawberry slices in between the pieces of bread—my favorite—before I'd even gotten the straw into my juice box.

"Back to school shopping," I correct myself, smiling at the way Maya had squealed with glee when our parents said she could buy her new outfits straight from Fifth Avenue. "Maya insisted I come, too, and I was fine until we got to the first store. There were so many people, and I panicked." My forearms tense, and Wren slides her thumb back and forth across my skin. "I hid behind a rack of fur coats. It was dark and quiet and warm. I fell asleep. I woke up a couple of hours later. There were cops and security, and Maya was crying. My mother, she . . . I think she was mad that I ruined the trip. We went straight back to the hangar after that. Maya didn't want to shop anymore." My tea ripples as I continue to spin the mug, yellow flowers loosed from the tea bag trembling against the surface. "She held my hand the entire flight home."

"Lee, I had no idea." Both of Wren's hands are on my arms now as if she can reach into the past to my younger self.

"I shouldn't really be complaining," I say past the lump

in my throat. "We were on a private jet flying across the country to go on a shopping trip. Rich-people problems, am I right?" My laugh is brittle and clatters through the room like bones.

Wren shrugs and swirls her spoon in her tea. "I mean, you've always been so outgoing and relaxed."

"Yeah." I clear my throat and lean back in my chair. "I got older and realized that learning to do well in a crowd was less uncomfortable than what I dealt with at home if I didn't."

Next to me, Wren is still, inviting, a soft place to land, and I continue to fall.

"Not long after the whole shopping disaster, my father got me a fidget spinner. He said it would help me focus on myself. Keep your body calm when your mind isn't," I say, my voice, a nearly identical match to my father's deep timbre. "I was so happy. For the first time, I thought he saw me. I thought he wanted to help." I glance down at my hands. Heat pricks my eyes, and I swallow my tears. "I got in trouble for not using it enough. For not improving my finger dexterity. It wasn't a gift for me, to help me. It was for them. For the Young family. For the dynasty, the cause, the ego of it all.

"From then on, I cared as much about the Young family as they cared about me. They had Maya, and she wanted everything they wanted and more. I became the spare, the second son, but now . . ."

"She's gone."

I nod. "And I have spent the past two years learning everything she'd learned in eighteen." I lean forward. "I want this, Wren. I want to win the Trials, earn a spot on the Lunar Council, and not for me, not for Titan or my parents or our family name. I want it for Maya."

The teakettle lets out a shrill whistle, and Wren flinches before unfolding her crossed legs and rushing to turn off the stove. The burner clicks off, and she grabs the handle of the teakettle.

"Ouch!" The kettle clatters against the metal stove grate as Wren snatches her hand back and presses her finger to her mouth.

"You okay?" I ask, abandoning my untouched tea to join her.

"I wasn't paying attention and grabbed the side of the kettle." She winces and blows on the tip of her index finger. "Think they have any Neosporin around here? What am I saying? They probably have a whole fancy hospital—" She stops as I take her hand and angle it toward the moonlight.

The pad of her finger is pink and swollen, a blister forming where the hot metal made contact.

My left hand's by my side, my fingers moving instinctually, plucking the chords of magick that vibrate within my chest as I focus my intention on healing the only person left on this earth who truly knows me.

Wren's lips part with a gentle gasp that blows warm against my hand cradling hers, and we both watch her puckered skin smooth and the angry color vanish.

Her gaze meets mine, her blue eyes twinkling in the rays of silver light that streak her face. "How did you . . ." A swallow ripples down her throat, and her lips move noiselessly, searching for words.

"Like I said, it's been a long couple years."

TEN

Wren

My alarm goes off way too soon, though I'm not sorry that Lee and I talked so late. I'm so glad there's not a country between us anymore that I do not care that my eyes feel sandpapery, and Aquarius Hall is empty and silent as I rush down the stairs and then jog along the cobblestone path that leads to the big circled courtyard and finally Moon Hall.

The cafeteria is already more than half-empty. I catch a glimpse of Lee's broad back walking out one of the rear doors. Luke, who I've decided to think of as the evil twin to Lily's good twin energy, is beside him, so I don't try to catch up with him.

"Wren! Here!"

Sam calls to me and I'm super relieved to hurry to her table. She slides a plate that has a greasy egg sandwich on it over to me. "Eat. Fast. And drink." She pours me some semi-warm but very strong English breakfast tea from a pot in the center of the otherwise abandoned table that's littered with dirty dishes.

"Thanks," I say around a mouthful of egg.

"No biggie. Lee said you two were up late talking, so I saved you some breakfast. If you eat fast enough, we can still make the Intro to Moon Isle lecture," she says.

In under ten minutes I bolt my food, gulp the lukewarm tea, and then wipe my mouth. "Ready."

Sam hooks her arm through mine and practically drags me from the deserted cafeteria. Moon Hall is huge, but Sam seems to know where she's going. I wish I had time to gawk at the gorgeous artwork and chandeliers that decorate the wide halls, but they blur as we race to an arched wooden door that's propped open and duck inside to sit in the back row seconds before a tall woman closes it. She strides up the center row of the big room that's set up like one of the lecture classrooms I visited when my uncles and I checked out college campuses last year. She climbs the stairs to the stagelike area, steps behind the podium, and smooths back her ash-blond hair. Her smile is friendly and even from the back row I can see how blue her eyes are.

"Good morning. I am Professor Scherer, a Taurus moon. Welcome to your first lecture at the Academia de la Luna, Intro to Moon Isle." Her smile widens as her eyes scan the mostly full room. "I'm glad to see so many of you here. Though some of you will probably know most of the information I'm going to give you today, a refresher is always wise, especially as the outcome of the next three months will set you on the path you will follow for the rest of your lives. So take notes and ask questions."

As I realize what Professor Scherer has just said I lean close to Sam and whisper, "You don't have to stay with me. You already know all this stuff."

Sam whispers back, "The professor is right. A refresher is always a good idea. . . ." She pauses and glances around the room. Her look turns smug. "Just like I thought. There's not one other Taurus moon in here."

"Because Taurus moons already know all this introductory stuff," I say.

Sam waggles her eyebrows and says, "Hubris is not my thing." Then she jerks her chin back at the professor and tells me, "Sssh, Professor Scherer is cool. She greeted us in Taurus Hall last night."

I settle in to listen and sigh as I remember that I forgot to grab anything to take notes with, but Sam grins at me and mouths, *I've got you,* as she hands me a pad of paper and a pencil she takes out of the backpack she's shrugged to the floor.

"Moon Isle is the site of the very first Academia de la Luna, founded in 1785," the professor is saying. "At one time it was our only academy, and because of the Elementals who guard the isle, it is still our most powerful campus, though we have cloaked schools worldwide."

A girl in the front row raises her hand. Professor Scherer nods and the girl clears her throat before she asks, "Um, don't the other schools also have Elementals?"

"Good question. No, they do not. Early in 1785 a Spanish ship sank near this island. All hands should have died, but for reasons we still do not fully understand the Elementals stepped in. They saved a small group from the ship. Among them was a lovely young Spanish aristocrat, Selene Perez. The Elementals took particular interest in her. Again, we don't know exactly why.

"What we do know is that the ancient Elementals were even more volatile than they are now. They wanted stability, more control over themselves, like the physical stability humans have. And the shipwrecked humans, especially Selene, wanted the ability to wield magick like the Elementals manifested. So the Elementals struck a deal with Selene. They would draw down the moon and channel its magick into four corresponding moon signs. These signs directly relate to the four elements, air, fire, water, and earth. Those special humans born under one of the four lunar signs were gifted powers and became Moonstruck. In exchange, humans swore to use some of that power to stabilize the Elementals, cloak this island, and protect them." Professor Scherer makes a little flourish with her hand. "And voila! The Moonstruck were born. Though there are Magicks all over the world, we remain fewer in number than Mundanes. The only Academia de la Luna with Elementals is here, which is also why the Lunar Council is here and why our leader, Celeste, never leaves the isle."

I feel a little jolt of surprise and elbow Sam. "Queen Celeste never leaves?"

Sam shrugs. "Not that big of a deal. It's not like she can't leave when she retires."

Another hand goes up and a student asks, "But if we're the only campus with Elementals, how do students at the other academies fully manifest their powers?"

"The Elementals only facilitated the transfer of lunar power for the first Moonstruck. Once the connection was

98 / P. C. CAST & KRISTIN CAST

set it became all about the moon and the four signs She blessed with power—one for each element to honor their role in the magickal exchange.

"Each academy has a team of powerful professors, gifted in wielding their magick. These professors create a . . ." The professor pauses, considering. "Let's call it a dome of power that covers its campus. The dome focuses moon magick, serving the same function as does the Elemental power that fuels this island. The concentration of powerful Moonstruck magick is a catalyst that brings to maturity young Moonstruck abilities. But of course there's more to it than just creating a hub of magick. Moonstruck who are coming into their powers need to exercise them to make them grow. That's why each academy holds Trials and why it is so important for you to attend and to practice your powers consistently while you're here. What you attain during your three months at the academy will serve as the magickal foundation for the rest of your lives."

My hand goes up.

Professor Scherer points at me. "Yes? A question there from the back?"

"Yes, thanks." I speak up so my voice carries. "What happens if a student's powers don't manifest?"

"Except for very rare anomalies, that is impossible. Yes, there will be varying degrees of magickal success among our student population and some will simply be more powerfully gifted than others, but all are Moonstruck and all are valuable members of our community. Your question does bring up another important topic, though. Can anyone tell me how a Moonstruck knows she, he, or they have awakened all their powers?"

Predictably, Sam's hand shoots up.

Professor Scherer smiles. "I see we do have another Taurus moon with us today." A few students laugh. "Yes, Sam. What's the answer?"

"Each Moonstruck will know when their powers have fully manifested because they will plateau. It's why the Trials are so important. Usually, the students who score the highest and advance through all three Trials have powers that are still growing and need more exercises to finish maturing," says Sam.

Professor Scherer nods. "Exactly."

A hand in the middle of the room rises and the professor calls on the student, whose voice is a little shaky as he asks, "S-so, everyone who doesn't make it to the third T-trial will only have weak powers?"

"Let's not call them weak," says Professor Scherer as she brushes a hunk of blond hair back from her face. "There are a lot of factors that play into moon magick. The temperament of each Moonstruck is important. For instance, Leo moons tend to find careers that are very public, as their abilities can calm and influence crowds. But what if a Leo moon is an introvert and so painfully shy that just the idea of being around crowds of people makes him uncomfortable? It wouldn't matter if he had been gifted with great power because to wield it would make him miserable. That doesn't make him less than, does it?"

A general shaking of heads and muttering of *no*s rustles through the room.

"My best advice is not to worry about how much power you've been given," continues Professor Scherer. "And instead focus on the whole package, which means manifesting your power and considering how you might wield that power so that your life is as productive as it is personally satisfying.

"Now, let's go over some of the basic hand positions that help us channel our magick. Remember, you may alter these gestures to best suit your own dexterity, but attaining dexterity is the goal. I cannot emphasize enough how important it is that you attain enough hand coordination skill that the gestures and channeling become second nature to you and thus are easily hidden from Mundanes."

The girl in the front row who asked the first question raises her hand again. "Professor Scherer, I've heard that some Moonstrucks become so good at channeling that they don't even need to use hand gestures. Is that really true?"

"It absolutely is true. The leader of our Lunar Council is one such Moonstruck. It is something to which we should all aspire. So, let's go over some of the basic gestures. And remember, practice often while you're here. Moon Isle is the only place you can safely do so in public."

I only half pay attention to the rest of the lecture. I understand the hand gestures are important, but they're also basic. I remember watching my mom and dad practice at home, and even though I never had any magick at all, I used to like mimicking my parents. So, while my hands follow the movement exercises the professor takes us through, inside my mind, over and over again I hear my question and Professor Scherer's answer. *What happens if a student's powers don't manifest? ... Except for very rare anomalies, that's impossible.*

I have to force myself to take slow, deep breaths. Is that me? Am I impossible?

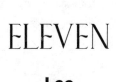

ELEVEN

Lee

"Dude, I'm telling you that I don't have to be a Leo to know the mechanics behind casting your 'special brand' of magick." I emphasize the phrase with air quotes as Luke crosses his arms over his chest.

"I get the distinct impression that you don't think my moon magick is as special as yours." He covers his heart with his hands as if he's been struck with an arrow. "I have to say, man, I'm wounded."

"You're *something* all right."

We're in the center of a stone-paved courtyard tucked behind the dorm halls and surrounded with statues of the four Elementals, sinister robes and all. Two clusters of other students are huddled throughout the wide court-yard, a trio of Scorpios who've challenged one another to a race that ends with depositing a giant boulder in front of their Elemental's statue, and a group of Taureans clustered together, discussing the magick only they can see.

I flex my fingers and hold out my hands, readying my-self to demonstrate the magickal signals in the same exag-gerated motions my father did when I first learned. "You have to get the basics down in order to channel your in-tent and make the signals more subtle. It's like breathing or sleeping—your body knows how it feels, how to do it without force, without thought."

"I'm not a complete virgin, Lee. I have cast before. And you don't have to go over the basics each time we train. Believe it or not, I do practice on my own." Luke points up to pines encircling the courtyard. "See those crows?"

I shrug. I can hear them more than see them, but I stay quiet as Luke lifts his hands and strums the air with a graceful sweep of his fingers. "You have been practicing," I acknowledge, my gaze resuming its search for the birds, magick crackling against my skin.

Out of the corner of my eye, I catch flashes of Luke's hands as they direct his magickal intention into the boughs of the swaying pines. With each motion, throaty *caws* sound until a murder of crows bursts from the trees, moving in sync with the precise flicks and twists of Luke's fingers. There's a surreal harmony to it, each bird soaring and dip-ping as Luke's hands dance in the air, fluttering like the wings of the murder above.

"Now take that magick that you feel in your hands and shrink it down," I instruct, miming working a ball of clay smaller and smaller until my palms almost touch.

Sweat glistens on Luke's pale white skin as he shakes his head. "It's too big."

"It's not," I say, stepping closer. "It only feels that way because that's how you're thinking about it. *You* are the magick. Your hands are the tools. What you feel, what we all feel when we cast, is just the moon's energy. It's always there. Even when we're not actively using our magick."

Luke's nostrils flare and his fingers tremble as he fights himself, his magick, the moon's power, and brings his hands closer together.

"Work *with* the magick," I remind him.

He grunts and releases a strangled breath as a rogue crow breaks away from the controlled group and dive-bombs the Taureans. One of the girls shrieks and rushes backward, batting the air above her head like it's swarming with bees.

Luke lets out a string of grunt-laden curses and widens his stance, trying to gain back control. But it's too late.

The Taurean has crashed into a Scorpio, distracted by the weight of the massive boulder he lifts overhead. With a startled gasp, he loses control of the boulder. It slams against the ground and rumbles like thunder over the cobblestones as it picks up speed.

Luke's lanky arms snap to his sides, and the crows shoot off like an explosion of buckshot as the boulder rolls toward the towering statue of the Leos' Elemental. It crashes into the stone pedestal, and for a heart-stopping second, everyone is motionless.

"It's fine. No harm, no foul," Luke breathes, clapping his hand against my back. "Hey, I'm pretty sure that's a pun."

Before I can answer, the statue begins to lean. We all follow it, each person in the courtyard listing to the side as if the movement is its own kind of magick. The Fire Elemental smacks into the stone, sending a plume of dust into the air and fragments of marble skittering across the courtyard.

"Shit," Luke and I say in unison as the sound of distant waves stirs the silence and the Scorpios' water symbol blazes neon blue over their heads.

It's 1:42 PM, but I swear I've been staring at the clock for ten whole minutes and the seconds hand has only managed to drop in agonizingly slow increments from 2 down to 6. Time ticks by so slowly I wouldn't be surprised if this two-hour lecture on career possibilities for Aquarius moons wasn't my first Trial growing and maturing my ability to regenerate and heal my body as I'm gradually worn down to nothing but raw nerves by this clock.

Tick. Tick. Tick. Tick.

I don't actually need to be here, but my father told me the importance of attending the Aquarius lectures to better know my people and the level of power they each possess.

Tick. Tick. Tick. Tick.

It's not good for me to keep glaring at the shiny glass clock face and golden hands glimmering in the low light like a cyclops's eye. I peel my gaze away and focus on the scarlet wallpaper. Coupled with the sleepy, campfire-like glow of the gilded sconces framing the rectangular blackboard, the room feels like a living thing. A heart contracting and relaxing in response to our breaths, our movements, our acknowledgment of Professor Turner as he informs the fifteen of us who've decided to attend this lecture about the numerous professions in which an Aquarius moon can excel.

I rest my elbow on the polished mahogany library table I share with one other student and drop my cheek against my fist before reminding myself that that's not what an attentive and engaged listener would do. It doesn't matter that I'm not the least bit interested. Like most things in my life, it's the front that's important—what everyone else sees.

Tick. Tick. Tick. Tick.

I flick my gaze above Professor Turner, whose cheeks are round with a smile as he delivers the punch line to another joke. People laugh, and I join in. Though Moonstruck are around the globe, our world is small. What I do here, how I appear to everyone around me, matters to the Young name and to Maya's memory.

Around me, everyone is flipping to another page in the worksheet handed out at the beginning of the lecture. I lean to my right, pretending to stretch, until I see which page Silas has his book open to. He glances at me, and I yawn, trying to sell the fact that I'm tired instead of simply not paying attention. Silas doesn't buy it. Instead, he frowns and turns in his chair until his back and the end of his long dark braid are to me.

I have to do a better job. I have to try harder. I have to channel my sister.

Quickly, I thumb through the pages until I catch up with the rest of the class. The instructor's deep, southern drawl swirls around the room, pouring like liquid into the chalk he uses to scrawl cursive letters on the blackboard, coating his brown fingers ashy white. It's not that I can't understand him or can't read the word he underlines twice. I could if I tried, but I have no patience for trying. Not when my thoughts are such a mess.

What if I plateau early? What if I don't make it past the second Trial or even the first?

Maya had not only made it past the first two Trials; she'd

maintained the top score. She would have won the third. I know it. So did Dean Rottingham. That's why he'd offered her an apprenticeship. She was destined for the council, destined for greatness. But now . . .

She's gone.

Wren's voice floats to the surface of my turbulent thoughts, a buoy I grab onto. Now, instead of thoughts of failure, of letting my sister down, of being the unworthy member of my family, I'm caught up in Wren, the way her bright blue eyes shone in the moonlight and her soft hand in mine.

I stare down at the printed pages on the desk. Text seems to lift from the paper, lingering in front of my eyes before bursting like bubbles, their residue sticky against my fingers. I pull my pen from my pocket and turn the packet sideways, words rushing out of me, calming my nerves like only two things in life can.

> *how funny to realize that love is not kind*
> *like learning home is not home*
> *air is not for breathing but for wearing tight around your*
>   *lungs*
> *it is a secret meant to bury*
> *this ravenous beast called love*
>
> *i will keep you safe*
> *hide away the secret, that once freed, will devour*
> *our friendship*
>
> *i will keep you safe*
> *feed it pieces of my heart*

until it is full
and I am numb

Silas nudges my shoulder, and I blink the poetic tunnel vision from my eyes. "Hey, man, the lecture's over."

I look around, and sure enough, we're the last two people in the room other than Professor Turner, who's busy organizing the contents of his briefcase.

"Oh." I scrub my hand down my cheek. "Thanks."

Silas grunts a response and leaves before we have to have any kind of real conversation. My chair slides noiselessly against the Oriental rug as I get to my feet, collecting my pen and papers before gliding out of the room in a haze of words and emotion.

I'm still in a poetic hangover when I leave Moon Hall's back entrance and plunge into the sun-drenched courtyard that stretches to the wooded area surrounding each moon sign's hall. I take a moment to get my bearings, dragging my gaze along the four paths that split off to each of the living quarters. My thoughts must be buffering, because I only now realize that the cobblestone circle that makes up the center of Crossroads Courtyard is slick with water. I rub my hand along the back of my neck. I'm not sure if this is weird or if I am.

"Not yet, but the Scorpios left for their Trial right after the Leos." I spin around to catch whoever's snippet of conversation I just overheard, but a couple of lectures must have gotten out at once, because there are too many people milling around the courtyard to know exactly who spoke.

My stomach growls, pulling my attention and focusing my thoughts. There's not another Aquarius lecture today, and I spent the morning practicing. I need to get more hours in, but I have to eat before I crash.

I scan the crowd, searching for Luke, but I see another familiar face instead.

I cup my free hand around my mouth and shout, "Ruby!"

They're across the courtyard, walking toward the stone pathway that leads to Scorpio Hall, head down and hands tucked into the pockets of the bloodred sweatshirt they wore last night.

"Ruby!" I yell again, but they don't look up.

I'm not sure if they can't hear me or just can't be bothered to slow down. Either way, I'm running across the courtyard, weaving around sculptures of moon phases and boxwoods shaped like the signs of the Elementals, and dodging groups of other students who aren't panic sprinting across the wide lawn.

"Ru—by." I catch up to them, but my lungs are burning, and I'm gulping down so much air that their name comes out as two separate words.

Their dark eyes flick in my direction, but they don't slow their pace even though I'm struggling.

"Your strides—" I take in another lungful of air and clear my throat. "They're really long."

Their wet shoes squelch, leaving behind hourglass-shaped outlines on the stone path as their narrow shoulders move beneath the red fabric. "That's why you ran all this way?"

My mouth twitches with a smile. Straight to business. I respect that. "You had your Trial this morning." I'm finally breathing normally, but I don't say more. I want Ruby to tell me any information they want without leading questions.

But Ruby only nods.

"Well . . ." I throw up my hand. I'm not annoyed as much as I am anxious. "What was it like?"

Another hike of their shoulders. "Does it matter?"

Does it matter? Are they serious?

"Whoever doesn't plateau and wins the third Trial is pretty much guaranteed a seat on the Lunar Council. It's basically how they choose their newest member."

Nothing matters more. I don't say that last part. I know other things do matter, and a lot of things can matter more than a place on the Lunar Council even if I can't think of any right now.

"I'm a Scorpio moon," Ruby says without looking at me. "You're an Aquarius. What I did in my Trial won't be close to what you do in yours."

"Yeah, but—" I dart in front of them and stand there like a pick. "Can we just stop for a second?"

Ruby crosses their arms over their chest and tilts their head to the side. "Lee, whatever answer or cheat code you're looking for, I don't have it."

I suck in another gulp of air, this time unable to breathe for a different set of reasons, and dig my fingers into my scalp. "I want to win, Ruby. I need to. More than I've needed anything."

Being on the council, leading our magickal world and the one beyond, is not only what I know my sister would have done; it's what I need to do to fix my family. We were never a perfect, loving, matching-outfits kind of movie family, but losing Maya has fractured us in a way only a success like this can mend.

Ruby's expression doesn't change, but I see a piece of them relax, unfurl as if they sense that this is something I've only shared once. And they'd be right.

"You have ink on your face."

My lungs unclench and a rush of air slips past my lips as I rub my cheek. Ruby shakes their head, the wide bridge of their nose wrinkling.

"I made it worse, didn't I?" I ask.

They pull a clean tissue from their pocket, and a wad of others falls to the mossy earth. I bend to pick them up, but Ruby is too fast. Before they stuff them back into their pocket, I see a flash of red. The same red as their sweatshirt. The same red as blood.

"Are you okay?"

"Cut my finger. It stopped bleeding before I got to the infirmary." Another hike of their shoulders, and I'm beginning to realize this motion means an array of different things. "I probably should've asked you the same."

There's a commotion in the trees behind me that pricks my ears. A high-pitched whine that I recognize too well. Wren and Sam emerge from behind a Douglas fir as wide as all of us put together.

"Look. It. Up!" Wren practically squawks at Sam, who bats the air beside her like Wren is an annoying gnat. "You know I won't stop bothering you until you do."

Sam stops, hugs a textbook to her chest, and looks at me. "I'm glad I found you. You have to save me."

"Simply look it up and I'll go away," Wren says, a burst of energy lifting her onto her toes. "I would do it myself, but I don't have my phone and I haven't even seen a computer since we got to this island."

"Does she do this to you, too? Annoy the crap out of you until you have semi-violent thoughts?" Sam purses her lips and narrows her gaze at our best friend. "Don't you know any other Taureans?"

Wren's brow furrows. "Lily's not a Taurus, right? She's a—"

"Leo," Ruby interjects.

"Thank you." Wren nods to Ruby. "So, no, *Sam,* I don't know any other Taureans. At least, none that I trust as much as you." She settles her hands on her hips, and I hide my laugh behind my ink-smudged hand. Whether or not Sam gives in, Wren won.

Sam stomps her foot and purses her lips, mumbling jagged-edged words as she gathers her long hair into the scrunchie that's around her wrist.

"*I love you,*" Wren singsongs as Sam's body stills and she stares straight ahead, a blank expression smoothing the frustration from her face.

"*Elegida,*" she begins, pressing the pad of her thumb against the tip of each finger, pointer to pinky and back again.

Elegida—that's what the Elemental said. I've been so lost in my own thoughts that I'd almost forgotten.

"*Chosen, as in the chosen one.*" Sam blinks, snapping out of her magick with a wiggle of her fingers. "I hope that answers your question, because that was a onetime thing. I refuse to be your public database while we're here." She releases her hair from her scrunchie, shaking it out like a mane. "And I love you, too."

Chosen? What could Wren and I be chosen for?

Wren is special, there's no doubt about that, but *selected . . . picked . . .* that's more than special. She only found out she had magick three days ago. Could that be what the Elemental sensed? But what does that have to do with me? What does that have to do with us? Are *we* chosen . . . *together?*

The question fuels my heartbeat.

"*Chosen?*" Wren's expression twists as she smooths her palm across her forehead. "What the hell could I be chosen for?"

Before any of us can respond, flames erupt from the circular center of Crossroads Courtyard. The loitering students take off running, frightened screams bouncing off the nearby statues. I step in front of Wren and Sam to shield them from the fireball engulfing the cobblestones. Ruby does the same for me. They're about a head shorter than I am and could get lost behind a toothpick, but that doesn't matter. Ruby is all coiled muscle and hit-first-ask-questions-later. They could best almost anyone in a fight, and I'm glad they decided the three of us are worth fighting for.

Another shriek from Crossroads pulls my attention. As quickly as they appeared, the flames extinguish, leaving behind curling trails of smoke and a scorch mark in the grass around the cobblestones.

"The Leos!" Wren gasps as she and Sam peek out from behind me.

The Leo moons have returned from their Trial, mud-caked and haggard. I stare at the swirling flames disappearing behind them. It looks like they were transported here by their fire Elemental, carried through the air and dropped right in the middle of the courtyard. There's a commotion in the center of the tightly packed group, and a familiar voice shouts over the growing murmurs of confusion and shock.

"Move! We need to get her to the infirmary." The crowd of Leos ripples, pushed from the center out as Luke continues to bark commands. "Get out of the way! Can't you see she's hurt?"

He emerges from the group, his red hair smeared with

mud, a girl's arm draped across his shoulders. She hops on one foot, her other hanging limp, twisted at an odd angle. Her short hair is dirtier than Luke's, and her face is so pinched with pain and covered in mud that I can't tell who she is.

A Leo I don't recognize follows them out, the girl's other arm clinging to his shoulders. They're her crutches, and it's times like this when I wish Moon Isle worked its magick all at once and I could've reached my full healer potential as soon as I'd set foot on the island.

The rest of the Leo moons seem to shake themselves, fully realizing that they're back on campus and not knee-deep in mud as Luke's trio limps into Moon Hall and toward the infirmary.

Other Leos begin to break away, and I realize those of us in the courtyard, living our lives as usual before the bomb of Leos went off, have inched forward, forming a crescent around the stunned arrivals.

I clear my throat and take a step back as Ruby surges forward, their hands stuffed back into the pockets of their hoodie. "Lily!" they shout, lifting onto their tiptoes.

Luke's twin rushes over. She smells like fire and sweat and the best parts of camping. She's one of the only Leos without a faceful of mud, but her torn and dirty jeans and the bright pink of her cheeks prove she was right there with them.

The hunger Ruby had eased returns, and I bite the inside of my cheek to keep from interrogating Lily about her Trial. It doesn't matter that Wren and Sam and Lily are all hugging and talking over one another about how wild that entrance was or that we're heading to the dining hall like Ruby's shoes aren't completely soaked and Lily's pants aren't caked with dirt. No matter how odd any of this would be out in the Mundane world, it's simply another day on campus at Moon Isle.

We're halfway to the dining hall; Wren, Sam, and Lily continue talking at once while Ruby follows the conversation with flicks of their penetrating gaze when Lily holds up her hands. "If I would have known magickally returning from a muddy swamp forest straight out of an apocalypse show would make me so popular, I would have done this back in high school."

We slow to a stop as the three of them laugh and Ruby and I share a confused expression. "No idea," I say with a shrug.

Lily combs her fingers through the ends of her long hair. "I'm so relieved we got out of there in one piece."

I open my mouth to ask the first of a million questions I have about the Leos' Trial when Ruby speaks up. "You should get some rest."

A soft smile smooths Lily's lips. "From the looks of it, we both should."

"I wonder who'll be next?" Wren loops her arm around Sam's and leans into her. "If it's Aquarius, I hope we get to eat first."

The neon-yellow air symbol appears over my head and then Wren's, washing us in golden light as a fresh batch of startled squeals erupts from behind us.

A cyclone spins above the middle of Crossroads, the Leos' dissipating smoke caught in the spinning gusts like the chains of Marley's ghost as the funnel crashes to the ground. The air clears, revealing a deep black cloak and amber eyes that seem to lock onto mine.

"Wren," I sigh. "Looks like you cursed us."

TWELVE

Wren

Being caught in the middle of the Air Elemental's weird tornado thingy isn't as unpleasant as you might imagine, though I'm pretty sure the fact that as soon as stuff begins whirling around us Lee pulls me protectively into his arms has a lot to do with that.

I smell ash even before the Elemental plops us down and disappears (predictably) like the wind. Growing up in the Pacific Northwest has given me much more knowledge about forest fires than I wish I had reason to know (climate change *is a thing*) and the scent of scorched forest has me holding on to Lee even tighter and burying my face in his chest.

He smells so much better than burnt trees.

Tentatively, I raise my head. The noon sun perches over Lee's shoulder, brilliant and golden, and I blink and squint. Lee moves his head to block the sun and looks down at me. He grins.

"Better?"

He's so considerate that I forget for an instant all about the Trial and the Elemental and the scent of charred earth and grin up at his kind, familiar face. My smile is reflected in his dark eyes and I'm suddenly very aware that I have my arms wrapped around his strong shoulders and our bodies are pressed together, fitting perfectly. Lee's gaze captures mine and his smile fades to be replaced by a much more serious look—a look I have a hard time putting a name to. I open my mouth to break the sudden tension between us by asking him if I have something in my nose.

"Welcome to your first Trial, Aquarius moons."

My face flames and I practically leap out of Lee's arms to turn and face Celeste. The Queen of the Lunar Council (Yes, I know, but I don't care. If you met her, you'd think of her as Queen Celeste, too. Seriously.) is standing with Dean Rottingham in the center of a circle of students, all of whom I recognize as fellow residents of Aquarius Hall. Except for Celeste, who looks magnificent in her moonlight-colored cloak, we're windblown and confused, and several of us—me included—nervously straighten our clothes and brush hair from our faces. Celeste's dark eyes rest on me for a moment before flicking to Lee. When her gaze returns to me I swear she quirks up her lip in a sarcastic little smirk. Her gaze moves on as she continues.

"As *most* of you know . . ." Again, her eyes find me and it's clear that I'm not part of *most*. "Being a healer is complex. There is an enormous variety of talents that encompass the skills of healer." Celeste paces as she talks, flicking her cloak around her as she moves. She's super intense and a lot less professor-like than the dean. Actually, the more I listen to her and watch her the more she reminds me of a non-cartoon version of Cruella de Vil (I mean, she does have the white streak in her hair!). And I'm *not* being dramatic. Her voice seems to always have a mean edge. I glance up at Lee to see if he notices, but he's staring adoringly at her. I sigh as she continues.

"Aquarius moons have to learn to heal the earth, its fauna, *and* the human body. These Trials, though dangerous"— she pauses and her gaze slides to me again—"will help you practice controlling and focusing your powers."

"Yes, exactly." Dean Rottingham nods and continues. "And the Trials will give us an evaluation tool that will lead us to understand which type of healing best suits each of you. You may work in groups, pairs, or alone. The choice is entirely your own, but whichever students do well enough in the first two Trials to reach the final Trial will have to work alone."

Celeste paces again, her dark eyes picking out individual students as she takes over for Dean Rottingham. "For your first Trial you are to choose a part of this burned and ruined forest and heal it."

Everyone's gaze moves from Celeste and the dean in the center of the circle to the blackened remains of the forest. It looks as awful as it smells. Everything around us has been utterly destroyed. Huge trees are now black splinters, shards of ruin where once there was life. It makes me shudder.

"As you can see, the forest around us has been badly damaged," continues Celeste. "This terrible fire is extreme, even for Elementals. Such a shame . . ." Her voice fades as she and the rest of us stare at the destruction.

"What happened? What made them do it?"

I don't even realize I've spoken my thoughts aloud until Queen Celeste's gaze snaps to me. I take a step closer to Lee as she narrows her eyes and her voice sharpens like the shards of burnt trees.

"The Fire Elementals' behavior screams of a lack of control. This, Miss Nightingale, is what happens when control and self-discipline are lost—chaos, destruction, and death!"

Okay, do you see the Cruella de Vil similarity now?

Dean Rottingham moves quickly to Celeste's side and pats her shoulder like she needs soothing. "Why don't you let me take it from here, Celeste? You're getting overly emotional." The sharp expression slides from Celeste's face and her gaze falls to the blackened ground at her feet, but not before I see a flash of anger in her eyes. Her lips flatten into a crimson line. As the dean continues I force myself to look away from her and concentrate on him. "Of course we all should be emotional about centuries-old trees being destroyed. We do not know for sure why, but two nights ago almost exactly at midnight the Fire Elementals lost control and burned the forest."

My mind latches onto his words. Two nights ago . . . midnight . . . That was when I was Moonstruck!

"Excuse me, Dean Rottingham." Lee's voice surprises me. "But can't we just ask the Elementals what's wrong?"

"That is an excellent question," says Queen Celeste as she nods approval at Lee. (If Lee were a cat he'd be purring right about now.) "We can communicate with the four Elementals who watch over each of our halls, but these others." She makes a sweeping gesture with her long, sharp scarlet fingernails. They flash in the sunlight, suddenly appearing wet and bloody. "They are not as well domesticated and are much more difficult to communicate with, though we are trying."

"Indeed, indeed," says Dean Rottingham. "But whatever upset the Fire Elementals is less important than the fact that, with your help, the forest is not beyond resurrection.

"Now, my best advice is for you to rely on your healer instincts to guide you. Listen within for how your gift will be best used. Focus on channeling—on control, as magick is of no use to anyone if it is not controllable." The dean's eyes flick to me and I feel my cheeks get hot. "The Trial ends at dusk, whether you have completed it or not. The Air Elemental will return to collect you. I cannot warn you strongly enough against attempting to make your way back to campus on your own. As Celeste and I have already explained, the only Elementals who can even modestly be considered domesticated are the four who are allied to the halls. The others are, as you can see, dangerous."

"Um, Mr., I mean *Dean* Rottingham?" A student named Kaia, the literal girl next door to me in Aquarius Hall, with long dark hair and skin so smooth and toasted brown it reminds me of a fawn, raises a trembling hand.

"Yes, Kaia, what is your question?" asks the dean.

"Well, if we don't know what's upset the Fire Elementals, is it safe for us to be out here?"

Celeste answers, but she's not looking at Kaia. Her dark eyes are staring at me. "The Trials are never safe. Get used to that fact."

The little hairs on the back of my neck lift. Something isn't right, and I don't just mean that it seems Celeste has some kind of problem with me. Okay, so the Trials are dangerous. I'm not exactly sure what that means, but there is definitely something off about allowing untrained students (students!) to be out here, alone and exposed to the literal elements, while literal Elementals are setting entire forests on fire! If the wild Elementals are so uncontrollable how are any of us safe? What would our parents think? Okay, yeah, we're technically adults, but I know Uncle Brad and Uncle Joel would never give their permission for me to be put in danger like this.

And then it hits me. Maya died while she was here! Everyone said it was an accident that she drowned. Was it really? Or was it more of the council allowing us to be in danger—deadly danger? My gut has been telling me since I first saw the island that there's more going on at the Academia de la Luna than just lectures and Trials.

Dean Rottingham clears his throat and adds, "Yes, well, that is true, but there are no Fire Elementals in this part of the forest today. You are safe from them as long as you do not wander outside the burn area. Any other questions?" When no one else speaks he nods and says, "Excellent. Good luck, and may the blessings of the moon be with you."

Dean Rottingham steps close to Celeste, claps his hands twice, and the Air Elemental appears above them. As the ancient creature whips up a tornado around the two of them the rest of us duck our heads and put our hands up to shield our faces from flying debris. From between my fingers I see the Air Elemental's glowing yellow eyes staring at me.

With a crack of thunder, the Elemental, the dean, and Queen Celeste are gone.

"That is the freakiest thing I've ever seen," blurts Kaia.

Her words unfreeze us and we laugh nervously as we begin to break off into little clusters of threes and fours and a few couples, while others, like Kaia, take off alone into the discolored forest.

I stand there, resisting the urge to pick at my lip. What am I supposed to do? I really want to attempt to use magick, but I have no idea how. I'm not like the rest of the students here. Their powers are part of them. They've felt magick often, even before they turned eighteen and it manifested fully. That's not me. That's Lee and Sam and Ruby and everyone else at this school. Lee's shoulder bumps mine. "Shall we take a stroll about the grounds, Lady Nightingale?" he asks in a really bad English accent. He offers me his arm, which I take, and then we head away from the rest of the group, stepping carefully over slivers of exploded trees.

As soon as we're out of hearing range of the rest of the Aquarius moons I clear my throat and try to reason with him. "Hey, I think we should talk about this."

Lee reaches out to move aside a long, sickly-looking vine, but it disintegrates into ash at his touch. He grimaces and wipes his hand on his jeans. "This is even worse than that fire in the Columbia River Gorge a few years ago. Remember?"

"Of course. One of us thought it was a good idea to hike it after the trail reopened," I said.

He looked at me and grinned. "That would be me."

"Yeah. Do *you* remember how pissed Uncle Joel was when I came home and my cream-colored overalls had turned to charcoal—permanently?" I shake my head. He's sidetracking me. Again. "Lee, I think it would be best if you and I split up here."

Lee stops so abruptly that I take a couple of steps past him before I realize he isn't with me. I walk back to him and look up into his frowning face.

"Split up?" he asks, his jaw clenching and unclenching like I'd just told him that poetry is frivolous and confusing (two things I sometimes think but will *never* say to him).

"Yeah. For the Trials. I'm just going to hold you back and I know how important it is to you to do really well."

Lee's jaw unclenches. "You're being ridiculous."

"No, I'm being for real. I have no idea if I actually have magick, or how to use it if I do. You partnering with me is like . . ." I pause to think of the perfect analogy that'll make him understand. "I know! Remember the dragon boat races in Portland that we watch during Fleet Week?"

His brow furrows, but he nods. "Yeah."

"Okay, you partnering with me out here is like making one of those sleek, fast dragon boats drag a rubber dinghy full of geese behind it during the race."

Lee snorts and starts walking again and I scramble to keep up with his much longer strides. "So now you're a goose-laden dinghy?"

"It's a metaphor," I say.

"Wren, I was there when you lit up by the fountain. You have magick. You just don't know what kind yet. That's what these Trials and the academies are for—figuring that out. . . ." He pauses and studies the area around us. To our left, he and I catch a glimpse of three Aquarius moons huddled around an area of blackened ferns. While Lee and I watch, they lift their hands and begin weaving patterns in the soot-scented air. "Come on, let's go this way." Lee heads away from the group and I follow him.

We walk on for a while and the ground gets rougher. We

half slide, half jog down a bank and pick our way carefully over the rocky bed of a dry creek and then clamber our way up the other side. Between breaths I try to reason with him.

"Lee, you heard what Dean Rottingham told my uncles. I may never get any magick, which means it's not even important that I pass these Trials. But you have a whole future ahead of you as a leader in this world—a really great healer. So, you should do this Trial on your own without my deadweight."

Lee puts out a hand and I take it and he helps pull me up the top of the dry stream bank. I look down at my white tee that has an outline of a porcupine on it and the words STAB RABBIT below it. I sigh. It's already covered with soot and ash.

"You're being dramatic. Again," says Lee as we continue walking.

"Huh?" I cup my ear with my sooty hand. "Did you say I'm being considerate? Again?"

He barks a little laugh as we detour around a stump that looks like a tree exploded from it. "You're not holding me back. Even if you weren't with me, I'd still be trudging through this forest trying to listen to my intuition tell me what I'm supposed to attempt to heal."

"See, I'm keeping you from hearing your intuition."

"Only because you keep whining," he says.

"I'm not whining," I whine. And then both of us laugh. "Hey, seriously, I know if I do have some kind of magick that I'll eventually figure it out. I don't want you to worry about that. But until I do I'm pretty much completely useless."

Lee looks down at me and I can't read his expression. He's not annoyed. He's not amused. It's almost like he's something adjacent to the two emotions. He blows out a long breath and says, "Wren, you're my best friend. That means I'll never think you're 'completely useless.'" He air quotes sarcastically. "You say you don't want to hold me back, then quit trying to get me to dump you and help me find something epic to heal."

"You mean it? I promise I won't be mad if you say no," I say, though I honestly don't want him to say no. Like, what am I going to do out here in this mess of a forest all by myself? But I lift my chin and give him my best *I'll be just fine if you say no* smile.

"I mean it and you can stop giving me that look. I know you don't want to be out here alone. Now, I beseech you sincerely, Lady Nightingale, stop vexing yourself and take a stroll around the . . ." Lee pauses to consider his words, grins, and says, "The Earl's delightful gardens with me." He offers me his arm.

"Well, you're welcome for all the help I will not be giving you." I drop into a graceful curtsey and take his arm. "Earl, though? Why can't it be a Duke?"

"I thought an Earl was the highest."

"No, no, no. A Duke is the highest of the five ranks of peerage. . . ." And I launch into an enthusiastic lecture on a class system that I very much recognize as archaic, but with which I am fictionally obsessed.

We walk far enough that I get through the peerage lecture and move on to a subject Lee and I love arguing about— British foods served with tea.

"I still don't get why clotted cream is so good on scones," he says as we start slide-scrambling down another steep bank.

"Because it's delicious," I say. "It just sounds gross." We

get to the bottom of the bank and this time there's a creek that hasn't completely dried up, so we move carefully from rock to rock and try to avoid falling into what's left of the muddy water.

"Oh, you mean the opposite of buttermilk." Lee makes it to the other side a little ahead of me and heads up the equally steep bank. "It sounds like it'd be delicious, but it's actually disgusting."

"Yes, exactly." Then I stop talking because I need to focus on getting up the bank. I'm almost on my hands and knees—and have completely given up on ever getting the mud and ash and black crap off my T-shirt—when Lee's hand is there, reaching for mine. With a sigh of gratitude, I take it, and he pulls me up over the lip of the bank, nearly lifting me off my feet. I stumble and almost fall, but he catches me.

"Whoa, be careful. You can actually get dirtier if you faceplant."

I look up at him and again find myself standing within his arms. *He's always here to catch me* drifts through my mind as I meet his familiar eyes. "My cool STAB RABBIT shirt is ruined."

"It's really not that cool," he says.

I laugh and impulsively hug him. "Thanks!"

He squeezes me tightly and then lets me go. "Thanks for letting you know how uncool your shirt is?"

"No." I smack his shoulder making a mental note about how high I have to reach up to do that and how ironlike his muscles feel. "Thanks for not changing too much during the time we were apart."

His brows go up. "What do you mean by *too much*?"

I mimic his snort and make a gesture that takes in his

tall, muscular body. "Well, you are like, six foot seven now, and that's definitely a change."

"Six four," he corrects me with a grin.

"Yeah, that."

His chest swells and he lifts his arms in a bodybuilding pose, showing off his biceps. ". . . I'm roughly the size of a barge." His deep voice does an excellent imitation of Gaston from *Beauty and the Beast.*

I know he's playing, but there's something so masculine, so grown about him that sobers me. Lee is handsome. I know it's a ridiculous moment to realize it, but now that I have I can't help but see him through different eyes. Eyes that are older. Eyes that appreciate how his strength and height and new maturity have taken him from my cute best friend to my seriously hot best friend, and now that I've acknowledged the change I have to acknowledge that I like it. Maybe more than a best friend should. Lily smiling at Lee last night in the cafeteria and Lee's nervous, babbling response lift from my memory. Lily knows how hot Lee is now, and Lee is obviously interested in Lily, too. Then I also remember how my stomach felt when I watched them.

No. I am not going to be one of those girls who has a guy as a best friend and becomes a jealous mess when he gets a girlfriend. My cheeks blaze as I think about what Lee would say if he could read my mind.

"Wren? What's wrong?"

I blink. Lee's staring at me. All the fun has drained from his face. "So, Lily's cute . . ." I blurt.

His eyes widen and he shakes his head like he's confused. "Okay?"

"You should talk to her," I say awkwardly.

Lee shrugs. "Yeah, she's pretty. I saw plenty of pictures of her before we met."

"What!" I don't even try to keep the shock from my voice.

He's looking everywhere but my eyes. "My father wants me to 'cultivate the right type of relationships,'" Lee does an excellent imitation of his dad. "I'm supposed to be friends with Senator Weatherton's son and his very attractive twin. My father's mentioned she's pretty so many times that I get the point he's really making."

I have to swallow to get rid of the terrible dryness that wants to clog my throat (and my brain). "Well. Um. He wasn't lying about Lily."

Lee's gaze is still scanning the forest around us. "Yeah," he says nonchalantly.

I blow out a breath and try again. "And I think she likes you."

His eyes find mine, but he doesn't say anything. He just stares at me.

I pick at the hem of my STAB RABBIT shirt, not able to keep meeting his gaze. "That's all. Just, uh, trying to be a good wingman. Or woman. Maybe you should ask her out. I mean, your dad would definitely approve. But whatever . . ." I sputter to a halt wishing I'd kept my mouth shut.

"I guess I'll think about it." He turns away from me and goes back to studying the burnt forest around us.

I clear my throat. "Cool. Uh, hey, I just noticed how late it's getting. We have to find something for you to heal, like right now. Remember what Rottingham said about not being out here past dusk?" When he glances over his shoulder at me I can see the hurt in his eyes, so I look quickly away. "Lee, check it out." I point behind him. "There's the fire line. Want to head that way?"

He turns and looks at the edge of the black forest and the verdant green that begins a football field length or so beyond it. "Yeah, that sounds good. You're right. We better hurry." He strides away, heading for the distant green. I follow more slowly, my stomach feeling heavy and sick. I've messed up and I don't know how to fix it.

When I catch Lee, he's standing in front of the scorched ruins of a tree. What's left of the trunk is so big that Lee and I couldn't have touched fingers around it. The fire split the tree and now part of the trunk is open. The strange remains of charred branches jut from the top of the trunk, looking spiderlike and a little frightening.

"This is it." He smooths the burnt skin of the tree with his fingertips. "I think this used to be a white oak. Although I'm not totally sure how I know that."

"It's perfect." I touch Lee's shoulder and he looks at me. "You can do this. You can heal this tree. I believe in you."

The ghost of a smile lifts the corners of his lips, though his eyes seem sad. "I can heal this tree." He turns back to the tree, rolls his shoulder, and cracks his knuckles. Then he begins with his hands down by his sides. His dexterity really is amazing. Like it's nothing, his fingers move quickly and perfectly. He folds his ring finger and pinky finger down with his thumb, leaving his first and second fingers pointing up. He flips his other hand so that his palms face the tree. Lee's movements are graceful. I'm amazed that his big hands move so subtly. He draws a deep breath and as he releases it he blows gently on the tree, like he's breathing life into it.

For a moment nothing happens and I have to stop myself from doing something, anything, to help him. *Should I cheer him on? Pace nervously? Hold my breath? Or should I mimic the magick sign he's making and try to help him?* Then there's a flicker from inside the burned, broken trunk and I feel an odd tug somewhere under my ribs. Heat blossoms within me as a yellow light, so dim that I'm afraid if I look away I won't find it again, begins to glow within the trunk.

"It's working," I whisper. "I can see something happening inside the trunk."

Lee grunts and closes his eyes. He takes another deep breath and releases it as if the tree is a giant birthday candle.

Again, I feel a strange pull. The dim yellow light flares and then turns green as a sapling lifts its head from the ashes of the tree and tremulously stretches a little shoot upward.

The magickal pull is inside me, like the sapling is inside the trunk, and it, too, is getting bigger.

I gasp and look at Lee. His eyes are still closed, so I whisper, "You're doing it, Lee. A baby tree just appeared."

Lee nods once, draws another breath that he releases, blowing at the tree. Enthralled, I stare at the little green shoot, wondering what will happen next. But nothing happens. The tug inside me relaxes, like a rubber band being gently released. My gaze returns to Lee. His eyes are squeezed shut. Sweat drips from his face, running in rivulets through the soot on his cheeks and down his neck to darken his shirt. His right hand is no longer forming a subtle gesture at his side. He's raised it—raised both of his hands—and they're shaking.

My gaze flies back to the sapling. It's starting to wilt.

Pure instinct moves me. I lunge forward and grab Lee's

left hand in my right one. "Keep going, Lee! You can do it!" When I feel that tug under my skin again, I think of nothing but the sapling and how much I want it to live and grow into a big, beautiful white oak. Within me the pull expands like I'm at the top of the first dip of a giant roller coaster. And then *whoosh!* The delicious but terrifying feeling bundled inside me releases, flying into Lee.

Yellow light flares around the tiny oak, and it's so bright I look away. When I finally blink my eyes clear of yellow spots, the sapling is bursting up, up, and up! It's not a tiny, spindly thing anymore. It's as thick as my wrist, and then my arm—and then Lee's arm as it reaches toward the sky.

"Lee, open your eyes!"

He does, his jaw falling. The sapling has become *a tree.* Like a green phoenix it soars from the ruined husk of the trunk, shattering it into charcoal ashes as, with the sound of an enormous sigh, the white oak unfurls its magnificent branches.

Lee and I stagger back. "I can't believe it!" We laugh and hug—and then realize that we have our arms wrapped around each other, so we awkwardly take a step away. Our eyes go to the tree.

"You were right. It's definitely a white oak, and it's beautiful," I say.

Lee's staring at the tree. Smiling, he uses the end of his shirt to wipe sweat and dirt from his face. "I think that's the coolest thing I've ever done. I felt so powerful! It's true. These tests really do help us come into our magick."

I wonder if I should mention the tug and the heat, but what would I say? *Hey, Lee, I think I might have somehow done something to the tree, too?* And totally poop on his party?

Plus, how do I know I did something? Yeah, I felt strange, but that's it.

"Wow, Wren, it's huge. A fully grown tree."

Lee's circling around the tree, and while he's distracted I half turn away from him to a much smaller version of a burnt husk of a tree by my feet. I bend my fingers into the same position Lee's had been in, draw a deep breath, think, *Grow, little tree, grow,* and blow on the trunk.

Nothing happens to the tree, and I feel . . . empty.

I glance up at Lee, who's still grinning up at the healthy oak. I draw another deep breath, concentrate harder, and blow— *Grow, little tree, grow!*

Not one thing happens. No flicker of yellow. No tug. Not. One. Thing. Disappointment washes through me. Do I or do I not have magick? How do I reach it if I do? It definitely doesn't respond like Lee's magick.

"Wren?"

I hear the question in Lee's voice and turn to face him, ready to try to explain that I was unsuccessfully trying to—

Fear rockets through me. There are five *things* charging out of the healthy, green forest. They're hulking creatures that, animal-like, are on all fours. Their thick bodies are part canine, part nightmare. Their chests are impossibly wide and they pull themselves forward with their massive front legs. Smoke billows from their bodies as their color ripples and changes from a gray to black to a strange rust color. Their eyes blaze with fire.

But the worst thing about them is the snarling sound they make as they race across the blackened grass, razor teeth glinting white while saliva sprays from their mouths.

They've reached the halfway point between us and the

greenbelt. The creatures pause and Lee backs to me. The instant he moves, their red eyes find us and they come together with an explosion of fire. From that burst of flame one creature emerges. An enormous dragon's serpentine neck arches as its horned head turns, seeking, until its red eyes focus on us. It opens its huge maw and roars, shooting flames in our direction.

"Run!" Lee shouts. He grabs my hand and begins to race back through the ruined forest.

The dragon follows, roaring as it spews fire. I cling to Lee's hand, running faster than I've ever moved in my life, but I can feel the heat of the dragon's breath. I smell burnt hair as my fuchsia ends singe and curl.

I should release Lee's hand. He's a lot faster without me. But he'd stop. I know he would. It wouldn't help to set him free; he'll never leave me. I only know I'm crying because my tears feel cool on my scorched cheeks.

We're going to die.

Thunder cracks around us and air, deliciously cold and damp, pours over us as amber-colored fog cascades from above. The dragon's roar turns to a shriek. The cold wind batters us. We can't keep moving forward against it. Lee and I turn.

The Air Elemental, *our* Elemental, swoops down from the sky, riding a cloud of mist. The Elemental hovers just a few feet off the ground, taking a stand between us and the dragon. The dragon snarls and screams again.

Our Elemental *laughs*. It's not an infectious, full-throated laugh. It's the kind of laugh that comes from a killer just before they strike. Our Elemental scoops its skeletal, clawed hands through the amber fog, gathering it into a glowing ball, and hurls it at the dragon. It hits the creature in its open, salivating jaws. The dragon shrieks and shatters into five lumpy forms that fall to the blackened forest floor, smoldering and twitching.

Our Air Elemental turns to face us, its black cloak swirling gracefully around it. It lifts one long finger and twirls it in a circle. The wind instantly obeys, forming a funnel cloud around Lee and me. I only have time to grab Lee's arm and then we're in the eye of the tornado, lifting and moving impossibly fast, only to be gently placed down in the center of Crossroads Courtyard.

The wind clears quickly, leaving Lee and me breathing hard and shaking. The Air Elemental hovers just in front of us. Its yellow eyes meet mine before it floats away.

"Wait!" I drop Lee's arm and run after it.

The Air Elemental pauses and drifts lower. I look into its hidden face.

"Thank you for saving our lives," I say. "Lee and I will never forget what you did for us."

The Air Elemental's colors of yellow and gold, amber and saffron swirl within the black cloak as it glides to me. I stand rigid, making myself stay still and not cringe back. Its cowl is so close that I'm lost in its yellow eyes. It smells like the breeze after a spring rain, like a foggy Pacific Northwest morning, like fall leaves carried on a current of crisp, cinnamon air.

In a voice that sounds like wind sloughing through trees it whispers, "*The strength of the maiden*," before it soars up into the darkening sky and disappears.

THIRTEEN

Lee

Psst! Ruby!" They're ignoring me (again), but I know they hear me. At this point, I just hope not everyone can.

Professor Douglas stops lecturing and peers over the rims of her black spectacles. "Lee, you're not required to be here. If you'd rather chat with your friends, you can see yourself out."

Luke is on the other side of the lecture hall, arms crossed over his chest and feet up on the long shared desk. He lets out a low *ooooh* like we're in kindergarten, and a few other students laugh.

"And Luke!" Professor Douglas's glare snaps to the

next offender. "Feet off the table, *now*. This is not your living room."

"Yes, ma'am," he grumbles, the wind knocked out of his sails.

"As I was saying," our professor continues, her cream-colored pantsuit, pale white skin, and light blond ponytail all blending together. A vanilla shake with black cat-eye glasses. "Of course, you'll need the *Moon Guides* you picked up on your way in, but I'll also distribute one Moon Isle practice orb. I'll be here if you have any questions, but I suggest you and your partner spend time troubleshooting before asking me to intervene. A professor will not be with you if you ever need to make a trip back to this isle or to any other, and I refuse to supply you with obvious answers." She tugs on the bottom of her suit coat and gives the class a once-over. "Well . . ." She throws up her hands. "Break into pairs."

I seize the opportunity, jump out of my seat, and slide across the top of the desk like it's the hood of a car and I'm in any action movie. I regret my quick movements mid-slide; not only is it not the move of a future CEO, but my muscles are sore from last night. Ruby's deskmate has gone off to partner up, and I land in the empty chair.

"Ruby," I whisper even though the room is abuzz with conversation.

"Lee." They shake their head and pull up the red hood of their sweatshirt, but I swear I see the faintest hint of a smile lift their cheek.

"I had my first Trial." I don't know why I've been so eager to share with Ruby specifically. I'd normally go straight to Wren, but she was there. She already knows what happened.

And what she said.

The thought makes my throat tighten and shoulders slump, and I push the embarrassing memory of being told by the girl I've wanted to date for the past five years that she'd love to help me win over someone else.

"We were at Crossroads together," Ruby says, their hands methodically moving in their pockets, and I'm reminded of something more important than the Trial.

"How's your finger?" I ask, gesturing to their buried hand.

They stiffen a little and won't face me. "It's rude to make comments about other people's bodies."

"Ruby." My voice is stern as I talk to their profile, obscured by the red hood. "You literally told me yesterday you were injured. I'm not making a comment. I'm checking on my friend."

"We're friends?"

"I mean . . ." I swallow. Clearly, my relationship gauge is nonfunctioning. "*I* think so."

"Okay."

"Okay," I say, but all I want to do is apologize, although I don't know what for.

"That was a positive *okay*," they explain. "A happy okay. Like, *okay.*" Their inflection is high-pitched and more of a squeak, and I sputter a laugh. "I have a hard time getting my tone to match how I feel."

I'm not sure what to say to this level of honesty, so I don't say anything. Instead, we sit in companionable silence and watch Professor Douglas hand out Moon Isle orbs from a wooden crate that looks like something off a pirate ship.

There's an ease to being with Ruby that I hadn't noticed until now. Yes, they're forward and honest, which is intense, but there's no padding or filler in the conversation, no need to talk simply to keep the silence at bay.

"Your finger," I say but only because it's worth mentioning again. "Is it okay?"

Ruby takes their hand from their pocket and flexes their fingers. The middle one is wrapped in gauze, fuzzy and tinged red with sweatshirt lint. "I didn't need stitches or anything, but they insisted I put on this giant wrap. The healer wanted to fix it completely, but it doesn't really hurt. And I want to remember."

"Remember what?"

They turn to look at me, and I think it's the first time Ruby's ever actually made eye contact. "What happened during my first Trial."

Their intensity squeezes my stomach, and I'm glad when Professor Douglas approaches with the crate.

"If anyone would like to check out an orb to practice on their own time, come see me," she announces to the class as she sets the crystal ball between us. She adjusts her glasses and is once again glaring at me from over thick black rims. "And I suggest you do so."

I want to tell her that I'm a good student, or I have been for the past two years, and remind her that I'm a Young, but even the thought makes me feel like a douche.

Instead, I smile and give an awkward nod.

Professor Douglas's pale pink lips thin into an unimpressed line as she lifts the crate from our table and moves on to the next.

The orb sits between Ruby and me, a glass ball the size of a cantaloupe. Inside is a terrarium complete with a mini version of Moon Isle down to the tiny conifers, dorm halls, and moat of ocean water rippling around the rock.

I touch the smooth glass, and the magickal cloak that protects the toy version of the island swells to life like a bag of microwave popcorn.

Ruby lets out a sound somewhere between a grunt and a question before opening their copy of *Moon Guide* and flipping through the pages.

I follow suit, turning to grab my *Moon Guide* from my table. The cover creaks as I lift it, the edges of the pages soft and feathered with age. Toward the beginning are two pages that detail the moon signs required for uncloaking Moon Isle.

"Your Trial . . ." Ruby's reading over their book, and it takes me a minute to realize they're talking to me.

"'Oh!" I'd completely forgotten that I'd literally vaulted over a table to tell them about yesterday.

I scoot my chair closer and lean in conspiratorially. "I healed a tree yesterday. Well, not just me. Wren helped. But we healed a whole entire tree."

"You're an Aquarius moon." Ruby takes off their hood and blinks at me. "You're supposed to heal things."

"Yeah, but that's not what I mean." I smooth my hands down my braids as I think of a better way to articulate what happened in the forest. "So, I can help you with the cut you don't want healed," I say, motioning to the hand they've kept stuffed in their pocket. "But not if you needed to regrow your whole finger. At least, not yet."

They nod, the ends of their black bob skimming their hood.

I take a breath to control the rush of adrenaline that surges through me as I recount the events. "But, during our Trial, Wren and I grew a tree from a stump. Not a sapling, but a fifty-year-old fully grown white oak."

"That's not possible. No one's magick manifests that powerfully that fast." Ruby shakes their head and goes back to skimming their book, unimpressed with the story they believe I've made up.

But I haven't. It's real.

As real as Wren joining my parents in thinking that I should talk to Lily. At least now I know where I stand. She doesn't want me the same way I want her. My love has been proven unrequited. My pining can come to an end. No more poems. No more hope. Not that I'll share any of that with Ruby. They'll have something practical and logical to say that will make sense but won't make me feel better.

Above us, a speaker crackles and a voice lilts from the intercom, "Wren Nightingale and Lee Young are requested in the dean's office. Wren Nightingale and Lee Young to the dean's office."

I feel the class's eyes on me as I close my book, stand, and give another tight nod to Professor Douglas.

"You're right," I whisper to Ruby as I squeeze behind their chair on my way to the door. "It shouldn't be possible, but it happened."

The combo of not wanting to keep Dean Rottingham waiting paired with the nerves wriggling like snakes in my legs forces me to jog the short distance to his office. I slow to a walk before I get to the open doorway bordered by dark-stained wood.

Poppy sits behind the mahogany desk in the reception area outside the dean's office, the fuzzy end of her sparkly pen wagging in the air as she writes. "He'll be right with you, Lee," she says without looking up.

I've talked to Poppy numerous times. She's not only Dean Rottingham's assistant but the only source of communication we have with the Academia de la Luna before arriving at Moon Isle.

Her soft, melodic voice matches the creamy pastels and tulle skirts she's so fond of along with the crafty headbands she wears. Today the thick band is decorated with smooth river rocks, dried herbs, and bits of moss. It makes sense. Poppy's a Taurus moon, an earth symbol. It also fits that, as a sort of human encyclopedia, she'd have such an important position.

Wren's shoes squeak against the shiny marble floors as she drags herself into the reception space.

I stiffen.

Is it me she doesn't want to see or Dean Rottingham?

There's still so much between us that I can't be sure. I frown down at her as she crosses her arms over her chest and taps her foot on the tile. Actually, there isn't anything left between us. Not after last night. These are the feelings I can ignore, throw away, clear out from my brain. We're just two people—Lee and Wren—two friends. Nothing more.

The solid wood door next to Poppy's desk swings open, and she stands. Her skirt is a cheerful cloud of pale green fabric that bounces as she ushers us into the dean's office and to the wingback leather chairs that face his large desk. Rottingham thanks her with a smile, and she floats back to the door, closing us into the room without a sound.

"I understand there was an incident yesterday with the Fire Elementals." True to form, Dean Rottingham doesn't waste time with pleasantries. Instead, he flips to a clean page of the legal pad that sits in the center of his uncluttered desk, smoothing his hand over the yellow paper as he plucks a pen from the holder near his vintage rotary phone.

Wren snorts. "If by *incident* you mean they almost killed

us, then yeah, we had an incident with the Fire Elementals."

Dean Rottingham's gaze flicks to the legal pad while he jots down a note, and I have the same uncomfortable twisting in my stomach I used to get in family therapy.

"I see," he says.

I grind my teeth to keep from launching into a *what she meant to say* . . . tirade. Wren doesn't need anyone to apologize, clarify, or make excuses for her. She knows what she's saying and how she's saying it. Nothing is by accident. Not with Wren.

My teeth are sandpaper in my mouth with the memory of last night's conversation. I catch Wren's eye, and she looks away quickly, turning to stone in her seat.

I must be Medusa.

When I look back at the dean, he's staring at me. I'm not sure if I missed a question, but I start tripping over myself for the right answer. Every year, he chooses an apprentice, a shadow. Two years ago, it was Maya. This year, it'll be my turn.

"We landed in the forest at approximately three PM. After receiving our instructions from Celeste, Wren and I partnered up and headed into the destroyed landscape." I'm suddenly militaristic, my spine ramrod straight, words flat and calculated. Deep inside my chest, something unclenches, and my lungs fully expand for the first time in years.

This feeling of . . . *emptiness* . . . ? No, I'm not empty. What's inside me I can grab and hold on to. I can take it out and show it off without the weight of emotion. I am full of feelings all the time, a raw nerve, a fresh wound. I funnel that passion and pain into my poetry. When I'm away from studies and my parents and their expectations that lurk in the shadows like living, breathing things, I tell myself these emotions make me better, stronger, more alive. But what does a sore do if left with no scab, no protection from the outside world? It festers, turns gangrenous, rots.

I recount our experience, including only the relevant information in the same matter-of-fact way I began, skipping over both the fact that the girl I've been embarrassing myself pining over told me to talk to someone else and the powerful moment with the tree. I want the recognition, need the recognition, and whatever advancements and favors might come from revealing that kind of intense magick. But I'm also aware that the part of my brain swollen with pride and ready to gloat sounds exactly like my father.

When I finish, I feel Wren's eyes on me, and I pass her a sideways glance while Dean Rottingham completes the rest of his notes. Her brow is furrowed, blue eyes bright and wide with questions. I take a breath to mouth, *What's wrong?* but swallow the urge before it reaches my lips. Instead, I shrug and return her furrowed stare with one of my own.

It's not that I don't care. I do. I always will. We're friends, but that's the thing. We're friends. *Only* friends. The sooner I understand that, the better.

"And the oak?" This time, the dean looks at Wren.

She stiffens, and her throat convulses with a tight swallow. "What about it?"

"Students do not usually possess such power so soon after arriving at the academy. Not even when working with another."

"But it's possible?" she asks.

"I suppose it *is* possible, however improbable." He taps the point of his pen against the pad and doesn't break eye contact. They're locked in a battle. One I don't understand, but I feel it in the air and in the magick that trips down my back and hums beneath my skin. "What was your role in the tree's healing process, Miss Nightingale?"

I search my memory for whatever he's trying to find, whatever she's trying to hide, but I keep coming back to my own hurt feelings and the way my arms and hands still ache from wringing every ounce of magick from my body.

The chair creaks beneath her as she fidgets. "It was Lee. I was just there for support."

"You did nothing to assist?"

She grabs the arms of the chair, her knuckles blanching.

"The Trials, like this school, are here to help us develop our magick," I say, unable to stomach how uncomfortable she is. "That's what Wren's doing. What I'm doing."

"I don't know exactly how the tree grew like it did," she continues, her grip relaxing. "But you said yourself that it's possible."

Dean Rottingham rubs the backs of his knuckles against his goatee. "That I did." With one fluid motion, he caps his pen and picks up the phone's receiver. He sets it on the desk and spins the dial twice before hanging it back up.

Behind us, the door opens and Poppy breezes in.

"Thank you both for your candor." Dean Rottingham stands and tugs the bottom of his waistcoat. This meeting is over.

Wren springs from her seat like it's made of spiders and bolts past Poppy without another word.

I rise more leisurely, adjusting my T-shirt as if it's a suit jacket I need to rebutton, before holding out my hand. "I'm always available if you have any other questions."

Dean Rottingham stands, taking my hand in a firm grip. "You and Miss Nightingale may work together in the next Trial, but you are on your own in the final. I look forward to seeing what you can accomplish."

He releases my hand, and I nod. This is the opportunity I need. Dean Rottingham is paying attention, and I will not disappoint.

On my way out, I pause next to Poppy and flash her my most practiced smile. "Thank you for your help." I glance at the bits of earth thoughtfully nestled in her dark hair, and my grin turns lopsided. "I like your headband."

"Thanks." Her cheeks pinken, and she gingerly touches the stones. "I made it myself."

"Nice." My smile falters when I pass by Poppy's desk and see Wren leaning against the doorframe, her arms crossed over her chest.

"What was *that*?" she throws at me the second we turn down the corridor toward Moon Hall's back exit. The lecture's over by now, so there's no use going back.

Hopefully Ruby checked out one of those orbs.

We're walking so closely that my knuckles brush her arm, and I'm jolted back to our current situation. "What was what?" I ask, stuffing my hand into my pocket before it betrays me and I put my arm around her.

"*I like your headband.*" She's making fun of me, but she does it in the voice she uses when quoting Colin Firth from her favorite rendition of *Pride and Prejudice,* so I take it as a compliment. "Who are you, and what did you do with Lee?"

I ignore the question. Wren wouldn't like the answer.

"The dean's right, you know?" I say instead. "That tree never should have happened. At least, not like that."

She halts a few paces from the double doors that will take us to Crossroads, her tennis shoes squeaking against the gold-flecked tile. "So, what? You think *I* had something to do with it?"

"No, I mean . . . I don't know." I rub my forehead, trying to soothe the first pangs of a headache. I have no idea what to think.

"This place is, like, the powerhouse of magick, right?" Her gesture takes in the ornate wainscoting in the hall around us.

"But magick is like any other living thing—it grows over time." With a sigh, I slide my fingers along my cornrows. "And not enough has gone by for mine to grow that much."

"I don't have any magick." Her arms are back over her chest, and her mouth is in a line so tight her lips flash white.

I take a deep breath, and my mind starts gathering all the words to detail how great she is, but I let them go on my next exhale. I don't mean to her what she has meant to me, and giving her all those adjectives to describe how magickal she truly is would be a waste of beautiful words. This time, I'll keep them. I'll use them on myself or on someone who actually wants them. More than that, I have to break this cycle we've been in since she sat across from me in the cafeteria five years ago and dunked her chicken nuggets into my ketchup because *we both have magickal germs in our families.*

"I gotta go." I walk to the heavy wooden doors and push

them open. Sunlight floods the hallway where Wren is standing, motionless as a tombstone. I force my feet forward and my eyes straight ahead and hold my breath until the doors click shut behind me.

FOURTEEN

Wren

The next day when the lecture ends and we're let out I feel like I'm a bird that got trapped inside a house and finally found the escape window. It's not that I don't like the lectures here. Actually, they're really interesting. The problem is that *everyone* knows so much more about being Moonstruck than I do, and I feel like I'm constantly struggling to make up for lost time. A great example is the headache that's currently pounding in my left temple. It's caused by the fact that I am the only person in our magickal Hand Positions lecture who didn't show up to class with a *Moon Guide* notebook given to them by their parents. (Hello! I had no magick, hence no book from my parents, who are—incidentally—dead, so they couldn't even have scrambled around last minute to pass that family heirloom to me!) It's the same feeling my trigonometry class used to give me—the sinking understanding that I'm in way over my head and definitely need a tutor. I would usually find Lee and ask for his help, but that thought makes my stomach hurt.

Since the Trial, Lee hasn't been Lee.

I'm pretty positive that's my fault and I know I should talk to him, but what am I supposed to say that will make it better? *Hey, Lee, I thought I was being a good friend when I talked Lily up to you, because that's what we are—friends. That's all we are. Right?* I mentally shake my head. No, the new Lee feels cold and unreachable. Could it be because after I told him I think Lily's into him, Lee realized that he doesn't really want me out of the friend zone?

Knowing for sure would definitely be worse than just wondering.

Yes, when it comes to Lee I might be a coward.

And then there's the weirdness that was the Trial. I know I felt something when Lee was healing the tree, but I have no clue what that something means. Add to that the weirdness of the Elemental whispering to me, *The strength of the maiden,* and I'm drowning in the odd, which normally wouldn't be a big deal because Lee and I would talk it out. But I can't talk to Lee, or at least I can't talk to this new, unapproachable Lee.

Should I have told Rottingham about the tugging feeling I had when Lee healed the tree? I thought about it while we were in his office and maybe I would have if Lee had said something, *anything,* about me taking his hand right before the little sapling burst into a giant oak. But Lee didn't say anything, probably because I'd had nothing to do with healing the tree. Probably . . .

I have an hour lunch break before I have to struggle through a lecture called Lifting the Veil, which, thanks to my neighbor Kaia, I already know is where they teach us how to uncloak Moon Isle. Great. *I need magick to do that.* So, as I contemplate my future failure I realize that my feet have carried me in the direction of Crossroads Courtyard. At the edge of the courtyard there's a group of students clustered around a glass-encased bulletin board.

"Wren!" Sam waves at me from the middle of the group and I head over to join her, trying to fix my face so I don't look as miserable as I feel. "Oooh! They just posted the standings after the first Trial," Sam gushes as the group gives me appraising looks before they move away from the board. She points to a typed list of names that are ranked one through twenty-five. "You and Lee are number two!"

A sizzle of shock shoots through my body as I read the list. At the number one spot is Luke the Douchebag Weatherford, with his sister, Lily, at number eight. Lee and I are number two, but since I'm not sure how to feel about that my eyes skip down the list looking for other familiar names.

"Ruby is number five," I say. "That's great and I'm not surprised. They're awesome. Are you pissed that you're number ten?"

Sam shrugs. "Nah. You know I'm not super competitive. Plus, I know what I did wrong during my Trial. I—wait for it . . ." Her eyes sparkle. "Overthought the exercise. Who knew?"

"Yeah, who knew?" I mumble and sigh, and then I realize that I'm being a really crappy friend. Sam *always* overthinks and I should've laughed or said something much more

Wren-like than *who knew?* I open my mouth to take my foot out of it and turn to meet Sam's gaze and see it's too late.

"What's wrong, Wreny?"

And just like that my eyes are filling with tears and I feel that hotness in the back of my throat that says I'm on the verge of a snot cry.

Sam hooks her arm through mine. "Come on. We're going to have lunch and you're going to tell me everything."

The dining hall is large enough that even though there are a lot of students eating it's easy for Sam and me to go through the lunch line, get big bowls of pho, and sit at a table far enough away from others that we can't be overheard.

"Okay, tell me," Sam says.

I pick at the pho with my chopsticks. "Something happened during my Trial."

Sam nods. "Something happened during *everyone's* Trial. Did you hear about Misti? She's a Leo moon. She went home. Her Trial almost killed her."

"Holy crap! I didn't even know going home was an option."

"Apparently, it is if you're almost dead. . . ." She pauses to chew a big mouthful of rice noodles and then says, "What happened during *your* Trial? I heard that you and Lee got called to Dean Rottingham's office."

"Do you hear everything?"

She grins. "Nope. Only everything important. What'd the dean want?"

I move my shoulders and nibble at some noodles before I answer. "He wanted to know how Lee managed to heal an entire tree."

"Whoa, that's some serious skill. But why are you upset about it?"

I blow out a long breath. "I'm not upset about that. The tree healing was pretty awesome. It's what happened before that that's freaked me out. Well, and after as well."

"You're not making sense."

"Okay, sorry. I told Lee that he and Lily should talk. Like, *talk* talk," I whisper dramatically.

Sam almost drops her chopsticks. "No. Just no. Lee belongs with you. I've been waiting for you two to realize you're more than friends for years."

I narrow my eyes at her. "I do not know what you mean."

Sam snorts. "So, you told Lee he should date Lily. Then what happened?"

"He got weird and he's been different since," I say miserably. Then I take a deep breath and everything I've wanted to say since the day before comes rushing out at once. "Lee seemed really embarrassed and it was awkward between us until the Fire Elementals showed up and turned into a big dragon that almost killed us—which it would have if our Air Elemental hadn't saved us and brought us back to school. Then I thanked it and it whispered something strange to me. And now Lee is not acting like Lee and I have no idea what's going on with the Air Elemental *and* I'm seriously struggling because I wasn't supposed to be here so I'm totally unprepared and now on top of not understanding how to manifest my magick, if I ever will, I think I've lost one of my two best friends." I end in a rush and have to swipe at the escaped tears dripping down my cheeks.

"Okay. That's a lot. First, here." Sam passes me a napkin and I clean up my face. "Next, why did you tell Lee that he should be with Lily? I thought for sure that you *liked* him."

"I do!" I pick at my noodles and avoid her gaze. "But Lily's really pretty. And she's nice. And apparently her parents know Lee's parents and . . ." My voice trails off as I take a big mouthful of noodles and try to figure out how to make sense out of something that now seems senseless.

She shakes her head. "No, I don't mean like him as a friend—as more."

"Oh." Then I realize what she's saying. "Ohhh." My cheeks flush with heat. "I'm not sure how I like him. We've been friends for so long, and that was great. But he's different now, and I'm not talking about the Trial. When I look at him, I don't see the kid I used to sneak out with to have epic rotten apple battles in the old orchard. I see a—" My words break off because I know what I see. I just don't know if I can or even should admit it.

"Just say it," Sam prompts gently.

"I see someone I might not just love, but someone I could be in love with." I whisper the words as I stare at my soup.

"Then why didn't you tell him that instead of trying to fix him up with someone else?" Sam asks.

"First, because my feelings are pinging all over. Do I *like* Lee or like Lee? Do I have magick or not? Do I belong here or not?" I sigh. "It's all of this." I make a sweeping gesture. "If I fail here, do I just go back to my Mundane life? And if I succeed here, do I just go back to the bookstore as a Moonstruck? Or do I go off on some magickal future? I don't know!" The words burst from me. "I think that's a big part of it. Right now thinking about my future is like trying to look through muddy water. Nothing is clear. But Lee's future is unclouded. He knows exactly what he wants and he is driven to succeed. He has been since Maya died, but here it's massively intensified. I know how important it is for him to place high in the Trials. What if I tell him I want to be more than friends and actually being with me messes that up? What if he's too busy worrying about me to excel like he should?"

"Don't you trust him?" Sam asks quietly.

"Yes, of course I do." I'm surprised at the question.

"Then why don't you trust that Lee won't put himself in a situation that's going to mess up his future?"

The answer comes immediately to me. "Because I know Lee. When he loves someone it's with his whole being, and right now his whole being needs to be focused on his future."

Sam nods contemplatively as she eats more of her soup while I drink an entire glass of water and wipe my face again.

Finally she looks up at me. "Wreny, I love you, but I think you're acting like you're in a Netflix rom-com cluelessly experiencing The Big Misunderstanding that keeps the hero and heroine apart. Give him a chance. Give *the two of you* a chance."

"I don't think that's an option anymore. Lee's not acting like my Lee. He's acting like some kind of rule-following action figure."

"Oh, please. You just told me that when Lee loves it's with his whole being. Do you think a guy like that can just flip an internal switch and shut off his feelings?"

I poke at my pho and shrug. "Maybe."

"Not hardly. Should I make a comment about Lady Nightingale having the vapors to get through to you?" she says with a quick Sam grin.

"Well, a Regency analogy is always a good idea." I almost smile.

"Look, just give Lee some time. It's not surprising that he's embarrassed. Trust him, Wreny. You two are good together. Don't mess that up because of some emotional confusion and a misplaced yet dramatically selfless sacrificial act." She lifts her hand to shush me and continues. "No, I'm done trying to get through to you about Lee. You're going to have to think about it and come to the right conclusion— which is obviously *my* conclusion—because I'm incredibly smart. We're moving on now to the part about you and Lee almost burning up."

"Oh, well, there's not much to tell. He healed the tree and some wild Fire Elementals attacked us. Our Air Elemental saved us, which was actually pretty cool," I say.

"And incredibly terrifying," Sam adds. "So what is it that the Air Elemental said to you when it dropped you back on campus?"

"It's bizarre, but it said, *The strength of the maiden,* and then flew away. This time Lee didn't hear it like he did when it called me *elegida*. You're the only person I've told," I say.

She blinks in surprise. "You didn't tell Lee or Dean Rottingham?"

"No, Lee and I went back to our rooms to clean up and then it was just too hard to talk to the new him. I really don't know why I didn't say anything to Rottingham." And I truly don't know why. I could say it was because I hadn't told Lee and didn't want to spring it on him like that, but that's not the whole truth. My gut wanted me to keep my mouth shut, and I listened.

"Well, I guess I get why you didn't tell Lee." She met my gaze. "I don't trust Rottingham, either, and Celeste bothers me."

"What?" Relief flooded me. "I thought it was just me!

Rottingham doesn't seem that bad, but Celeste is border-line Disney villain."

"Cruella de Vil?"

A giggle escapes me and my whole body begins to un-wind. "Yes!" We laugh together and I feel a lot more like myself. "So, why did the Air Elemental call me *elegida* and then say that stuff about the maiden?"

"It said, *The strength of the maiden,* and nothing else?"

"Correct," I say. "What does it mean?"

"Well, we already know *elegida* means 'the chosen.' Let me check out this maiden thing." Sam takes a deep breath and closes her eyes. Her right hand is lying on the table and I watch as she curls her pointer finger down so that her thumb holds it, leaving her three other fingers extended, like she's a baseball umpire calling the third strike.

I feel something small flutter with warmth under my rib cage, but it's gone in an instant.

Sam opens her eyes and leans forward. "A maiden is typically defined as a virgin."

I nod. "Yeah, I know all about that from my love of Romancelandia."

She mirrors my nod. "Of course. But did you know that many cultures attributed power to virginity? An excellent example is the Vestal Virgins in ancient Rome who watched over the goddess Vesta's eternal flame. Their connection to the goddess was severed if they had sex. They were also killed, but let's hope that doesn't have any bearing on what the Air Elemental is trying to tell you."

"Gruesome," I say, feeling a little sick. *Yes, I'm a virgin. No, I don't want to remain one forever.*

"Well, that's just one example of many. Virgin blood has been thought to be sacred. Virgin oracles were revered and remained untouched so they could commune with what-ever god or goddess sent them signs and portents."

"Please tell me the Air Elemental isn't saying that I'm a chosen virgin." It sounds ridiculous as I say it, yet a chill of foreboding skitters across my skin, making me shiver.

"Sadly, it seems that's exactly what it's saying. Hang on. Let me put the two together—*elegida* and *the strength of the maiden*." Again, Sam positions her hand and closes her eyes. I can see her eyeballs darting back and forth like she's deep in REM sleep. My chest feels warm, but not like when I was with Lee in the forest. It's just a brief beat of heat that dissipates as soon as Sam opens her eyes and meets mine. "That's weird."

"What?" I ask.

"All right, stay with me here. Do you understand that Taureans, past and present, magickally gather and store information?"

"Kind of like the internet, right?"

Sam nods. "Right. Kind of. So, that information stays in our Taurean database. And, like the internet, it's basically out there forever—it never goes away."

"Yeah, I get that. It's why I won't send naked pics to, well, *anyone*. Definitely not worth the risk," I say.

Sam snorts and then continues. "Well, the truth is that if someone has enough time, knowledge, and skills, they can disappear things from the internet. Same for our Taurean database, though I promise you that's a lot more difficult than messing with the worldwide web.

"Which makes it very strange that when I searched for those two things together, *elegida* and *the strength of the maiden,* I kept coming up against oddly broken links, crazy rumors like *it's all a video game*."

"A video game? That makes zero sense," I say.

"Yeah, I know. There were other strange things, with one similarity—it seems that when I link both things the Air Elemental said to you it breaks my Taurean brain's connection to our magickal network, which has never, ever happened to me before." Sam frowned and picked at her lip.

"I don't understand," I say.

"Neither do I, and I *really* need to understand." Sam's eyes shine with such intensity that it's a little intimidating. "So it's time to go back to the basics, or as I like to think of it—The Dark Ages."

My brows go up. "What are you talking about?"

"Books."

"Books?" Then I get it. "Ohhh, *library* books."

"They're archaic, but there are no glitches in them. Plus, it makes sense that the information an Elemental is trying to tell you would be discoverable on this island."

"Well, yeah, and there is a really big library right here in this building," I say.

Sam grimaces. "Along with a card catalog no doubt."

I smile at my best friend. "So we're going to find a book."

"We're definitely going to find a book," Sam agrees. "Instead of going to dinner at six, let's meet at the library. It'll be empty then. Better for snooping around."

"Okay, deal."

Sam gives a long-suffering sigh. "I suppose it'll be good practice for me in case I wash out of the Trials and I'm sent somewhere primitive."

"Like the Midwest?" I offer.

Sam shudders. "Exactly."

FIFTEEN

Wren

Sam stomps her foot and crosses her arms over her chest as she glares at the massive card catalog. "I cannot stand how slow this thing is." We've already pulled out several long drawers with their little sleeves of library cards with their brief descriptions of books and the corresponding Dewey decimal number under which they're filed in the seemingly endless shelves of the enormous library. White cards for the *many* books we've browsed through and discarded litter one of the gleaming wooden tables like feathers from broken wings.

I look up from a book titled *Women to Reckon With* as I put it on the to-be-reshelved cart with the rest of our rejects.

"And by *this thing* you're talking about an inanimate card catalog?"

"Yes. Why aren't you a computer?" Sam scolds it.

I cover my laugh by clearing my throat, though Sam shoots me a look that says she is not amused by my amusement. "Okay," I say. "We've been here for hours. You're not going to any lectures tomorrow and none of the ones I want to attend are early, so let's take a break and go to Aquarius Hall. Grab some snacks and then make notes about which categories are big zeros so we can regroup and come back tomorrow."

Sam blows out a long breath. "I'm all for the break and the snack, especially if we go to my hall where there's a big charcuterie board wrapped up in the fridge begging to be eaten, but I have to tell you, Wreny, I honestly don't know where else to look."

I glance around us at the immense library. It's like something the Beast would've built for Belle, complete with rolling ladders, beautiful reading tables with bright, individual lights, *and* comfy window seats built under each of the leaded-glass windows. "Sam, you cannot seriously tell me that we're done looking through all of these books."

"Of course not, but not all of these books make any sense for us to check out. It's just that we've struck out in the categories where we should find something about being a chosen maiden. Sure, there are more books we can look through, but I'm not feeling very hopeful."

Sam looks so dejected that I wrap my arm around her shoulders as we wind our way back through the stacks toward the entrance. "Hey, you're just bummed that it's taking us a lot longer than it should to find anything. You'll feel better after some charcuterie."

Sam sighs. "Charcuterie does make everything better."

I nod. "Exactly. Just like tea and biscuits."

Sam snorts. "No, absolutely not like tea and biscuits."

We round the end of one stack and the main librarian's counter comes into sight. It's a beautiful piece of polished wood that curves into a big crescent shape behind which is an ornately carved desk. Behind the desk are lots of holding shelves for books that are on the academy's recommended reading lists. I was just wondering where the librarian had gone and feeling slightly guilty about leaving so many books on the reshelve cart *when one of the bookcases behind the desk swings open and out steps the librarian with Dean Rottingham.*

My arm tightens around Sam's shoulders and I pull her back behind the stack as I peer through the shelves to see the bookcase click closed behind them. "Ohmygod! What is that?" I whisper to Sam.

"I know, right? The librarian with the dean is really cute."

I give Sam's shoulders a little shake and turn her to face me. "Not the librarian. Did you not see where they came from?"

Sam shrugs. "Yeah, from the wall behind—" Her eyes go big and round. "Holy crap! There's a secret door behind the counter!"

"Sssh!" I whisper, and freeze as my gaze snaps back to the dean. Rottingham had been deep in conversation with the librarian, but at Sam's outburst he glances up and I swear he looks straight at me. I hold my breath, not sure why my gut is telling me to stay hidden. I expect Rottingham to call my name and ask me questions I will not want to answer, but after just a few seconds his gaze returns to the librarian. I grab Sam's hand, take a step back, and whisper, "Sam, what if there are more books inside whatever super secret room that door leads to? *Restricted books*."

Sam cocks her head to the side. "It would make sense. Someone has gone to a lot of trouble to be sure *the chosen one* and *the strength of a maiden* are a dead end, so it's not like they'd leave books explaining those phrases out here where anyone can read them."

"We have to get inside that secret room," I say.

The dean's voice booms to us, "Well, Steven, is that yawn because I'm boring you?"

"Never, Dean Rottingham!"

Sam and I peek through the stacks at the two men as they move from behind the crescent moon counter.

"Oh, I'm just kidding, son," says the dean with a little chuckle. "But some coffee will fix you right up."

"Yes, sir, it will, and I have some freshly brewed dark roast in the break room."

"That sounds excellent. Do you mind if I get a cup to take back to my office with me? Sadly, I have a pile of paperwork that seems never-ending."

"Oh, absolutely!" The librarian begins to head toward a wooden door labeled STAFF ONLY, but the dean stops after just a couple of steps.

"Steven, is the room secure?" Rottingham motions toward the space secreted away behind the shelf of books.

"Yes, sir." The librarian nods and pats his hip pocket. "Although I wouldn't be too worried. The library isn't typically a hotbed of intrigue." He hides his laugh with a sputtering cough as Rottingham's gaze narrows.

"Secrets are meant to be kept, Steven," Rottingham

says, placing his hand on the young librarian's shoulder. "I hope the council hasn't made a mistake allowing you to guard some of ours." The dean doesn't wait for a response. He opens the door to the break room, the librarian chasing after him, muttering apologies.

As soon as the door closes behind them I turn to Sam.

"Come on!"

Sam and I race from the stacks and run to the counter, skidding to a stop behind the desk directly in front of the panel that had recently been a door.

"Do you see anything? A knob or button or something?" I ask as I study the section of shelves.

"No, but in movies, the release mechanism is tied to a book. Here, let me try."

I move aside and Sam runs her hand over the spines of the neatly shelved books. She puts her face close to them and then starts pressing her hand firmly against the spines before tilting the books out a little.

Sam huffs in frustration. "Nothing's happening. Here, Wren, you start on that shelf and I'll—"

I tap Sam's shoulder and point up. Above our heads the words RESTRICTED BOOKS have just appeared in the same yellowish-golden glow that embossed the names on the doors of Aquarius Hall. Below it, just about at our eye level a keyhole materializes, also glowing.

"Whoa! We definitely need to get in there," says Sam.

Quickly I riffle through the librarian's desk. The key isn't hard to find. It's one of the old-timey skeleton keys attached to a heavy iron ring, and it's sitting right on top of a lopsided pile of papers. I grab it, turn, press my hand to the books, and put the key in the lock. "It's a fit!"

"I thought he said it was secure . . ." says Sam.

"I guess we're just really lucky, but now is not the time to stop and analyze."

Sam grins, but when she glances back at the hidden door her face pales. "Wren, look."

I follow her gaze to see that the glowing RESTRICTED BOOKS has disappeared and been replaced by a single word, ELEGIDA. Shock flushes through me making my hands sweat and my stomach clench.

"Yes, sir, it's always good to see you, too." The librarian's voice drifts to us. "Please visit anytime."

Sam and I duck down. Not that that's a smart move. All the two men have to do is walk our way and we'll be caught, especially with the glowing neon ELEGIDA behind us.

"Thank you for the coffee. Have a good night, Steven."

I'm relieved to hear the big library doors close behind Rottingham. I whisper to Sam, "You gotta distract Cute Librarian. I'm going in there. Now!" Still crouching, Sam flips her hair back, rolls her shoulders, and cracks her knuckles like she's preparing to participate in an extreme sport. "I'll take one for the team." Her gaze returns to the hidden door I'm leaning against and the glowing ELEGIDA. "But I think you need to stop touching that and stay hidden until I lure him away with my feminine charms."

I crawl away from the hidden door and duck down behind the desk as Sam rushes around the counter.

"Oh, hey, are you the night librarian?" Sam's voice has risen several octaves, and I clap my hand over my mouth to keep from laughing.

"I am. I'm Mr. Knight." Sam must have looked appropriately amused at the name, because he adds, "Not like the time of day. *Knight* with a *Kn*. How may I help you?"

Sam's flirtatious laugh makes me bite my lip. "Ohmygod, *totally* ironic! And I do need your help. I'm super intrigued by the island, so I thought I'd check out some books on Moon Isle, but I'm pretty confused about that card catalog thingy. Which category should I look under?"

"That's understandable and no problem. You're going to want to look in the eight hundreds, which is where the books on history and geography are shelved. Would you like me to show you?"

"I would!" Sam says loudly and enthusiastically. "Are the eight hundreds right up here or . . . ?"

"Oh no, they're back farther in the stacks. Come this way."

"Your coffee smells really good. Coffee fascinates me, you know, like most Pacific Northwest girls. Do you grind your own beans?" Sam's voice fades as the two of them head to the rear of the library.

"Good job, Sam!" I whisper as I straighten and hurry to the bookcase. It looks like a normal shelf again until I press my hand to the books and ELEGIDA glows above me as the keyhole reappears.

I don't hesitate but put the old key into the lock and turn it. With a little click, the bookcase swings outward just enough for me to slip inside. I'm momentarily disoriented because it's so dark, but when I take one more step, wall sconces burst into flickering flames. It looks cool but doesn't seem very wise because *there are books everywhere.* It is only about the size of my dorm room, but the walls are lined floor to ceiling with books. There's a modest wooden desk in the middle of the room. It's piled high with books. There are a couple of side tables scattered around the room. They're also covered with books. There are even books on the floor, stacked in tall columns like precariously leaning skyscrapers.

I go to the desk first to see if there might be a card catalog or some kind of filing system, but all that's on the desk are books and dust. A lot of dust. I pick up one of the books and dust rises around me in little motes that sparkle in the flickering sconce light, causing me to have a full-on sneezing fit.

I'm still sniffling as I walk to the nearest shelf and let my gaze move across the spines of the books, trying to see if they're in any kind of order—Dewey or alphabetical.

They are not.

"This room is a total mess," I mutter.

Feeling hopeless I quickly return to the entrance and start at the bookshelf on my right, determined to move methodically around the room as I search titles. And then I realize that many of the books don't have titles! Or authors! Or anything on the leather spines except metallic decorations that range from interweaving flowers to geometric designs.

"I am never going to find anything." I suppress the ridiculous urge to cry. Like that'll do me any good? *Don't lose hope. Just do your best.* I'm in the middle of my internal pep talk when I feel it—warmth blossoms under my rib cage and my heartbeat speeds up. I stop, a little dizzy, as I try to think through the strange blooming heat when the sensation changes, shifting into a tug. It's so damn weird! It's like there's a heating pad pressed against my chest and someone is pulling on its cord. It's a lot like the tug that I felt when Lee healed the tree, only it's less intense, though not less insistent.

"Okay. Okay. I get it. Maybe." I close my eyes, draw in a

long breath, and when I let it out I relax, keeping my eyes closed but allowing my feet to move—to follow the tug. I walk slowly, trying not to think, only to feel and follow until I run into a bookshelf. I open my eyes, ready to declare defeat, retreat from the room, and find Sam so we can figure out our next move, when just below my eye level something flickers yellow along the leather spine of a big, old book.

There are no words on the spine or the cover, but as I pull it from the shelf the warmth that tugged me forward flares through my fingers, zapping me like static electricity. A yelp of surprise squeaks from me and then the heat disappears leaving me holding the book. I let it fall open and my breath catches. Silver ink runs across thick, hand-pressed paper pages. I can see it just fine, but I cannot read it. Sequences of numbers and letters and even symbols skitter across the pages like I'm watching an invisible person writing in code. And then, in the middle of what looks like gibberish, one word forms that I can read: *ELEGIDA*.

Seeing it there, glowing silver, startles me so badly that my hands tremble and I almost drop the book. As I fumble with it a slip of paper slides from between its pages and falls to the floor. I pick it up. It's folded in half. Scrawled across the blank half page is one sentence: *DON'T READ IN THE DARK!*

"Like reading in the dark makes any sense at all?" I mumble to myself as I unfold the sheet of paper. I'm surprised to recognize it as a handout like the one given to us in the Lifting the Veil lecture today.

And then my eyes find the student's name at the top of the paper, written with the same hurried script as the single sentence. *MAYA YOUNG*.

For an instant my mind goes blank and I can't process

what I'm reading, and then a shudder passes through me. This was Maya's paper. This was Maya's book!

Through the open secret door I hear Sam's very fake, very shrill laughter.

"Oh, crap!" I put the sheet of paper in the book and then stuff the book inside the front of my overalls, thankful that I'm wearing a T-shirt and not a crop top under them, and rush for the door. I slip out of it and use my foot to close it behind me. It clicks softly. I drop the key on the desk where I found it and haven't quite made it around the counter as Sam and Mr. Knight come into view.

The librarian's brow furrows. "Oh, well, hello. We don't allow students behind the counter. May I help you find a book?"

"That's my friend." Sam moves quickly toward me as I step from behind the counter. She suddenly looks like a headlight-trapped deer when her eyes dart to the waistband of my overalls and I realize the book is too big to be hidden.

I wrap my arms around my middle and bend over as I moan. "Ugh, Sam. I know you want to do research, but I think I'm going to be sick." I make a loud, disgusting retching sound that has the cute librarian turning the color of curdled milk.

"Oh no!" Sam rushes to my side, putting herself between the librarian and me and wrapping her arm securely around my waist. "Let me get you back to your room. I told you that tuna smelled off. Do you have any ginger ale? That should settle your stomach. It always helps mine." She keeps talking as she steers me past Mr. Knight and to the door. Over her shoulder she calls, "Thank you for the scintillating discussion on different types of coffee beans. Who knew there were so many?"

"Come back anytime," his voice drifts after us. "I'm here most nights. Maybe we can taste test some different strains of my freshly ground beans next time."

The door to the library closes firmly behind us. Sam and I sprint down the empty hall as I hold the book close against my middle.

"You found it!" Sam says after we burst through the back doors of Moon Hall and slow to a normal pace, heading toward Crossroads Courtyard.

"I did and wait until you see it. It is not what I expected. It's going to take a genius to crack the code," I say.

Sam's eyes sparkle in the moonlight. "Good thing you know a genius."

"Good thing . . ." I pause and sober. "I found something else, too. A note. Written on the back of a lecture handout."

"Huh, that's weird. A student had a book from the restricted area? Maybe a professor left it there?"

"Um, no. It's not just any student and not just any book." I take a deep breath and as I let it out say, "The handout has Maya's name on it. And the note is written in her handwriting."

Sam's eyes look huge. "Maya? As in Lee's Maya?"

I nod. "And the reason I picked this book is because magick drew me to it."

"You're serious? You're not exaggerating?"

"I promise I'm not exaggerating. Sam, we can't say anything to Lee about this."

"Agreed."

"Plus, we don't even know what this is yet." We start walking again. I still have my arms crossed protectively over the book. It feels warm against my skin.

"What does Maya's note say?" Sam asks.

"*Don't read in the dark*," I say.

Sam scoffs. "Who would read in the dark?"

"Right? Maybe she was doodling?" Even as I say the words my gut is telling me there's way more to it than that.

"I don't know, Wren. Maya was a Taurus moon, right?"

"Yeah." I nod.

Sam speaks slowly, like she's reasoning aloud. "Not to sound all full of myself, but even the doodles of a Taurus moon have meaning."

"That's what I thought," I admit.

"Well, let's get something to eat and then check out that book. . . ." Sam pauses and adds, "But not in the dark."

"Sounds like a plan." We pick up our pace and I try to shake off the strange someone-just-walked-over-my-grave feeling Maya's note has given me. I bump Sam with my shoulder. "Soooo, are you going back to the library for more scintillating coffee discussions?"

"Never. I will never go back. I don't even drink coffee. It tastes like mud, no matter how much sugar and cream I add to it." Sam shudders delicately.

"Oh, but he's *so cute*." I bat my eyes.

"Shall I remind you of the time you said Ryan Gosling was cute?"

It's my turn to shudder. "No. Never. I will never go back."

We link arms as we head for Aquarius Hall and I try not to freak out about the dead girl's note between the pages of the strange book I hold tightly against me—like I can imprint it on my skin, absorb it, understand it and whatever is really going on at the Academia de la Luna.

SIXTEEN

Lee

It's the Fourth of July. The past three weeks have gone by in a blur of endless training that's left my hands aching and has me wishing I could have spent this summer in Fern Valley going from crashing in our movie room to getting in Wren's way during her shifts at Pages.

But that was what the old me would be aching for.

The new me, the me firmly in place from now until I'm six feet under, is happy to have a break in training and to be in the stands witnessing the end of a lacrosse game organized by the Scorpio moons. My pal Ruby is killing the other team. Not literally. Although their impressive physical display makes it clear that it's better to stay on their good side.

Lily's on her feet next to me, shouting Ruby's name and screeching encouragement. "Did you just see that? Ruby scored again. They're unbelievable."

I can't help but laugh. Lily's completely lit up with excitement and has the ability—without using her magick—to make everyone around her happy just by being happy in their presence.

Luke's on my other side, moving his straw up and down so fast in the plastic lid of his fountain drink that it's whistling.

Lily brings a cloud of cinnamon and spice with her as she settles back onto the bleachers and crosses her arms over her chest. "You can leave, you know?" she says, her glare burning through me straight to her brother.

"Wow, Lil, thanks. I'm so glad to finally have your permission," he grumbles, and takes a long drink from the straw.

I run my fingers along my scalp and apparently let out the groan I thought I'd only uttered in my head, because they're both staring at me. Caught between the narrowed gazes of these two fiery redheads—two people who were, at first, an assignment but are now a couple of my closest friends—makes me sweat more than the summer heat.

As if scheduled, they both erupt into laughter, Luke clapping me on the back while Lily sags against my side, vibrating with giggles.

"We suck," she says, wiping tears from her bright eyes.

"Next time, tell us to shut up," Luke adds, standing and stretching his long, lanky arms overhead.

"Or squirt Luke with a spray bottle." Lily shrugs. "It works better on him than it does on the dogs."

"Germ," Luke says, leaning over to swat the air above her head.

"Dweeb," she counters, sticking out her tongue.

My chest tightens, and I rub the cage covering my heart. Maya and I were less Lily and Luke and more Bunsen and Beaker, but I would exchange that for Lily and Luke's worst days. I just want my sister back.

Luke snaps his fingers, returning me to the present. "Gotta make the rounds."

"I'll find you after the game," I say, aware of the fact that there's a fifty-fifty chance of seeing him again today. Over the past three weeks, I've learned that *gotta make the rounds* is the phrase Luke uses to transition from normal, chill guy into the senator's son. I'm not sure which version of Luke my parents wanted me to be close to, but I know there's only one I like to be around.

"He's off to make someone's life miserable." It's Lily's turn to groan as she watches Luke squeeze down the packed aisle and jog down the bleacher's stairs. "I don't know why he has to be like that. Like, you're my brother, and I love you, but when you're a douche I want to squeeze your head until it pops like a zit. You know what I mean?"

Her eyes widen, and her jaw drops, and I know what she's about to say even before she does.

"It's fine, Lily," I say, lungs squeezing.

"I am so sorry, Lee." She presses her fingers to her mouth as if she can shove the words back in. "I know about Maya, but I totally—"

"Seriously, Lily, it's fine. We're good. No need to apologize." After a certain point, hearing people say they were sorry about my sister was worse than if they'd said that she's dead.

"Well, I feel like an asshole," she whispers more to her-self than to me, but I wrap my arm around her shoulders and scoop her into an awkward side hug anyway, tendrils of her spice-scented hair tickling my cheeks.

"At least you don't smell like one."

She chuckles and playfully pushes me away. A part of my chest relaxes, and I'm light-headed as air is once again able to slip freely into my lungs. She and Luke don't know how Maya's death has changed my family . . . has changed me. In moments like this, they think they understand because they can imagine and empathize, but it's impossible to know how someone's absence baptizes those around it, cleanses them of who they were. Washed clean of Past Lee, I have taken his place. And it's a thing I've only shared with Wren.

As if summoned, I see a flash of pink two rows down. I spot Wren and Sam as they shrug and point to their laps at an open book that looks like it belongs in a museum.

There's another reason I've become so dedicated to my training, and I'm currently staring at the back of its head. It's been three weeks since she and I were in Dean Rot-tingham's office. Three weeks since I left her standing in the hallway and let the doors close in her face. Three weeks since we've been able to spend time alone together or say more than a few stilted words to each other. We're not us anymore. But I guess we never were.

I clench my hands and wince at the dull ache.

I'm not mad, just disappointed. I've managed to lose the girl of my dreams and my best friend all at once. Worse, I have no clue what to do to fix it. Actually, the worst part is that I don't think Wren wants me to. Lily leans over and nudges me, and I realize I've been staring at the back of Wren's head for the past five minutes of the final quarter.

"Earth to Lee, come in, Lee."

I clear my throat and with it my mood. "Ruby looks good out there." It's only a partial lie. I know Ruby's doing great even if I haven't been watching. "Thanks again for asking me to go to the game with you," I blurt, and hope she doesn't notice the rings of moisture soaking through the pits of my tee.

"I'm so glad you came." Lily pulls the scrunchie from her wrist, scoops her fiery hair from between her shoulder blades, and knots it into a pile on top of her head. "I was worried you'd spend the whole day cooped up in Aquarius Hall practicing dexterity or meditating to better manifest your magick."

"I don't meditate, but that does sound like a lecture one of the professors would give. Maybe you have a future at the academy."

She frowns wrinkling the constellation of freckles that dot the bridge of her nose. "No thanks. I don't know what I want to do, but I do know that it won't deal with teaching, math, or politics. But don't tell my mom about that last part. She doesn't exactly know that I won't be following in her footsteps."

Out on the field, Ruby catches a pass and fires the ball into the top right corner of the net. Lily grabs my hand, and we jump to our feet, our excited shouts blending into the roars of the cheering crowd. She wraps her arms around me and hops up and down. She's trying to get a "Ruby! Ruby!" chant going, but people are already sitting back down. Lily and I are among the few left standing, my arm slung across her sun-kissed shoulders, when Sam and Wren rise from the bench. Out of the corner of my eye, I see Wren stuff the old, dirt-colored leather book into her oversized crossbody. She follows Sam, squeezing past the others in their row who are so focused on the final minutes of the game that they don't seem to notice the heavy book in Wren's bag slam against their knees.

Sam and Wren stand on the stairs for a moment, shielding their eyes from the afternoon sun as they lean into each other, whispering and surveying the stands. Wren's eyes meet mine, and my stomach falls into my shoes. She takes one step up and then another, and now she's on our row, her short sunflower-yellow dress bursting with life against her pale skin.

Every time she looks at me is like the first time, and I don't know if I can stay out of Cupid's path if she keeps staring at me like that. My palms start sweating, my heart aching with unspoken words, and I drop my arm from around Lily's shoulders. I know what it looks like. At least, what Wren thinks it looks like, and I want to shout that she was wrong. That Lily is harboring her own secret crush and it has nothing to do with me.

"Lily! So glad I found you." She reaches into the pocket on the outside of her bag and pulls out a small envelope. "Sam said you're the one in charge of gathering donations for the Pacific Northwest Orca Preservation Society. I've seen you a thousand times, but I keep forgetting to give this to you."

Lily takes the envelope and pulls Wren against her in the same bouncy hug she just gave me. "You're the absolute best," she chimes, releasing Wren and stuffing the envelope into her back pocket.

"Thanks, and I, uh, I didn't mean to interrupt your date." Wren tucks a strand of hair behind her ear, and I know her well enough to spot the light pink blush racing up her neck.

"It's not a date," I blurt, and immediately want to punch myself.

"Oh." Wren's smile is thin and twisted, and she won't meet my gaze.

Sam clears her throat, her hands on her hips. Her round eyes ping-pong from Lily to me to Wren and back again. I wish I could stop sweating for two seconds. "Well, we're going to skedaddle. We have some . . ." Her gaze finally falls away, landing on the rectangular bulge in Wren's bag. "Research to do. See you at tonight's festivities." She grabs Wren's hand and drags her away.

I watch Wren leave, and it's like the sun is setting as she walks down the steps and disappears around the side of the stands in her bright yellow dress.

Lily grabs the bottom of my shirt and tugs, and I realize I'm the only one standing.

"So, you still haven't had a real conversation with her?" she asks as I take my seat.

"With who?" I feign ignorance and check the scoreboard. Only one minute left in the tied game. Only one minute until I can satisfy the urge squeezing my calves, the urge to run down the stairs and chase after the center of my universe.

"Seriously?" Lily's red brows lift, and she purses her lips. "Look, Lee, you have got to get out of your own way. You're in your head way too much. Just talk to her. The worst thing that can happen is literally what you're experiencing right now."

"You're one to talk," I say, getting defensive instead of

dealing with my emotions. "You're doing exactly what I'm doing with—"

"Okay, rude. And no, Lee, I'm definitely not being angsty and awkward and avoiding the person I'm into." Lily brushes back a strand of hair that's fallen from her bun and fixes her green gaze to the field.

"I'm sorry, Lily."

She places her hand on top of mine and squeezes. "You should be. You should also talk to Wren. You're a big guy. There has to be a little courage in there somewhere."

A whistle blows, and our section of the stands erupts once again.

"Ruby scored!" Lily screams and jumps to her feet. "They won! Ruby won!"

Regardless of which Moon Isle team they rooted for, everyone is out of their seats and rushing to the field.

I swallow a lungful of air and push myself away from the hot metal, joining the chorus of clanging footsteps down the bleachers and onto the grass. A cheery smile hangs from my lips and a mouthful of compliments waits on my tongue as I look for Ruby and Lily. Not being ready to face my fears with Wren reeks of Past Lee, and I'm not sure that's a bad thing.

SEVENTEEN

Wren

I think I'm obsessed." I blow out a long breath as Sam joins me on one of the benches surrounding Crossroads Courtyard.

"With me?" Sam drops into a quick curtsey. "Milady! I'm flattered."

I roll my eyes at Sam, who sits beside me. I hold up the leather book that has practically become part of me over the past three weeks. "I love you, but I was talking about this book." The moon lamps that dot campus flicker on at that moment and the indecipherable silver script on the front of the book glistens like mercury. "Not that my obsession is getting me anywhere."

Sam takes the book from me and it falls open in her lap. She frowns down at the silver lettering that runs across the pages. Once in a while we can make out a word—often that word is in Spanish—but mostly it just looks like gibberish. "It really is frustrating. I've never come up against something like this." Her fingers trace the moving ink. "I honestly don't know what it is. I still don't think it's a code, though. Code cracking is something I'm very, *very* good at, but I cannot find any continuity to this."

"Well, I think I figured out something new about it, though it's not going to help," I say, taking the book from her and opening it to a page she and I had bookmarked last week. Throughout the book Maya had written notes in the margins and at the top and bottom of the pages—and a lot of her comments are disturbing. Scrawled throughout the book are annotations like: *This isn't what they're teaching*; *new info!*; *this is not good*. Sometimes Maya only wrote one word, but those single words are just as troubling. *What?!* . . . *No!* . . . *Bizarre!* are sprinkled inside the mysterious old book in Maya's handwriting. The problem is we can't understand her notes because we can't read the text! But this time it's a little different. There's a single word written at the top of the page, *FRACTURADA!* It's in all caps, with an exclamation point and an underline.

"Look at this." My finger traces under a sentence fragment about halfway down the page that says: *but when the power is held by only one, the Conduit, it ensures* . . . From there the pretty cursive writing returns to an indecipherable mixture of letters, numbers, and strange symbols.

"Oooh! That's good! At least we can read it for a change." Sam claps happily.

"Hang on. There's more." I flip the page. At the top

Maya had written: *This isn't what they're teaching*. And I point at more silver gibberish toward the bottom of the page. "Last night when I was waiting out here for you before we went to the dining hall I'm one hundred percent sure that right about here I could suddenly read the words joined with *the maiden* and *elder*."

Sam squints at the unreadable script. "But it's completely illegible."

"*Now* it is." I turn back to the page that Maya had annotated with the single Spanish word. "And last night this was all nonsense, but today they're complete words. Sam, I swear it's like the book changes every time I open it." I turn the pages slowly, watching the silvery ink slither past, as beautiful as it is mysterious. "I really wish Maya was still alive or, at the very least, had written more notes in this thing."

"I do, too, but we're going to figure it out."

I just chew on my bottom lip, because figuring out this book seems more impossible now than it did a few weeks ago.

"Okay, so the book changes, or at least our ability to understand it changes. We need to figure out what changes it and why." Sam looks up from the book to me. "So be sure to check it several times a day, every day."

"You're feeding my obsession," I mutter.

"Do you have a better idea?"

"Absolutely not." I sigh.

"Also, let's start marking the pages with sticky tabs when we can read words and phrases. We'll number the tabs and record exactly what the book says. That way we'll know for sure what's changing and what isn't. Maybe we just need to put together the lines we can read and eventually they'll form something coherent." Sam digs through her back-pack for a notebook and a little plastic pack of sticky tabs.

"That's a good idea," I say.

"I don't know why I didn't think of it earlier."

CRACK! BOOM!

Sam and I startle as the warm-up for the big fireworks show sounds in the distance. I press my hand against my chest. "I don't mean to sound un-'Merican, but the Fourth of July is my least favorite holiday."

Sam cocks her head and asks, "Too loud?"

I nod vigorously. "Way seriously too loud. Plus, fire-works are not environmentally friendly."

"I agree. Think about all the freaked-out animals."

"Grace Kelly has to be drugged for twenty-four hours *at least* or she does nothing but Frenchie death yodel and shake." My breath catches and I'm surprised by the wave of homesickness that washes over me.

Sam hooks her arm through mine. "I know. I miss home, too."

I open my mouth to tell Sam that I'd talked to my uncles earlier on the archaic landline phone in Aquarius Hall, which made me miss home even more, but a loud "*Got-cha!*" from somewhere behind us interrupts me. Sam and I turn on the bench in time to peer through the pines to see a guy I recognize as one of Luke Weatherford's Leo moon buddies pulling a brown bag from the middle of a thick group of ferns. Sticking out of the top of it are the ends of Roman candles and rockets. He shoves the bag in his backpack and sprints past Crossroads Courtyard to Luke and a group of guys who pound him on the back before they race away toward the beach, laughing uproariously.

"Juvenile delinquents," Sam says.

"Where the hell did they even get fireworks and why can't they just be happy with the stuff the school's going to set off?" I shake my head. "I only like sparklers. That's it. Seriously."

"What about the big fireworks they're going to set off over the water pretty soon? Do you hate them, too?"

"I only mildly dislike them," I say. "Grace Kelly hates them enough for both of us, and then there's . . ." My words choke off as my heart jumps up into my throat. Lee's jogging across campus. He has a blanket over his shoulder and he's heading toward the beach where we're all supposed to gather for the fireworks. I sigh dramatically when he doesn't even glance my way.

"Okay, I'm done." Sam abruptly packs away the notebook.

"What?" I turn semi-innocent eyes to her.

"I refuse to continue our work relationship until you go talk to him. You're martyring yourself, and you're not supposed to do that until after you have children."

"Talk to who?"

Sam snorts. "Don't even."

My shoulders bow. "I can't help it. I miss Lee."

"Please. You can *definitely* help it—you just *won't*."

"Sam, he won't talk to me." I blink fast as tears fill my eyes. I hate crying, but since Lee and I have been so weird around each other it seems like I'm always only one stray thought away from bawling.

"Time for some tough love, Wreny." Sam turns to face me. When I don't look at her, she crosses her arms over her chest and waits.

I know her. If I don't say something, she'll just glower at me. Forever.

"Fine. Time for some tough love. Let me have it." I also cross my arms over my chest, though I realize I look pathetic instead of stern.

"Good. Listen up because after I say this the topic of Lee will not be spoken of again—" I open my mouth, but with a glare she shushes me and continues. "*Until* you actually talk to him, which means more than the *hello* and *hey, what's up* non-talk words you've been firing at him for the past three weeks before you find an excuse and run away."

"I don't *run*." I pout.

"Run, walk briskly—same-same. And you know what I mean. So, here goes. Wreny, it is obvious to everyone—"

"People are talking about me?" I squeak.

"I'm using hyperbole. Shush and listen. It is obvious that you hurt Lee when you rejected him. Then you—"

"But I didn't reject him!" I interrupt again.

"You told him to be with someone else. Wren, that's a rejection." She raises her voice and keeps talking when I open my mouth to argue. "Then you compounded that hurt by avoiding him. For three weeks. You've treated him like he's an acquaintance when the truth is he's been your best friend for the past *five years*."

"*You're* my best friend," I say softly.

"Yes, I'm one of your best friends. You *had* two of them up until three weeks ago when you rejected Lee and then continued to reject him."

I scuff the toes of my shoes on the cobblestones. "He's been spending a lot of time with Lily."

"Actually, he's been spending a lot of time with Luke and Lily," corrects Sam.

"Yeah, and a bunch of other new friends who are not me." Even I can hear the pathetic whine in my voice.

"So? You've been spending a lot of time with me." She holds up her hand when I start to protest. "What did you expect him to do? Sit in his room by himself and pine away? It's been *weeks*. Plus, he and Lily aren't together. Ruby told me. Lily says he's still obsessed with you."

I look up from the cobblestones as my stomach does a little flip-flop. "Really?"

Sam rolls her eyes. "You know I wouldn't lie to you. You have two choices. One, let Lee go and be okay with it. Or two, *talk to him. Tell him why you rejected him and give him the opportunity to respond honestly.*"

"You think maybe I haven't ruined everything between us?" The flip-flopping in my stomach rises into my chest.

"I think you still have a chance at fixing your mistake, but the window is closing. Either way, you gotta end this sad-sack stuff. You've been picking at this broken relationship like a scab. Fix it or leave it alone and move on."

"That is a disgusting analogy."

"Thank you." Sam stands. "Now I'm meeting Ruby at Scorpio Hall. We're going to watch the fireworks. Are you coming with us or are you going to do the right thing?"

"When you put it like that I think there's only one thing I *can* do." I stand and wipe the butt of my yellow sundress off and run my fingers through my hair. "Do I look okay?"

Sam studies me. "That dress is cute. Your hair's kind of wild tonight, but I have a feeling Lee will like that. Put on some of that lip gloss you like so much that smells like strawberries and you're good to go."

"I'm nervous."

Sam grins. "Good." She takes the cobblestone sidewalk that heads in the direction of Scorpio Hall and calls over her shoulder in her best RuPaul imitation (which really isn't good at all), "Good luck and *don't* F it up."

I'm going to do this. I'm going to do this. I'm going to do this. The mantra plays around and around in my mind as I stuff the book into my crossbody and fish out my lip gloss, slathering it on and breathing in the strawberry scent like it's a balm for my nerves—which it isn't because I have to wipe my sweaty palms on my dress.

I've decided. Or been tough-loved into deciding. Either way I'm going to talk to Lee. Now. And I mean *really* talk to him. I brush back my hair and head for the beach.

The ferns and pines give way to sandy dunes and clumps of tall grasses as I get near the water. The dock is at one end of the little cove area that fronts the school. There is only a small beach that's adjacent to the dock. Sandy dunes lead down to the beach, which forms a crescent moon. One tip of the moon holds the dock. Then there's a little swimming area that ends at the other curved tip of the crescent. It's the only area on Moon Isle where we're allowed to swim. More dunes and grasses separate the approved beach area and the rest of the coast. There are big, red-lettered signs at the end of the beach that read RESTRICTED. ABSOLUTELY NO ENTRANCE. But I don't care about what's beyond the beach. I've caught sight of Lee and the flip-flopping in my chest drops back into my stomach and switches to nausea. He and Lily are sharing a blanket spread out on one of the last dunes. Most of the other students are already on the beach, but I can see the genius in Lee's choice of location. It's not as packed and he'll have a clear, *romantic* view of the fireworks when they start—as well as more privacy than the crowd on the beach.

My feet stop moving and I stand there, watching Lee and wishing Uncle Joel was here to give me a pep talk like he used to before every one of my volleyball games (*I'm short, but I serve like a demon—which is a good thing*). On the plus side, Lee and Lily aren't all snuggled up together. On the negative side, I hate that their names make such a cute alliteration. I watch as Lee points down at the beach and says something, which makes Lily laugh. It's a full-on, head-tossed-back, for real laugh. I can hear it from where I'm standing. It's musical and pretty and when Lee joins her I want to turn around and sprint away.

At that moment Lee glances over his shoulder, like he could feel my pain and hopelessness. Our eyes meet. The laughter in his snuffs out and for a moment I can see his sadness so clearly that it makes me gasp. Then Lily says something and he turns back to her.

Instead of making me run, Lee's look of raw pain pulls me to him. *I* did that. I caused him that pain. I'd like to say I only just realized it, but I'd be lying. I knew I'd hurt him. I just didn't want to face that hurt, which is unfair to Lee. I've also been terrified that if I really talk to him I'll find out that we are through—as best friends, as anything except the acquaintances we've become, which is also unfair to Lee. I need to face this.

I make my feet move again and walk directly to Lee and Lily.

Lily sees me first. She looks up and smiles. "Hey there, Wren. Wanna join us? It's almost dark enough for the fireworks to start."

I study her face for signs that she's annoyed or pissed, but Lily is just Lily—friendly and kind. (The opposite of her twin.)

Lee doesn't say anything.

I clear my throat. "Hi, Lily. That's, um, really nice of you, but I need to talk to Lee. I'm, um, sorry to interrupt your—"

"No problem." Her smile widens. "I think you and Lee talking is a good thing."

My gaze slides to Lee. He's watching me silently. "Can we talk? I promise it won't take long."

Lee nods, though he still doesn't say anything. With a familiar athletic grace, he stands and gestures for me to lead. I pause for just a moment, hoping that he'll bow, call me *milady,* and offer me his arm.

He doesn't.

"Um, okay. Uh. This way," I mumble awkwardly and head away from the crowd and along the dunes closer to the restricted area and a big patch of tall grasses that will give us a little privacy. I stop by the clump of grass, turn to face Lee, and take a deep breath.

I don't know what the hell to say.

I look up into his brown eyes and blurt, "Hi."

"That's what you called me over here to say?" He doesn't sound pissed, just confused and sad.

I look down at the dune. "No. Sorry. I'm nervous."

"You shouldn't be nervous to talk to me." His voice is low and soft and my gaze finds his face again. His lips lift in the hint of a smile, though his eyes are so, so sad. "It's okay. Just say it."

And I suddenly realize that he thinks I'm going to officially end things between us. "Oh no! It's not that!"

"Not what?"

"I don't want us to break up." As I say the words my voice hitches and my vision starts to blur as my eyes fill with tears.

"Break up? Wren, we're not together. We haven't been together for weeks. And we've never been together like that," he says.

"I know!" Tears spill down my cheeks and I wipe at them. "And I hate it. It's my fault." I have to stop talking to sniffle and take several breaths as I unsuccessfully try to stop crying. "I'm so sorry about everything. About telling you to date Lily. About avoiding you for weeks. About being a truly awful friend."

"Hey, it's okay." Lee takes a little step toward me and starts to reach for me, but his hands fall to his sides. "I know you just want to be friends." He shakes his head and runs his hand over his neat braids. "I should have been honest when I started to feel more for you. I didn't want to ruin things between us, which it seems I did anyway. I've had all this time to think about it. I miss you, Wren. I miss my best friend. Can we go back to the way it was before?"

"I have messed this up so bad. Lee, what I'm trying to tell you is I *do* feel more than friendship for you."

Lee blinks several times and then he shakes his head. "I don't get it. Then why try to get me to be with Lily? And why have you iced me out for weeks?"

I wipe my face again, take in another big breath, and in a rush I say, "Because I've been confused about my feelings. Things changed so fast. You're gone two years and then suddenly you're back and all tall and sexy and manly. Then I'm Moonstruck, but weirdly. And that same day I'm at the Academia de la Luna, a place I never thought I'd be with my best friend who I'm having lots of feelings for—like, more than friend feelings. I wanted to tell you, but I've been afraid of getting in your way and screwing things up for you! I don't have any magick, or at least not any like everyone else—and I mean *everyone* else. I know you, Lee. If we're together you're going to want to protect me—take care of me—put me first. But you can't right now. You have to excel here so you can have the future you want."

His brow furrows. "Wait. You told me to be with Lily because you think it'll mess up my future to be with you?"

I sniffle and nod.

A burst of laughter explodes from his lips. He puts his hand to his mouth, like he's trying to keep the laugh in, and then he gives up and *giggles*.

I'm utterly miserable and I feel my face getting hot. "Why are you laughing at me?"

"No, no, no. I'm not laughing at you. . . ." He has to pause while he gets his mirth under control, though his brown eyes continue to sparkle. "Well, maybe I'm laughing at you a little. Wren, since when do you need protection? Or to be taken care of? Or to have my world revolve around you?"

"Well, um . . ." I pause and gesture around us. "I'm not exactly in my element here."

"So you want me to babysit you?"

"No!"

He finally stops laughing. His gaze traps mine. "Then tell me what you do want."

I know my next words will change everything, though I can't tell whether that change is going to be good or bad. "Lee, I want you. I want us. I've missed you so much. I should have trusted you. I should have talked to you, even if that meant I was going to hear something that would break my heart. That's why it's taken me so long to come to you." My voice is a whisper and Lee moves closer to me, so close that I can smell the familiar scent of the bergamot lotion he likes so much—he smells like home. "Because I'm a coward. I've been afraid if I told you all of this you'd say that we should just be friends, which is okay because being just friends is better than being nothing. I couldn't stand it if we were nothing. I can't—"

Lee's hands cup my face, wiping away my tears with his thumbs. "We could never be nothing, Wren. Never." I can't look away from him. "I love you, Wren Nightingale," he whispers.

"I love you, Lee Young," I whisper back.

"You think I'm tall and sexy and manly?" His thumbs caress my cheeks as he smiles down at me.

"I don't think it. I know it," I say. Relief and joy shiver through me as Lee's expression shifts from teasing to intense. His hands slide through my hair to cradle my head. Lee bends and I tilt my face up to meet him—to meet his lips.

He's going to kiss me! My Lee is finally going to kiss me!

There's a crack and a whistle, and then several pops and booms as the fireworks light up the sky, framing Lee perfectly, *just like in season one of* Bridgerton*!* I want to shout, *Flawless!* so loud that the fictional queen hears me, and for one very weird moment I think I have shouted. Screamed? Shrieked? Lee freezes just before his lips touch mine. His body tenses as the sound comes again. Reluctantly, we step apart and glance around us because a girl is screaming so loud that we can hear her over the fireworks.

EIGHTEEN

Lee

I break away from Wren, and the warmth of her drains from me as I increase the distance between us. I rush over the dune, my flip-flops sinking into the sand, warm with the rays of the newly set sun. Another scream sounds, cracking in my bones, shooting slivers of panic through my limbs. I run to the peak of the dune, blades of grass stabbing my shins.

A ball of neon yellow zips through the night sky, throwing stains of lemon-colored light across the craggy rocks jutting out from the foam-capped waters below.

I stop next to the red restricted-access sign, and my muscles turn to ice beneath my skin. Instinctively, I reach for Wren, and she's there, like she always should have been. Like she always *would have* been if I'd gotten over myself. But now is not the time to review the past.

Down on the beach, a group sets off fireworks. Shrill whistles screech from a fountain of sparks shooting at least twenty feet into the air. They're beyond the safety of campus grounds and have upset the Elementals.

This land is not yours. It is not ours. It belongs to the Elemental factions.

Dean Rottingham's warning slips across my memory while the false sun morphs, throwing wisps of golden light into the night air as it takes the shape of a massive owl. A shadow dangles from its beak, something moving . . . something *alive,* but the raptor is too fast, too wild, for me to know exactly what.

The yellow orb splits into three, and I can see each one clearly now.

"Air Elementals," I whisper, and squeeze Wren's hand tight, images of the fire dragon and the memory of the heat of its flames bringing sweat to my brow.

"Oh god," she gasps, lifting her arm to point to the sky, to the shape the creatures toss between them. "They—they have . . ."

Her voice fades, swept up into the steady crash of waves against the deadly rocks. She can't bring herself to say it, and it's clear why.

The shadowed shape is lit by each of the Air Elementals burning bright yellow against the indigo sky as they toss it between them in a gruesome game of Hacky Sack. *It* is a person.

I feel Wren start to move, to lean forward, to run down the slope of the dune to the group below. I hold on to her tight, her buoy in the tide of death that's sure to wash over us all. My feet never inch past the restricted-access sign and neither will hers.

They got themselves into this. Heroes are only heroes in movies. In real life they're defendants or cold in a mortuary fridge. Without Maya there to carry the family torch, I can't be reckless.

"We have to do something." Wren is breathless beside me, her words erupting in tiny gasps.

"No," I say. "We don't." The ice has melted now, washed me clean of any panic. I know what to do.

My gaze trails over the obvious warning sign.

And what not to.

Another scream echoes off the cove's battered rocks, and my gaze flicks down to the craggy shore below and the group huddled at the water's edge.

"Let him go!" a girl shrieks. I can't make out who she is, who any of them are, with the disco balls of light swirling in the sky.

Behind us, footsteps dig into the sand as professors rush up the dune.

"We have to—" Wren takes a step forward, and I pull her two steps back.

"We have to stay here. We have to stay safe."

She stares up at me, her blue eyes shimmering with unshed tears, and for a moment I think she'll fight me, that I'll have to throw her over my shoulder and run from the beach like her life depends on it, because it might. And I'm not willing to take that chance. Then her brow furrows, and I don't know if it's her heartbeat I hear or mine, but I do know that we're both in the same place—lost in the memories of years ago, haunted by the people we couldn't save.

I pull her close, my throat raw and tight, fighting back the tears I never let myself cry.

Two of the Elementals break off, shooting stars dive-bombing the group that strayed too far from safety. They're screaming now, but my mind is trapped two years in the past, and I can only hear my mother's piercing wails and her knees smacking the white tiles of our foyer when the dean told her my sister was never coming home.

A sharp gust of salt-tinged air burns my eyes. I inhale, and I'm back in the present. I comb my fingers through Wren's hair and focus on how warm she is against my middle. I ground myself in this moment, no matter how horrible it may be, because it will always be better than the past.

The Elementals blitz through the sky as the panicked group rushes from the restricted area and scrambles up the other side of the dune, hands and feet clawing at the sand.

Dean Rottingham blows past us, Professor Douglas and two others I don't recognize on his heels. His fingers work, hands beating the air around him in a series of movements I've never seen in my *Moon Guide*.

The group of students escaping the beach break the line the dean and professors have formed on the other side of the sign, pushing and shoving one another to get to safety, to the place they never should have left.

One of them crashes into me, spraying sand across my legs. I reach down as he pushes himself onto his hands and knees and help him up.

The side of Luke's face is coated in sand. "Thanks, man." He spits out a mouthful and runs a shaking hand through his red curls.

A crowd has gathered, gasping and shouting each time one Elemental throws the body to another.

"Luke, what happened?" I ask. "Why'd you go past the sign?"

"We, uh, we didn't think it'd be a big deal." His face is drained of color, his eyes wide and frantic. "I didn't mention it because I didn't think you'd come. You always follow the rules. I didn't think . . ." His vacant gaze looms over the onlookers as his trembling fingers brush his cheek. "We snuck some fireworks. We're so close to campus, I didn't think . . . They came out of nowhere and grabbed Wyatt and—"

He's cut off by the crowd's collective gasp as the Elementals go quiet, frozen overhead, and the wind picks up, gusting hurricane strength, searing us with ocean spray and pelting us with rocks. Each Aquarius Air Elemental swells, their neon bodies pulsing brighter, brighter until I'm forced to shield my eyes.

I glance at Dean Rottingham and the line of professors bracing themselves against the gale, arms outstretched, fingers plucking strands of magick.

I curl my arm around Wren and hold her close as my gaze picks through the crowd, searching for Celeste. I can't help but think that, if she were here, this would already be over and Wyatt would have two feet on the ground instead of hanging like a doll from the claws of these wild, ancient beings.

"Lee!" Sam's voice slams against me on the back of another punishing gust. Her hands are in the air, and the top of her head bobs up and down as she shuffles through the crowd, Lily's fiery tangle of hair and Ruby's scarlet hood not far behind.

They squeeze through the crowd and huddle around Wren, Luke, and me. I push into the people behind us, not wanting anyone I care about to step over the invisible line that separates safety from chaos.

Lily gives Wren and me a quick embrace before throwing herself onto her brother. As they hug, their heads together, wind twirling through their hair, it's hard to see where one stops and the other begins.

Energy pops against my skin as more academy professors push through the throng, their magickal intent focused on the creatures.

My attention returns to the sky. The Elementals hover, each pulse of light an exhale of power that rushes over us in strong gusts. They're communicating, heads swiveling, teeth gnashing, in an unspoken language all their own.

There's a swell of pressure against us as the crowd parts and a cloaked figure sprints to Rottingham. Celeste claps her hands onto the dean's shoulders, her cape sparkling in the neon lights.

He raises his hands above his head, and this time the magick shoots from his fingers, lashing the sky with a rippling wave of energy.

Beside me, Wren stumbles, and I hold her up as the weight of reality threatens to crush her. Celeste is here now. She will save Wyatt. She will save us all.

The Elementals' gazes latch on to the dean. The wind ceases blowing, and if anyone was talking, they aren't now. Another tear of his fingers through the air, and another whip of magick slashes the sky.

The creatures who own this land, who should not be approached or antagonized, release Wyatt. His body falls, falls, falls, so long there's hope he might fly. But he doesn't.

Dean Rottingham and the professors lean forward, focusing all their magick into reaching him before he crashes. But they don't.

Wyatt Jackson smacks into the rocks, carved into earthen swords by the Pacific's rabid waters. We all gasp, stealing Wyatt's final breath, making it a piece of us.

My gaze returns to Celeste, but she's no longer there.

Wren presses her face against my chest, the warmth of her tears sinking into my skin. I hold her against me. I want to say something, *anything* to take away her pain, but all I can think about is Maya. My sister died on this campus, drowned in this sea. And I'm lost again. Back in my house with the doors that no longer shut right and the paint that's always chipped in the corners no matter how many fresh coats are applied. I'm back in the moment my mother answered those sharp knocks. I'm back with the bowed heads and the dean's serious voice, and the house that will never forget the way that she screamed.

NINETEEN

Wren

It's eerily quiet in the dining hall. Professor Scherer led the other teachers in hastily rounding us all up and guiding us inside Moon Hall, where we're sitting in little groups, waiting for Dean Rottingham to speak to us. I'm strangely exhausted. I feel like my legs are noodles and my brain is foggy. I'm indescribably glad that Lee's hand is holding mine and we're sitting so close that our shoulders are pressed together. But having him beside me doesn't keep terrible images from flickering through my mind—Wyatt being tossed back and forth in the air, caught in enormous beaks and talons while he screamed in pain and terror, and then dropped—impaled on jagged rocks, painting the sea-foam waves scarlet.

I rub the spot above my heart, still feeling the heat that had blossomed painfully there when Celeste had rushed to the dean and grabbed his shoulders. Why had it felt like my chest was going to explode when she joined Rottingham and the other professors? And why had she been the only one to collapse after Wyatt was dropped? I only got one glimpse of her as a couple of professors carried her into Moon Hall and I swear it looked like her dark hair had suddenly turned white. But that had to have been a trick of moonlight and confusion. Right?

And why am I so damn tired that I have to keep blinking to focus my vision while I fight the urge to curl against Lee and fall asleep? *Fall asleep! After what just happened? What is wrong with me?*

"It's so hard to believe," Sam whispers. She's sitting at my other side.

From beside Sam, Ruby says softly, "It was gruesome. Really awful."

A sob from a few tables over from us pulls my attention. A group of Leo moons, looking glassy-eyed with shock, huddle at two long tables they've pushed together. Even Luke has deflated. Lily is sitting beside him with her arm around a brunette girl I recognize as the one who had started the screaming on the beach. She's sobbing and shaking.

"That's Hannah," Lee says. "She's Wyatt's girlfriend."

I look up at Lee and realize how difficult this must be for him. During the weeks we weren't talking he'd gotten really close to Luke and Lily and the Leo moons. I thread my arm through his and scoot closer, wanting him to know that I'm here for him, now and always. "Nothing like this has happened before," Sam says.

"Seriously?" I ask. "But why would—"

The wide double doors to the dining hall open and Dean Rottingham strides in with Professor Scherer.

"Good. Now we'll find out what really happened," says Lee.

I follow his gaze and he's looking hopefully at Dean Rottingham like he's an oracle. I want to tell Lee that I highly doubt that anyone is going to be straight with us, but press my lips into a tight line. Now is definitely not the time.

They face the room. Professor Scherer is so pale her cheeks have blanched to the color of cottage cheese. In contrast, Rottingham's cheeks are splotches of crimson and his eyes look strangely bright—not crying bright. Excited bright, which makes me shudder. Lee squeezes my hand and I lean into him, soaking up his strong, warm presence.

"What just happened to Wyatt is a tragedy," begins Professor Scherer.

The kind-eyed professor barely takes a breath, but Rottingham's hard voice fills the brief pause. "We have questions and will be conducting interviews with several of you."

"Yes, of course." Professor Scherer nods. "But we want you to be aware that tomorrow there will be counselors available for any student who would like to speak with one. Let me encourage you to take advantage of this offer. Our Aquarius moon healers can and will help you move forward from this horrible accident."

"Accident?" Sam's voice is shockingly loud. "It didn't look like an accident."

Rottingham's glittering hazel gaze skewers her. "Samantha, isn't it?"

"Yes."

"This is Moon Isle. Things, especially difficult, *accidental* things, are rarely as simple as they look."

The dean turns his gaze away dismissively, but Sam continues. "It didn't just *look* like a group of Air Elementals attacked Wyatt. They did attack him, not accidentally. Then they dropped him. *On purpose*. Killing him."

I'm so proud of Sam that I want to cheer.

Dean Rottingham's eyes narrow. "The Elemental did as I commanded. It let loose the boy. . . ." He pauses to shake his head and blow out a long breath, like he has to reset his thoughts before he continues. "The fact that it released Wyatt so abruptly is shocking and unfortunate."

"So does this mean our last two Trials will be canceled?" Sam asks.

Professor Scherer opens her mouth to respond, but the dean beats her to it. "*Absolutely not*." He enunciates the two words sharply, verbally slicing across the dining hall to Sam. "The purpose of this school is not simply to help you hone, control, and manifest your magick. It is also to prepare you for the real world, and the real world is filled with loss and tragedy—as some of your fellow students are already too aware." His eyes slide to Lee and rest on him gently as he lets out a long, sad breath.

"He isn't wrong," Lee murmurs.

"It would not be productive or fair to the rest of you to alter or end the Trials, but we will definitely increase security. . . ." The dean pauses, clears his throat, and continues. "Wyatt was in the restricted area. As we have explained from the day you arrived, unless you are actively participating in a Trial, you must remain within the clearly marked campus limits. As horrible as this accident is, it could have been much worse. Wyatt was not the only student who crossed into the restricted zone tonight—he is simply the only one who died because of it."

Hannah's sob is heartbreaking. Sam and I exchange a look that says neither of us is buying whatever it is Rottingham is selling. Then four more professors I don't recognize rush into the dining room. "They have silver moon insignias on their jackets. They're members of the Lunar Council," Lee says in a hushed voice.

The council members halt just inside the open doors. Standing so close their shoulders almost touch, they cup their hands, pressing their fingers together to form an O shape. A familiar heat spreads under my ribs, expanding with each of my heartbeats as first Lee and then Sam and Ruby breathe out long sighs. An almost-visible wave of soothing energy washes across the dining hall. Hannah stops sobbing. The Leo moons blink like they're waking from a bad dream and rub their faces.

"Those council members," I whisper to Sam. "They're Leo moons."

She nods slightly and whispers back, "They're calming us."

Not me, I think but don't say. *I can feel what they're doing, but it's not soothing me. It's just making my chest hot.*

"Now, that's better," says Dean Rottingham. "Please go to your halls."

"Our halls?" Hannah's voice is shrill. "B-but what about the Elementals? They'll be there. In our halls. What if they attack us?"

"The four Elementals who reside on campus will not

harm you," says Rottingham. He throws a look over her shoulder at the council members and more heat tugs at my chest. When the dean continues, his voice is pitched to sound fatherly and soothing. "Hannah, you have nothing to fear as long as you do not leave campus. Do you understand?"

Hannah's sigh is shaky, but she nods. Luke hands her a napkin and she blows her nose.

"Yes, that is *much* better." Dean Rottingham nods. "Our Leo moon council members"—he gestures at the four people at the head of the room—"will join you so that you will rest easily tonight. Tomorrow Aquarius moon healers who specialize in tragedies such as this one will arrive to further help you. My thoughts and prayers, as well as Celeste's, will be with you."

"Where is Celeste?" I'm not aware that I've spoken my question aloud until the dean's gaze stabs me.

"Resting. What happened on the beach was highly upsetting. The leader of our Lunar Council cares deeply about all of our students. It is not surprising that she is currently indisposed." Without another word he turns and strides from the dining hall.

"Thoughts and prayers," Sam mutters.

"What?" Lee asks.

"Oh, nothing. Just talking to myself," she says, not looking at me.

As a group we walk slowly from the dining hall, through the glittering foyer of Moon Hall, and make our way through Crossroads Courtyard where we split up, following a council member to our individual halls. I'm incredibly tired. It's like my charge has died. I have no bars. I need to shut off.

Most of the Aquarius moons cluster in the big common room, looking lost and not saying much. Our council member is a tall woman with long, wavy dark hair that rests on her broad shoulders.

"Come on in, kids." She smiles warmly as she enters the big rec room. "I think it's a good idea to do some energy work before you go to your rooms. Dean Rottingham has extended lights out tonight until midnight so we have plenty of time."

Lee squeezes my hand. "That's a really good idea," he says as he starts guiding me into the room.

I stop, tugging on his hand so that he pauses with me near the wide staircase. "Lee, I'm really tired. I'm just going to take a long bath and then go to sleep. This has been a lot for me." I meet his brown eyes. "I know you understand."

"I do. But the Leo moon will be able to help—be able to make us feel better." He touches my face gently and I press my cheek into his palm.

"I'm already better." Not used to lying to Lee, I say the words quickly. "Really, I just want a bath and a bed."

He slides his arm around my shoulder. "I get it. I'll walk you to your room and then come back down. I can use more of what the Leo moon is sending us."

The grief is clear in his eyes, darkening them and making Lee look a lot older than eighteen. I know what's surfacing within him—memories of Maya—just like memories of Mom and Dad feel so close to me that I can almost reach out and touch them. Almost.

Lee and I walk slowly to my room. At my door I turn in his arms and we hold each other. He rests his cheek on the top of my head, soothing me a lot more than the Leo moons did.

"This isn't how I wanted today to turn out," I tell his chest.

He lifts his head and looks into my eyes. "We're together, though. We can handle anything if we're together."

Lee's embrace is a promise of a better future because in that future we'll be together. I hold on to that promise as I slide into my bath and finally let myself think about my parents while the salt of my tears mixes with the lavender-scented bubbles. I remember the way Mom and I used to have special Mommy-Baby Day where we'd hang out, just the two of us, getting manicures before we had high tea at Portland's bougiest five-star hotel, where we'd stuff ourselves with tiny crustless sandwiches and dense, delicious scones. And about how every single night Dad used to read to me at bedtime, even when I was well past picture-book age, and then kiss me good night and whisper, *Wren Nightingale, always remember that you are smart and beautiful and you can do anything you set your brilliant mind to.*

TWENTY

Wren

"Okay, students, huddle up so I can give you your tickets and some last-minute instructions." Rottingham's voice has me turning quickly to face him and I stumble as our little ferry bobs in the gentle swell of Seattle's waterfront. Lee grabs my elbow to steady me, but my crossbody smacks into Kaia, the Aquarius moon whose room is next door to mine.

"Ohmygod! I'm so sorry, Kaia."

She sweeps back her thick dark hair. "It's okay. But what do you have in there, a brick?"

"No, just a big old book that feels like a brick whenever her purse thing hits you," Lee tells her with a wry smile.

Kaia just grins and moves closer to the other students huddling around Rottingham as Lee whispers, "Why do you carry that book everywhere? It's so heavy it's practically a weapon."

I shrug. "I'm beginning to wonder. I can't even really read it," I mutter as Lee and I move with the group toward Rottingham and I shift the weight of my crossbody on my shoulder.

"All right, these are all general admission tickets, so you can choose your seats once you're inside." Dean Rottingham holds up a handful of tickets. On either side of us the other three ferries from the academy have docked and I see professors motioning for their students to gather around them, too. The dean's voice sharpens and when my gaze returns to him he's giving me a stern look as he continues. "Remember that you are attending the Mariners game as an exercise. You are to divide yourselves into groups and work together, but each group must have at least one Leo moon. Your assignment is to support the Leo moon in calming the section of the stadium nearest your group. Although you all do not have the ability to influence a crowd, you do all have magick. When we work together, everyone's power is strengthened. Everyone benefits. It is imperative you remember to be subtle. We never coerce or force Mundanes. We simply guide and soothe. There will be professors stationed throughout the stadium with me, watching and assessing your progress. Tomorrow your group will turn in a short essay about your observations and reactions to today's exercise to Professor Douglas, so taking notes is wise. Good luck."

Rottingham quickly passes out all the tickets and then we follow him from the ferry and begin walking along

Western Avenue toward the Mariners stadium. The three other groups from the school move with us and it's nice to hear everyone laughing and talking. It's been a week since Wyatt's death. Several students left Moon Isle after parents were notified about the "accident." (Sam and I hate that Rottingham and the professors insist we call it that.) School has been weird and tense until today's ferry ride to the city, but now an air of *ooooh, field trip!* buoys our spirits and I've seen more grins in the past few minutes than I have all week.

I look around trying to spot Sam and my hand brushes against Lee's. I sigh happily as his hand closes around mine. I thread my fingers with his and feel my cheeks heat as his slow, intimate smile says he'd like to be kissing me.

"I think I recognize that look," I tell him.

"Oh, you think you do, do you?" He waggles his dark brows.

"I do." I lean into him, glad things are back to being easy between Lee and me, and even though we haven't actually kissed—yet—I'm sure I know what that heat in his smile says. I sing softly, "*Kiss me, out of the bearded barley; Nightly, beside the green, green grass.*"

His smile blazes. "Okay, so you *do* know that look."

I laugh with Lee as our joined hands swing with our steps. Our friendship built a foundation for this next step with us, and that foundation is strong. I used to wonder what it would be like if Lee and I were more than friends. I thought it'd be awkward. I was absolutely wrong—and I'm so glad I was! Lee and I already had the shorthand communication skills best friends develop, and now that we're dating and really together, that has translated to an intimacy that makes me feel so safe in this new relationship with Lee that sometimes I have to stop myself from expecting the sky to fall or something else horrible to happen because *I'm just too happy.*

But that's crap. Being too happy isn't possible. It's the way things should be. Right?

I notice Lee's looking around us like he's searching for someone. "Do you see Sam? I'm too short. I can't find her."

"I think I saw her back there." He uses his thumb to point behind us. "She was on the last ferry that docked. Don't worry. We'll wait for her inside the stadium. I was looking for Celeste. I don't see her anywhere."

Before I can impart information from one of the many lectures I've attended, Kaia speaks up. "The leader of the Lunar Council doesn't leave campus until she retires, remember?" Kaia falls into step beside me, carefully avoiding my lethal crossbody.

"That's right." Lee rubs his forehead and frowns. "Guess I was thinking about the fact that I don't think I've even seen her on campus since *that night.*"

I know for sure Lee hasn't seen her because Sam and I have talked about the fact that Queen Celeste has been conspicuously absent from any lectures, gatherings, or even from the dining hall since Wyatt's death, but that's not something I want to talk about with Lee today. I do not want to dim the brightness of everyone's mood.

I tug on Lee's hand. "Hey, let's hurry! The light's getting ready to change." We sprint across a street and the stadium fills the sky. Its facade is brick and glass. The rest of it reminds me of a weird spaceship, partially open to the air and humming with activity.

"You've been here before, right?" I ask as we move slowly forward in the line to enter.

"Nah, I was never into baseball enough to drive all the way up here. Plus, my mom loves the Portland Thorns and Dad is wild about the Blazers, so that's where we go." He keeps staring up at the stadium. "This place is massive."

"I want popcorn," I say. I realize that my opinion is not the popular one, but the reason I didn't remember that Lee hadn't been to the Mariners stadium before is because, other than volleyball, I really don't care about sports. At all. I do, however, care deeply about popcorn. Especially the kind with lots of butter.

We push our way inside and I'm steering Lee toward a concession stand from which popcorn and butter aromas waft tantalizingly when Sam, her arm hooked through Lily's, rushes up to us.

"There you two are! I thought I'd never find you in this crowd." Sam shudders slightly and bumps her shoulder into Lily's. "I don't know how you Leo moons do it. This kind of stuff is way too peopley for me."

Lily lifts one smooth, bare shoulder. She's wearing a pretty green tank that matches the color of her equally pretty eyes. Her fiery hair is pulled into a high ponytail, which makes her neck look long and graceful (because it's long and graceful). Her cream-colored maxi skirt is tulle. She has on wedges that make my feet hurt just looking at them. Lily belongs between the pages of a high-fashion magazine. Lily is smiling at Sam. "I think if you're born a Leo moon you're almost always also born an extrovert. I mean . . ." She jerks her chin in the direction of a cluster of Leo moons, her twin in the center. Luke's leading them in some kind of raucous Mariners cheer that a bunch of strangers immediately and enthusiastically join.

"Hey!"

The four of us startle as Ruby seems to materialize be-hind us. I clutch my pearls. "Sheesh, give us some warning."

They frown. "I wasn't sneaking. You were busy watch-ing the Leos. You know, you really should practice better S.A. when you're in a big place like this."

"S.A.?" Lily asks.

"Situational awareness," Ruby and Sam say together. And then Sam shouts, "Jinx!"

Ruby sighs. "Damn. Beat me to it. But only this time."

"We shall see." Sam grins.

Ruby snorts and then raises one brow. "This is a good group. We'll do well."

Lee nods. "I agree. Let's go find seats and get ready to soothe the savage beast."

We head toward the nosebleed seats that are general admission. Everyone is talking and laughing—even me, though I keep side-eyeing Lily. Not because I don't like her. Actually, what I know of her I like. She's authentic and smart. My stomach feels weird around her because of those three weeks when Lee and I weren't talking much. She (and her brother) hung out with Lee a lot. I know he likes both of them. I could definitely take or leave Luke (mostly leave), but Lily is nice. Ruby and Sam like her. I like her, but my messed-up stomach says that I'm worried that there are unsaid things between us, which means I need to talk to Lily so there's no awkwardness in our friend group. (Shit.) As we pass the last concession stand before we enter the seating area, I clear my throat and metaphorically put on my big-girl panties.

"Lily?" She turns to me. "I'm going to get some pop-corn. Would you come with me?"

"Oh. Sure."

Lee's watching me and I pretend I don't see the question in his gaze. "Anyone else want anything?" I ask. "Lily can help me carry the stuff to our seats."

We take everyone's order and then get in line as Lee, Ruby, and Sam disappear through the giant, mouthlike opening. I do not wait. I blurt, "I want to talk to you about Lee."

Lily's brows go up. "Lee? Well, okay, but you know him a lot better than I do, so if he's doing something mystifying or annoying I don't think I can help."

"Yeah, well, um, that's not it. Okay. Um." I realize I'm speaking nonsense and start over. "Lily, I want to be sure you are okay with me being with Lee. I know when he and I weren't talking you two—"

She raises her hand, palm out. "Stop. Lee and I are friends. That's all we've ever been or would ever be, even if you two weren't together. That night a week ago . . ." Her words trail off as the horror of that night drifts up, dark and terrible, from our memories. She clears her throat. "Well, I don't want you to think anything was going on between us. It was just Lee and me hanging out together because we're friends and he was lonely and I was sick of dealing with my brother and his idiot group—as usual."

The rush of relief I feel almost makes me dizzy. "So, you and I are good?"

"More than good, I hope. I want us to be friends."

"I do, too!" I say with perhaps too much enthusiasm, but Lily smiles anyway.

I'm carrying two bags (large) of popcorn (buttered) and Lily has the cupholder thingy for our drinks, and we're *excuse us* and *sorry, coming through*-ing our way to where Sam is flailing her arms when Luke's voice slaps us.

"Lily! Get over here!"

Lily stops. She sighs. She glances down several rows to the right, as close to the good seats as the general admission can get, where Luke is standing in the center of his usual gang of followers—mostly guys with a few girls I can't help thinking of as groupies. (*Why anyone would want to be a groupie to that douchesack I'll never understand.*) His hands are fisted on his hips and he's glaring at Lily.

"He looks pissed," I say.

"Luke only has three looks," she says. "Pissed, sarcastic, and charming. Pissed is the one I deal with most. I'll bet you can guess which look I deal with least. Can you carry the drinks? I better go see what he wants. He's really good at causing a scene."

I balance one bag of popcorn on top of the other. "Yeah, no problem." And grab the handle of the drink holder before I make my way carefully to our group.

"What's up with Lily?" Sam asks.

I nod toward where she and Luke are standing. "Luke called her. Okay, I don't know her very well yet, but she seems as nice as he is awful."

"She is really nice," says Sam.

"Luke Weatherford is definitely awful." Ruby takes a Coke from me.

Lee moves his shoulders and frowns a little. I secretly watch him as I hand out our snacks. He hangs out with Luke. Not like the guys who always cluster around Luke, but the two of them talk. I know Lee is helping Luke practice his magickal hand sign dexterity. I wonder about that. Lee is usually a really good judge of character, and it seems like Luke is an ass.

Then I remember the Leo moons returning from their

Trial and how Luke helped the girl who was so severely injured that she ended up going home. Maybe Luke's less awful than I/we think. That would definitely explain why Lee's friendly with him, and Luke is the only student who placed ahead of him in the first Trial. His mother's a senator and friends with Lee's parents. Lee's also ambitious and driven to succeed. Hm . . .

"Maybe the good twin/bad twin thing is true," I say, sneaking more looks at Lee, but he's drinking his Sprite and munching on popcorn as I sit beside him. "Okay. So. What's the plan?"

"Well, the Mariners are playing their rivals, the Astros," explains Sam. "Which means that tension in the crowd and on the field will be pretty high."

"That's good for us," adds Lee.

"They'll need to be calmed," says Ruby, nodding as they stare at the two teams who are still warming up.

"What do we do?" My voice sounds small.

Lee bumps my shoulder. "It'll be okay. When Lily gets back we'll basically just support her when those tensions Sam was talking about get bad." Lee glances down at Luke's group. "Here she comes."

Lily walks quickly up the stadium stairs toward us. Her head is bowed, like she's being very careful not to miss a step, but as she joins us she looks up. Her face is bright pink and tears are tracking down her cheeks. Sam jumps up and hurries to her, pulling tissues out of the ridiculous fanny pack she wears because she swears they're "back in style."

Ruby is on their feet, too, fists clenched at their sides. "Tell us."

Lily sniffles, hiccups a little sob, wipes at her face with the tissue, and sits between me and Ruby. "It's nothing.

Just the same old thing. Luke wants me to partner with him. And we *are* stronger together. But he can be so mean, so ruthless and driven." She says the last sentence in a whisper, sobs again, and blows her nose.

"He cannot make you do anything. Not here and not on Moon Isle," says Ruby.

Lily hiccups and nods. "I know. That's the problem. He's used to being able to get me to do what he wants. Our parents—they're not terrible or anything like that, but they always insist Luke and I do everything together." She shakes her head. "I hate it. Mom would say stuff like *you can make your brother become a better man.*" Lily looks up at us and her face is bleak. Her tears have washed away the makeup under her eyes to reveal dark circles. "It's not true. I can't *make* him do anything just like he can't make me do anything. And he doesn't want to be a better man. He likes being exactly how he is and doesn't want to change."

"It's not women's jobs to make men better," I say. "Ever."

"For real," says Sam.

"Never," agrees Ruby.

We look at Lee.

"It's not possible for someone to make another person better. That's boomer logic," says Lee. "The person with the problem has to fix it themself."

"*Shinjitsu,*" Ruby says firmly.

"Truth," Sam translates.

"Yeah, I understand that and have been refusing to partner with him. The problem is that he makes sure I'm isolated. He either gets anyone I start hanging out with to like him more than me—or he is so crappy to them that they stop wanting to be around me. It's lonely standing up to Luke."

Lily looks small and very young with her shoulders bowed and her head lowered. I feel a tug of sympathy. *She really is a nice person.* "He can't do either to us," I say firmly.

Lily lifts her head to look at me. Her eyes are bright with tears. "Really?"

"Absolutely," says Sam.

Ruby snorts. "His nonsense stops now."

"We like you best," says Lee.

"He can't intimidate us," adds Ruby as they crack their knuckles.

"We'll be your friends," says Lee.

"We can do better than that," I say. "We'll be your family."

Her face blooms with a smile. "Promise?"

"Promise!" the four of us say together.

"Have some popcorn." I offer her my bag. "Butter fixes everything."

Lily is so relieved that she's giddy, and I quickly find out that when Lily is giddy she's hilarious. She launches into a running commentary about the two teams' uniforms, rating them like it's New York Fashion Week in a perfect Christian Siriano imitation. I'm having such a good time that when the first tension sparks on the field it doesn't even register with me.

"Luke's group got it," Lee says, jerking his chin in the direction of Lily's twin and the students clustered around him. Professor Douglas makes her way to their group and nods like she's pleased with them before returning to her seat with Rottingham and two other professors, who are sitting not far from us to our right.

"That's okay," says Sam. "We need to wait for something bigger anyway."

"Agreed," says Ruby.

Lily rolls her shoulders. "I'll be ready."

My stomach clenches, and I raise my hand tentatively.

"The girl in the pink sundress has a question," Sam says in her best professor voice.

"You know you don't have to raise your hand." Lee grins at me.

"Sorry," I say. "Nervous."

"Hey, don't be," Lily says. "We've got your back."

Okay, I'm really liking Lily.

"Thanks. I'm confused and I didn't want to ask Rottingham because he already thinks I'm a screwup."

Lee speaks up right away. "He does not."

Ruby snorts.

I raise my brow. "Ruby's right. Anyway, I get that we're supposed to support Lily, our Leo moon, as she soothes the crowd, but that's so abstract. What exactly does it mean? Are we going to somehow use our—or rather *your*—powers to boost hers?"

"Oh, I see why you're confused." Sam's practically bouncing up and down in her seat. There are few things she likes more than helping someone understand a difficult concept. "It's not possible for any Moonstruck to boost another's power. This exercise is about focus. Lily is going to handle soothing the crowd as only a Leo moon can do. But the rest of us are going to *focus* our individual powers on the same person or group of people Lily targets."

Lily nods and continues the explanation. "So while I'm calming with my crowd control powers, Lee is going to focus his healing powers on the same people."

"Right," Lee takes up the telling. "I'm going to concentrate on sending healing energy to soothe their stress or anger."

"At the same time I'm going to focus my super smarts on the same people, coaxing them to use their intelligence to think through their anger," says Sam.

"I will send them my strength," adds Ruby. "So they find the courage to contain their anger."

"Oh, I think I get it! It's not about boosting a Leo moon's power. Instead, we're working together to make Lily's power more effective," I say.

"Exactly." Lily grins. "There are almost always representatives from all four moons at large gatherings like sports games, concerts, et cetera. The better all the moons work together the more effective the outcome."

"That makes a lot of sense." I'm relieved that I understand. "So, here's what I think will be best for us to do. Lee's our Aquarius moon and we don't need two." I hold up my hand when my friends start to speak. "No, let me finish. All of you know my powers haven't actually shown up yet and I'm just in Aquarius Hall because of Lee. When you all start your focus-power stuff I'm going to do something I'm truly good at. . . ." I pause and reach into my crossbody and take out a notebook and a pen. "I'll take notes about every detail of what happens so that our essays will be accurate, detailed, and super easy to write."

My four friends are silent for several breaths and then Sam nods. "That's not a bad idea. And Wren's right. We already have one each of the moons, so it's not like she's leaving us hanging."

"It's logical," says Ruby.

"It's smart, especially because I'm a crappy note taker," says Lily.

Lee wraps his arm around me and hugs me. "Told you it would be okay."

I lean into him and go back to stuffing my face with buttery popcorn and giggling as Lily resumes her fashion commentary, this time imitating Nina Garcia.

It happens in the top of the ninth inning. The Astros had been trailing by one and only had one out left. Apparently (as Lee explains to me), had they not scored, the Mariners, being the home team, would have won then without having to play another half inning, which is a really big deal because Seattle almost never beats Houston. But in a super close call an Astros player manages to slide into home seconds before his teammate is tagged out.

The Mariners fans lose their minds. It seems the entire stadium surges to its feet, one living, angry organism.

"Let's do this," says Lily, her long hair brushing my shoulder as she sweeps it into a ponytail.

I dig through my bag and pull out my notebook. With it open on my lap, I jot down how my group shakes out their hands, like they're warming them up. They watch Lily, who moves quickly. Holding her hands in her lap, she presses her middle fingers down with her thumbs. The three of them mimic her. Then Lily presses her hands together so her raised fingers, bent middle fingers, and thumbs touch. The gesture is graceful as well as powerful. The three raised fingers look like towers or teeth, pointed out toward the shouting, jeering crowd.

I feel a tug beneath my ribs. Warmth builds there, like I'm lying on the beach and the sun is heating my body.

Immediately I can tell their magick is working. The people in our section remain on their feet, but they stop shouting, frown down at the field, and mutter.

I'm noting all the reactions, and the fact that Lily's face is turning pink and sweat is beading her upper lip, when more shouts erupt from the field. I look to see that the manager of the Mariners has invaded the umpire's personal space and is shouting at him—which, of course, sets off the Mariners fans. Again.

Lily's groan pulls my attention back to my friends. Her hands are pressed together so tightly that her fingers are bloodless. Sweat trickles down her neck and soaks the ribbed collar of her tank, turning it from seafoam green to dark moss.

Lee, Sam, and Ruby don't look much better. Their eyes are closed. Sam's lips are moving as she whispers something to herself. Ruby's sweating almost as much as Lily. I'm frantically noting everything when Lee opens his eyes and looks at me.

"Wren, you have to join us. We need everyone. This crowd has been drinking all afternoon. They just thought they'd won for the first time in years. They are not going to settle easily."

"But I—"

"Just try." Lily scoots closer and sends me a beseeching look.

"Okay. Okay. I'll try." I put down my notebook and shake out my hands. My shoulder presses against Lily's, and immediately heat begins to increase in my chest. "What do I focus on?" I have no idea what I'm doing as I hold my hands together, mimicking the others. I think it's going to be awkward, but the lectures and the movements Sam's been making me practice have definitely helped. My fingers find the correct sign easily.

"Throw everything you have out of yourself while you think about being calm, serene, soothing." Lily's voice shakes as she instructs me.

I close my eyes and think about the heat that continues to build under my ribs. Incredibly, I feel my new connection to Lily. I draw in a deep breath.

Calm it down right meow. It's just a game. You're probably still going to win. It's just going to take another half inning. It'll all be okay.

And then I imagine that the heat roiling under my ribs is steam I can exhale. *Go help Lily,* I tell it. The heat flows out of my body like I've opened a faucet.

Lily's body jerks, and she sucks in a breath. And then I hear something else.

People are laughing.

Lily's voice is filled with joy. "We did it!"

"Holy crap!" Lee says.

Sam giggles.

"*Shori!*" Ruby shouts.

I open my eyes. In our section people are laughing and slapping one another on the back. Many of them are already seated. My gaze travels around the stadium. *No one is shouting anymore.* Not anywhere! People are yawning and stretching, laughing and motioning for the peanut and beer sellers to come back around. Our entire section is already seated again, murmuring to one another as they smile and congratulate one another on a great game.

My gaze is caught by the one spectator who isn't seated. It's Dean Rottingham. He's staring directly at me. As my gaze meets his slowly, deliberately, he smiles.

My friends are laughing and high-fiving one another. I pull my gaze from Rottingham and smile and high-five them back. After we settle, I bump Lee with my shoulder. This time I have to say something. Not just about the heat I feel when magick happens around me, but I need to talk to Lee about Rottingham. He's always watching me. Sam thinks he's creepy, too. Lee will listen to me. Lee will believe me.

The wattage of Lee's smile is intense. "Was that the coolest thing ever or what?"

"Yeah. Awesome. Hey, can I talk to you?"

"Sure, what—"

The crowd roars (in a good way this time) and I can't hear anything Lee's saying. I practically shout into his ear, "Let's go out for a sec."

Lee nods and stands. He holds my hand as we slip past our three friends. I think I feel Rottingham's gaze on me and glance at him. Sure enough. He's staring at me. As I pass Sam she points her chin in Rottingham's direction and mouths, *Creeper.*

As soon as we're out in the relatively deserted hall Lee twirls me once and laughs. "We rock!"

I smile up at him, still holding his hand. Before I can say anything, he surprises me by saying, "Wow! When you joined us our power really kicked into high drive. Totally makes me feel like we can do anything. Hey, I wonder if there's any way the five of us could work together in the future. You know, like after we're done at the academy. Maybe we could be involved in special crowd-calming assignments. I'll bet my parents and Lily's parents would talk to Dean Rottingham about it. It's unusual for a group as inexperienced as we are, but . . ." Lee finally registers that I've stopped smiling and started chewing my lip—a sure sign something is wrong. "What is it?" he asks.

I'm just going to say it. I'm going to start by telling him that there's something off about Rottingham. How, like today, he's always watching me and that my gut and Sam's says there's some weird stuff going on at the academy. Not for the first time I wish I could let Lee in on the fact that the old book I'm obsessed with was Maya's, but Sam and I have talked about it. No way would that information do anything but mess with Lee's head.

I draw a deep breath and as I let it out I say, "Lee, I think that Rottingham is—"

"There you are, Mr. Young!" Like I conjured him, Dean Rottingham strides up to us.

I drop Lee's hand and take a step away from him.

"Miss Nightingale." The dean nods to me and then all of his attention focuses on Lee as he continues. "That was quite an impressive show in there."

Lee seems to grow even taller. "Thank you, sir. It was a team effort."

"Of course. Of course." Rottingham waves his hand dismissively. "Mr. Young, Lee, you're aware that every year I choose two apprentices to train with me during the last two months of the season."

My stomach clenches.

"Yes, sir. Maya was lucky enough to be one of those interns."

Rottingham nods. "Maya was smart, a hard worker. Like you."

Even though I'm not touching Lee, I can feel the excitement radiating from him.

Rottingham keeps talking. "Almost every year, one of my interns goes on to win the final Trial and is guaranteed a prestigious position within our rankings. Sometimes they choose a professorial position. In the case of an Aquarius moon a campus healer or even my own assistant is a possibility, just to name a few. A seat on the Lunar Council isn't even beyond reach."

Lee swallows audibly.

"Lee, I would like to formally offer you one of my two intern positions. It is extra responsibility, but I wouldn't make the offer if I didn't believe you could handle it. Do you accept?"

"Yes, sir! I'd be honored. I won't let you down. I give you my word on that," Lee says solemnly.

Rottingham extends his hand and Lee takes it in his firm grip. "I have no doubt about that." His eyes slide to me again and it's like he's staring into my soul. Like he knows that my stomach is clenching so hard that I want to puke. That I am on to him. He opens his mouth to say something, but a huge cheer from the stadium interrupts and then ecstatic Mariners fans start pouring from inside. ". . . back at the ferry!" Rottingham shouts before he's caught in the tide of people.

Lee grabs my hand and I stick close to him as we wait behind a big concrete pillar until Sam, Lily, and Ruby emerge and we flail our arms to get their attention.

I make my lips form a smile. There's too much going on around us for anyone to notice that it doesn't reach my eyes, and for once I'm glad Sam's on the Taurus boat instead of with us. There's no way I could keep up my fake happiness with Sam around. And Lee would see through my charade if he looked hard enough, but Rottingham takes him aside and for the whole trip they have their heads together like Lee's already on the Lunar Council. Lee looks so proud, so serious and intense as he basks in Rottingham's attention that my clenching stomach becomes one big knot of sick.

I can't tell Lee about my suspicions that the dean isn't what he seems to be. I won't be responsible for ruining everything Lee's been working toward and is finally achieving.

As we cross through the magickal barrier that hides Moon Isle from the Mundane world, I stare out at the roiling water and wonder what else the island and the academy are hiding.

TWENTY-ONE

Wren

The next morning I pound firmly but not too loudly on Sam's door. Taurus Hall is as fancy and gorgeous as Aquarius Hall (actually, the Taureans have better snacks), and I like Sam's hallmates, which is why I'm trying to be quiet *and* get Sam to open the door. It's early—almost two hours before the first lecture starts—but I can't wait any longer. It was hard enough not to blurt everything out last night.

I knock on Sam's door again.

And why *didn't* I blurt everything out last night to Lee or Sam? It's definitely not like me to keep stuff from them. Of course I can't say anything to Lee about Rottingham now that he's the dean's intern. And I wanted to talk to Sam about what happened in the stadium, but our group was so happy after our successful exercise that I felt like I'd look like a massive jerk if I'd announced, *Hey, I don't think it's actually that you guys are so powerful. I think it's really that I have the ability to amplify your power.* Because yes, that has to be what happened, and I need Sam to help me prove it.

I knock again, only louder this time.

"What? It's too early. Go away, whoever you are." Sam's voice is grumpy and sleepy. Sam is not a morning person. It's one of the things I love about her.

"It's me!" I shout-whisper through the door.

I can hear movement within and then the door opens. Sam has an oversized tee on that proclaims NEVER TRUST AN ATOM, THEY MAKE UP EVERYTHING. Her dark hair is sticking out like she's been electrocuted. She grabs my wrist and pulls me inside as she fires questions at me. "What's wrong? Is someone dead? Again?"

"Nothing's wrong and no one is dead." I shake my head at her. "I forgot how gruesome you are in the morning."

"You know how to make me all better, though." Sam looks expectantly at the steaming cup I'm holding.

"I absolutely do. Hot chocolate. With marshmallows. Lots of them." I hand her the cup and wonder, not for the first time, how she can drink something so rich and sweet first thing in the morning.

Sam takes a sip. "You do an excellent job of getting the marshmallow-to-chocolate ratio correct."

"Well, it's important," I say. (It is, but it's also too early for chocolate.) I realize Sam's staring at me as she continues to sip her drink and I blurt, "I think I've figured out my power."

The sleepiness instantly clears from her eyes. "That is fantastic. What is it? You're a Leo moon, aren't you? After yesterday, it makes perfect sense. I've been thinking a lot about it. We need to look at your birth chart. There might have been an eclipse, or some other lunar phenomenon, which is why . . ."

Her words fade when she realizes that I'm shaking my head.

"So, not a Leo moon," she says, tapping her chin and narrowing her eyes at me as if I'm an algebraic equation that needs to be solved.

"Not a moon at all, but if I'm right it's a lot easier for me to show you rather than tell."

"Now I'm intrigued." Sam sits on the end of her bed. "Are you going to sit down or pace? You look like you're on the verge of lots of pacing."

I sit beside Sam, though I can't stop my feet from tapping restlessly. "I'd like to pace, but I need to be close to you. You'll see." I blow out a long breath. All of a sudden I'm super nervous. *What if I'm completely wrong?* I mentally shake myself. That's why I'm here, waking Sam up instead of Lee. Since Lee and I are together I'm less eager to embarrass myself in front of him—not that I've ever actually enjoyed embarrassing myself in front of him. "Okay, I need you to access your Taurus powers."

"Easy. Anything in particular you want me to focus on?"

I shrug. "Sure. How about Moon Hall and its history?" I give her a cheeky grin. "You know, because as you said to Cute Coffee Obsessed, you're sooooo interested in the history of Moon Isle."

Sam rolls her eyes. "Smart-ass." She puts the half-empty cup of hot chocolate on her bedside table before she returns to sit beside me. Sam cocks her head to the side like she's peering at something only she can see (which is accurate) and forms a V with her right hand. "Okay, I've accessed information on the school. Now what?"

"Now this." I hold out my hand. She grins at me and takes it. The instant my skin touches hers the warmth that started to bubble beneath my ribs when Sam accessed her magick begins to build. I concentrate on that warmth and, as it shifts into heat that spreads throughout my body, I exhale and tell it, *Go help Sam.*

Have you ever gotten an I.V.? I had terrible food poisoning once and I'll never forget the feeling of the warmed fluids flowing into my cold, dehydrated body. The sensation of my power flowing into Sam is a lot like that, only more intense.

Sams gasps. Her body jerks, but I keep a tight hold on her hand. I'm watching her face, so I don't see it right away. All I see is her shock as she babbles, "Ohmygod, ohmygod, ohmygod!"

"You feel it, right?"

"More than that. Look!" With the hand I'm not clutching, Sam points up.

And suddenly it's like we're on the starship *Enterprise*! Hovering just above us multiple holographic images glisten in the air. There's an entire schematic drawing of Moon Hall, complete with floating notes. It's like a history book has opened in 3-D in front of us.

"Wreny, this is amazing!" Sam stares at the images. She makes a little gesture with her free hand and the schematic moves, increasing the magnification so that it's more detailed. "Truly incredible. I've known a few Taurus moons who are so talented that they can sometimes manifest images from their minds, but they're all adults who have trained and practiced for decades." She pulls her gaze from the hologram. Sam blinks and her face lights with understanding. "You're boosting my power!"

I nod, gripping her hand even tighter. "Yes. It starts as heat here." I tap the middle of my chest. "At first I couldn't figure out what was going on. I've felt it several times since I got to the island, but I've been homesick and confused."

"And then you and Lee weren't talking and that messed with your head," Sam added.

"Totally. Plus, the rest of you have felt your magick growing since you were little. I've just started feeling it, so I thought that maybe that was what was going on. My magick was trying to manifest. And then it happened during the Trial when I grabbed Lee's hand just to show him support when he was trying to heal the burned tree. I felt the heat and it seemed to flow from me into Lee, but when I tried to make a plant grow by myself there was nothing. No heat. No growing plant. So I didn't say anything."

"Yeah, I can see why you wouldn't. But yesterday that changed, right?"

"Right. I didn't know what I was doing, so I guessed. My arm was touching Lily's, and I gathered the heat and I told it to help her," I say.

"And it definitely did," says Sam. "But you still didn't say anything."

I look down at our joined hands. "It wasn't a good time. We were all so happy, and then Rottingham asked Lee to be his apprentice and I got lost in all of the celebrations. Plus, I really needed something like this"—I jerk my chin at the hologram still glistening in front of us—"to make me one hundred percent sure."

Our gazes return to the schematic of the school.

"Sam, is this really what you see in your mind when you access your powers?" I ask.

"Yeah, it is. Cool, right?"

"Amazing," I say. My gaze catches on an area near a section of the blueprints labeled ATTIC. It's the only part of the entire hologram that's fuzzy. I blink several times, but the image doesn't clear, so I point at it. "Hey, why's that area up there all blurry?"

Sam squints at the hologram. "Huh. That's weird. But not too surprising. As much as I wish I was actually computer infallible—I'm not. Our Taurean database is dependent upon Moonstruck and their ability to learn, comprehend, and retain information. Sometimes things don't come in completely clear. And, Wreny, what we're doing." She lifts our joined hands. "Is completely new. Moonstruck are *not* supposed to be able to boost each other. Ever."

"Am I a freak?" I ask softly. I don't feel like a freak. Actually, I feel powerful, but this is all so new to me that Sam's words are a balm on my frayed nerves.

"No! You're a miracle," Sam corrects me sternly. Then she's grinning and wriggling in excitement. I mean, if she were Grace Kelly she'd be Frenchie snorting all over. "This is so incredible! We have to tell Dean Rottingham."

I wrinkle my nose. "Creeper Rottingham? I don't know, Sam."

"Hey, there's no doubt that he's been watching you, but he is our dean and he's on the Lunar Council." Her eyes widen. "Maybe that's it! Maybe he knows there's something really special about your powers and that's why he's been such a creep."

"I guess," I mutter, definitely not convinced, though I do see her point.

"Oooh! I wonder if I'll get some kind of extra credit for helping you figure this out."

"Do you need extra credit? We don't even get grades."

"I know, but I *like* extra credit." Sam takes one more wistful look at the hologram before letting loose my hand and rushing to grab jeans and her I'M NOT WEIRD I'M LIM-ITED EDITION T-shirt. She's rushing around the room, pulling on clothes and brushing her hair and teeth as she shoots questions at me. "So you feel the power as heat?"

"Yep."

"Since you stepped on the island?"

"Actually, I felt it going through the cloaking," I say.

Sam nods, spits out toothpaste, rinses her mouth, and asks, "Do you feel it every time someone uses their magick?"

I shake my head. "No. Yes. I don't know for sure. I've spent most of the past month and a half ignoring it because I thought it was what everyone feels."

"It's definitely not what anyone else feels." Sam snaps her fanny pack around her waist. "Ohmygod, Wreny, the Elemental has been trying to let you know that your power is special!"

I feel a sizzle of shock. "I hadn't even thought of that!"

"But it makes sense. Come on, we need to tell Dean Rottingham all of this." Sam turns to look back at me from her doorway. "What?"

"Sam, I still have a bad feeling about Rottingham."

"Hey, I know this is new and even scary, but what you just did is major. Rottingham is not the coolest person we've ever known, but it's his job to guide us into our futures. We have to tell him, Wreny. It's the right thing to do."

"I think he already knows," I say.

"What do you mean?"

"Yesterday when the thing happened."

"You mean when your boost let Lily calm an entire stadium," adds Sam.

"Yeah, that. Well, Rottingham knew. He was staring at me—like *right at me*. He didn't even glance at you or Lee or Ruby or Lily. He didn't look at Luke's group, and they were closer to him. He just locked eyes with me *and smiled*."

Sam laughed, opened the door, and pushed me through it. "Of course he smiled at you. You're super powerful! This is just more proof that what we thought was him creeping on you was actually him recognizing your growing magick. It's going to be okay. You'll see. Now that we've figured out your power you can start practicing it and learning to control it." She almost dances beside me as we leave Taurus Hall and head to Crossroads Courtyard.

I'm not actually listening to Sam. I'm glad she's excited. I'm relieved I know what kind of power I have, but I can't shake the heavy feeling in my gut that's anchoring me down and making it impossible to be giddy like Sam.

And I can't get the dean's Cheshire smile out of my mind.

It's still so early that the only person/being we see is the Air Elemental as it moves slowly toward Aquarius Hall. When it passes us, I smile up at it and say, "Good morning."

The saffron colors in its cloak swirl prettily and it nods its cowled head in response.

Sam's shooting me sideways looks and after it's out of hearing range she says, "Elementals don't usually do that."

"Do what?"

"Respond to students . . ." She pauses and adds, "Well, the truth is I don't think I've ever heard anyone say good morning or even hello to one before."

I shrug. "Just being polite."

"Uh-huh, sure."

I ignore her semi-sarcastic response and we're silent as we enter the main campus building and take the wide curving stairs up past the second floor to the top story where the professors' offices are located. Dean Rottingham's office overlooks the front of the school with a great view of the dock and beach. Our feet echo down the empty hall as we make our way past closed offices to the dean's, and as we get closer to the gleaming wooden door and the golden DEAN ROTTINGHAM plaque, voices can be heard.

At first it's not clear where they're coming from, but it's a man's and a woman's voice and they're definitely arguing. We slow as we reach the door and realize the voices are coming from within the dean's office. It's so quiet in the hallway we easily tell who is arguing—Dean Rottingham and Queen Celeste. Sam and I freeze. They have to be close to the door because we hear them so clearly it's like they're standing right in front of us.

"I do not understand what the problem is. You've identified her. Now take care of it." Celeste's words are sharp. They slice through the door and skewer us.

"It's not that easy and you know it. These things take time," the dean says.

"Time? Look at me. I do not have *time*."

"Yes, I admit that you're dealing with some, um, issues, but we just dealt with a student's death. If we are thinking of the good of the many, we must remember that *all* of our students and their families will be adversely impacted by another accident so soon."

My stomach clenches and a wave of nausea washes through me. He can't be saying what I think he is.

"Quincy, I'm dealing with more than *some issues*." The sneer in her voice drags out the two words. "There shouldn't be a change until my presence begins to be suspicious. Have you forgotten that when there's a new regime *everything* is different afterward—the council and the school's dean and his very well paid, very cushy position?"

"No! I would not forget that."

"Good, then stop acting so damn squeamish. You know what must happen. There can be only one."

Beside me Sam gasps, and then slaps her hand over her mouth as Rottingham and Celeste go silent. I hear the *tap-tap* of shoes, reach out, and pull Sam's hand from her mouth before I turn and lift my fist to knock and—

The door opens. Dean Rottingham's eyes widen when he sees Sam and me and he takes a quick step forward, blocking our view into his office, but not before I see a flash of white. *Celeste's hair! Is her white blaze wider?*

"Miss Nightingale, Miss Hopp— I'm sorry, but I don't have office hours until this afternoon." Dean Rottingham's face is pale except for the two bright blotches of red that paint his cheeks.

I smile and make my shoulders relax. "Oh! I'm super sorry, Dean Rottingham. Sam and I are definitely early birds."

"That's right," Sam chirps. "Gotta catch those worms."

"I do like to encourage students who are go-getters," says Rottingham, locking his gaze with mine. "But I'm in the middle of a rather important meeting right now and cannot be disturbed. Perhaps you'd like to make an appointment to see me between classes this afternoon? My secretary will be in after breakfast. She can help you with that."

"Oh, sure!" I nod with a ridiculous amount of enthusiasm. "But maybe we'd be wasting your time. Do you have to approve an after-hours study group?"

"Right," Sam says. "Like, do we need you to sponsor us?"

"Ladies, this isn't high school. You are all legally adults. Think of it like college. You don't need permission or a sponsor to get together to study. It's why our media center is open twenty-four-seven." He seems to be speaking to both of us, but his gaze never leaves mine.

"Oh, gosh! Sorry!" I say, already beginning to back away from his door. "That was really naive of us."

"Yeah, it's hard to think like college students when we haven't been out of high school for even two months," adds Sam.

"That's understandable." The words the dean says absolutely do not match his intense expression. It's like his eyes are boring into mine.

"Hey, we're really sorry to have bothered you so early. It won't happen again, right, Wren?" Sam says as she backs away from the door with me.

"Totally," I say. Rottingham hasn't so much as glanced at Sam.

"But thanks for the information, Dean." Sam grabs my hand. "We'll let you get back to your meeting. See you later."

"Yeah, bye," I say as, hand in hand, Sam and I turn and walk (not run even though I really want to run) back down the hallway.

I can feel Rottingham's gaze on me all the way to the stairway when finally his door clicks shut—and Sam and I sprint down the stairs.

"Sam! Sam!" I whisper frantically as we rush from the building. "Tell me they weren't talking about me. Tell me!"

Sam's brown eyes meet mine. I see worry there but also her sharp intelligence. "I can't tell you that, but what I *can* tell you is we have now been warned."

TWENTY-TWO

Lee

The sun is fully awake in the sky, the final pastel streaks of cotton-candy orange draining from the clouds like the last drops of juice from a glass. With each blink, a bleach-white spot claims my vision, and I know I should stop staring at the sun, but I'd rather look at it than what's below.

"Lee?" Wren's hands cover mine, and I'm finally able to tear my gaze from the sky. "You okay?"

Beneath me, the raft cuts through the water, and I focus on Wren's delicate fingers and painted nails and ignore the fact that we're tied to four other rafts being pulled farther and farther away from land.

"Yeah," I say, or at least I think I do. I'm using so much of my energy to banish the ghost of my sister that I can't be sure I've spoken.

Laughter swirls in the air around us, blown back from the raft hooked to ours. Jenny and Eliza have their hands raised, their ponytails whipping the air. I lean slowly, carefully, to see around them. There's an array of reactions from the people on the three other rafts, although I'm sure the pensive and serious expressions pulling on their features come more from stress about the Trial than fear the ocean will swallow them whole.

Only the top ten from the previous Aquarius Trial participate in this one. Two souls in each raft. Whether or not they're all working in pairs is a detail I missed. Honestly, I barely remember getting into this glorified inner tube. From the moment the ten of us were instructed to report to the dock, my memory is a blurry, mushy thing. Luckily, I have Wren to guide me when I'm lost.

In the second raft back from the speedboat towing us like a mother duck with her ducklings, Paul half stands, his hands outstretched on either side to keep him steady as he points up ahead. I follow his motion, and a rock drops into the pit of my stomach.

"Wren . . ." Now I'm pointing. One by one, we all are.

Ahead, the rippling surface of the ocean has a rainbow sheen rimmed in rusty orange. The smells of gasoline and rotten eggs hit us. I shake my head as if it's not going to get worse, as if we're not headed right for it.

The speedboat slows and turns, making an exaggerated U around the slick until it's even with the raft Wren and I sit in. I adjust my position on the air-filled cross tube, and my shoes slide along the thick plastic as shiny as a trash bag. For our sake, I hope it's sturdier.

I feel eyes on me and crane my neck to look toward the speedboat. Dean Rottingham stares at me, at Wren, at us. I release her hand and clear my throat, straightening my spine and cracking my neck as if I'm ready for this Trial. More than that, I'm amped. Nothing can stand in my way. If I act like it, maybe it'll be true.

"You disappeared this morning." I force the words out, hoping that the dean will notice how cool, calm, and collected I am instead of the way my legs shake. "I went to your room, and you weren't there."

"Oh, I was, uh, I was with Sam."

She's not looking at me, but to be fair, I'm not looking at her much, either. My gaze keeps drifting to the speedboat and Dean Rottingham. He's talking to Professor Douglas, but shouldn't Celeste be here? She was at the last Trial.

"Lee, I—"

The raft bobs, and I pop my knuckles and force out more words. "It's really the only time I've missed my phone, you know?"

It's imperative I act like everything's fine. I'm not sure of the exact rules around being Dean Rottingham's apprentice, but I can't lose this opportunity. I push on, determined to be normal.

"Not because I wanted to be on my phone instead of with you. I wanted to text you. To find out where you were. Not that you can't be with Sam. You're your own person. You can do whatever you want with whoever you want. *Whoever? Whomever?*" My cheeks are hot, and I'm literally blabbering, but I can't stop. "Point is, you can hang out with anyone. I just wanted us to get breakfast together."

I clench my jaw to keep any more nonsense from spewing out. Between being in an official relationship with Wren and trying not to think about my sister's final moments in this very ocean, I'm surprised my mouth hasn't chattered away like one of those dollar-store windup toys.

"That would have been nice." Wren blushes, her cheeks so perfectly petal pink that my heart skips a beat. This . . . *she* is what I should be focused on. Not the sky, not my fears, not Rottingham. Wren is my soft place. My stable place. When I focus on her, I have no choice but to be my best self, to keep her safe and happy. It's the least she deserves.

"Students!" Dean Rottingham's clap echoes off the rippling waters, and Wren and I turn our attention to him. "Welcome to your second Trial. Only five of you will continue to the final." He glances at each of us, but I swear his gaze lingers on Wren. She chews her bottom lip. She must feel the same. "Untether your raft from your peers. When the Trial is underway, you may use the oars beneath your seats to move about the spill."

Eliza launches into action, nearly throwing herself overboard to untie the nylon rope that connects their raft to ours.

Professor Douglas stands and tugs on the bottom of her neon-orange life jacket, and I realize too late that she is the only person wearing one. "Your second Trial is focused on healing fauna, specifically the sea creatures that have been exposed to these toxins. It's also well within an Aquarius moon's power to heal the sea from this type of spill as Aquarius moons can heal all organic matter, although I'm not positive as to each of your individual healing abilities.

Some of you may have already plateaued." Her lips tip into a tight smile as she pulls down the life vest that's crept up to her ears.

Where's Celeste?

"Yes, well, thank you, Professor Douglas." Dean Rottingham clears his throat, and I know I'm not the only one wishing for the leader of the Lunar Council. "A team of more seasoned healers is on the way along with an ecological cleanup crew and representatives from the pipeline company. Until they arrive, this is your Trial. I expect—"

Paul's on his feet again, but this time I don't need to follow his extended hand to know where to look. A dim streak of neon blue pierces the sludge before disappearing under the speedboat.

Next to us, Eliza shrieks and jumps back. Their raft lurches side to side, throwing oily seawater into their boat.

"There is no reason to be alarmed." Dean Rottingham's tone is stern but calm, authoritative and knowing. "We expect the Elementals to assess the situation. After all, this is a part of their home. Much like other creatures in the wild, they are more frightened of you than you are of them. However, I will remind you to be cautious."

Paul's still standing as he throws his hands into the air in a dramatic show of disagreement. "They sure weren't scared of Wyatt."

"Their behavior that night was unheard of," Rottingham insists with the lift of a salt-and-pepper brow. "No one at the academy, including the leader of the Lunar Council herself, expects an event like that to be repeated. We would not put any of you in overt danger."

"In addition," Professor Douglas says, "the farther from

the isle, the less power the Elementals have and the less possessive they are, and we are quite far out."

I feel the tension ripple off Wren like the oil on the waves. I lean forward and squeeze her knee. "You okay?"

She brushes her hair from her face, and with it whatever was bothering her. "Yeah," she beams. "I'm always okay as long as I'm with you." She tilts her head to the side. "You know, we've never actually gone on an official date."

I rub my palm against my thigh and try to concentrate on what she said instead of what I feel, but it's no use. The pressure of this Trial, of everything it means for my future, is back. My pulse throbs in my ears, and I'm terrified I won't live up to what everyone expects when water swells next to our raft. Neon blue breeches the slick waves, throwing black ooze into the air. I pull Wren against my chest and shield her as Jenny and Eliza's raft soars into the air along with the whale-shaped Elemental.

I don't hear Wren's scream above the noise of the Water Elemental's body crashing back into the sea, but I feel it crack against my skin. Waves surge over the lip of our raft, and I hear the screams now, but they're not only Wren's.

Jenny and Eliza are in the water, each frantically swimming in opposite directions of their sinking raft. Eliza splashes toward us, and I don't think. I'm up, crawling around Wren and lunging over the cross tubes to get to our classmate.

I reach out, my sleeve dipping into the water. Black sludge clings to the fabric as I extend my long limbs, getting to Eliza before the Elemental returns. My nerves are on fire, my magick zinging through every inch of me as I reach for her. She clamps her hand around my wrist, and I reel her in. Wren is right next to me, pulling the other side of Eliza's oil-coated body out of the water as the beam of electric blue surges out from beneath our raft.

My heart pounds in my chest, the muscle crawling up my throat as long neon fingers grab the back of Eliza's shirt and wrench her from my grasp. Her nails dig into my forearm, ripping the skin. Freeways of blood pool against my dark flesh, but I don't feel the pain.

I watch, helpless as Wren spills over the side of the raft, pulled down by Eliza. Fear so cold and sharp death itself must be near spears my chest as I try to grab onto any part of her.

"Lee!" My name turns to bubbles under the water's inky surface.

I throw myself forward and reach into the black tide. I feel hair and fabric, and then her hand is in mine.

"Wren!" I shout at the surface, but I can only see my terror mirrored at me in the oil, backlit by pulsing neon blue. "Don't leave me!" I shout, squeezing her hand in mine while using every ounce of myself to bring her back to me.

Wren's fingers are torn from my grasp, and I launch forward to follow her under, but there are hands on my back, around my shoulders, holding me in place.

"Wren! *Maya!*" I yell for the love of my life, but I also cry out for my sister, because the girl beneath the water is Maya and she's Wren and she's all my hopes and dreams and reasons for being pulled down beneath a slick skin of oil, claimed by the Pacific Ocean come to life.

TWENTY-THREE

Wren

I don't have time to panic when Eliza's grip on my forearm pulls me from the raft and I plunge under the water with her. It doesn't matter that it's the middle of July. The cold of the Pacific Ocean is a full-body slap. I only have time to scream Lee's name before I hold my breath and close my eyes as I'm yanked through the slimy black film and down into the depths. I struggle to save Eliza. I'm a strong swimmer and I should be able to kick us back to the surface, but the Water Elemental hasn't released her and with the strength of the whale form it's taken, the creature continues to sink and to drag us down with it.

Now I panic.

I frantically try to free my arm from Eliza's vicelike grip at the same time I tilt my head back and stare at the inky surface rippling above me. Something breaks through the oil. *Lee's hand!* With all my might, I kick hard and reach for Lee. My fingers tangle with his. His hand closes around mine, but we're slippery with water and oil—and the leviathan Elemental surges down again, ripping my hand from Lee's.

No! I scream in my mind. I blink to clear my vision and stare down, shocked that I can see so well. The Water Elemental's huge bulk is only the length of Eliza's body away from me. It's glowing a neon blue that lights up the ocean around us so that I can see it and Eliza with perfect clarity. Her eyes are wide and filled with panic. She's staring at me. Her mouth opens and she screams, releasing bubbles and precious breath. She begins shaking her head frantically back and forth, like she's denying the whole situation. Her face is colorless. A few more bubbles escape from between her lips and I know she's drowning. *We're* drowning.

I have to do something. I can't die like this. Uncle Brad and Uncle Joel will be devastated. And Lee . . . Lee might not recover if a second person he loves is taken from him by the ocean.

I need help!

My gaze returns to the glowing creature. One long blue tentacle has snaked from its massive whale-shaped body and is wrapped around Eliza's waist. The water around Eliza is stained scarlet and I realize the suckers on the tentacle have torn her skin.

Eliza is an Aquarius moon—a healer.

There's no heat within my chest, but I know the power

is there. I have to believe the power is there, just waiting to be awakened.

I stop trying to pull my arm from her grip. I stop kicking for the surface. Instead, I turn my hand, grasp Eliza's forearm, and use that grip to propel myself down to her. I put my face close to hers, point at the blood surrounding her, and mouth two words: *Heal yourself!*

She's almost gone. Her body is convulsing, but she's still conscious. Her eyes close and her free hand forms a simple shape, thumb and forefinger pressed together, and I feel a tiny bud of warmth beneath my ribs. I latch onto that bud and as my vision starts to gray and tunnel I think, *Help Eliza! Heal her! Save her! Save us!*

Heat explodes within my chest and shoots from the center of my body down my arm and through the hand that grasps Eliza's forearm. A yellow light blasts from her and me out through the water. There's a terrible shriek and the Water Elemental's tentacle unwinds from around Eliza. In a rush of blue light and surging current, she's propelled up past me, the force of the power tearing her loose and rocketing her to the surface.

As Eliza surges up, the light that surrounds her spreads throughout the water. It engulfs the dark, sticky oil and in a great maelstrom of current and pressure and power pulls it down, down, down toward the distant ocean floor.

Feeling like my lungs are going to detonate, I struggle against the strength of the incredibly strong backwash, kicking with all my might toward the glimpse of blue sky somewhere above me.

Suddenly the whalelike Elemental is there—right in front of my face. In the space of one of my frantic heartbeats its body fractures, becoming a school of neon-blue fish that circle me so fast they create a mini whirlpool with me in the center of it.

I have no more air. I have to open my mouth. I'm going to suck in water and drown. I don't want to give up, but I'm stuck, trapped by this feral Water Elemental. I close my eyes, relax my body, and silently ask the three men I love to forgive me as I open my mouth to die.

Air rushes into my burning lungs!

My eyes open. I'm levitating in the center of the whirl-pool. Neon-blue water swirls around me creating a bizarre water tornado that is open all the way to the surface. It's like a straw only instead of sucking liquid up it's allowing me to pull air down so that I can breathe. I gasp, cough, and *breathe again.* I don't have time to figure out how I'm going to get up to that delicious surface because the school of fish shift again, coming together to form a vaguely hu-manoid figure. It's blue and misty gray, but hard to focus on as its body is so watery and unsubstantial that it's like trying to visualize one current flowing into another. It has a face like a melting candle from which two sapphire eyes lock with mine. It presses toward me, breaking through the water barrier that whirls around me. In a wash of fishy breath it screams, "*Fracturada!*" before it swims away, col-lapsing the wall of water.

I tumble head over feet as I struggle to right myself. Even though I'd been able to steal a few breaths, my body is slug-gish and my brain is woozy. And I'm cold. Really cold.

I cannot give up. I cannot give up.

I force myself to stop struggling and float for a moment, and the ocean quiets around me as yellow light blazes above me. Above! I know which way it is to the surface!

I kick and kick and kick—and finally break the surface, gasping and coughing.

"There she is! There she is!" Lee's voice shouts from somewhere to my right.

I sputter as a wave pushes water into my face, making me cough again as I try to blink my sight clear. Warm air brushes against first my face and then my chest, and the rest of my body is also blanketed in heat as I'm lifted from the water. My vision clears to reveal that I'm hovering in the air above the cluster of rafts. The Air Elemental, *my* Elemental, is holding me in its arms like I'm a child. Its head is turned so that the dark cowl of its robe hides its profile.

"Th-thank y-you," I say through chattering teeth. "I w-wouldn't have been able to tell which way the surface was if you hadn't sh-shown up."

Slowly the Elemental turns its head. I try to focus on its face, but I'm trapped in its gaze. The Elemental's eyes aren't glowing yellow. Instead, they're more amber, like a big cat's. And they're kind. As we stare at each other, those amber eyes become more human, more filled with compassion. It's cradling me with one incredibly strong arm. It lifts the other arm and passes it over my body and I'm suffused in warmth. My shivering stops. My teeth don't chatter. My lips don't feel numb with cold. I smile.

"Thank you. Again. It seems I've been thanking you a lot. I'm Wren. Do you have a name?"

The Elemental's body jerks, like what I just said is a shock. Its kind amber eyes are still locked with mine. "*Wren,*" the Elemental whispers to me. Its breath is warm and smells like the foggy woods of the Pacific Northwest—pine and growing things—but its voice is echoey and pixelated, like we're talking through a phone with really crappy service. "*There can be only one,*" it says.

"What do you mean?" I ask softly.

"*Bring her to me!*" Dean Rottingham's voice whips up from below us.

The Air Elemental responds instantly. It turns its gaze from me and soars down, placing me gently in the center of the speedboat beside Lee.

"Oh god, Wren!" Lee pulls me into his arms and I cling to him. Over his shoulder I see the Air Elemental disappearing into the sky.

Rottingham steers the speedboat back toward the other rafts as he calls to Lee, "Open the first-aid kit under the front seat and wrap Wren in the hypothermia blanket."

Lee moves from my side and then returns quickly with a crinkly silver blanket that he burritos me into. He rubs my arms and back through the blanket.

"Wren, are you injured?" I look up at the dean as he weaves around Professor Douglas and Eliza, who is also wrapped in a silver blanket. She looks pale and is shivering, but she meets my eyes and sends me a shaky smile.

"No." The word comes out too whispery, so I clear my throat and try again. "No, I think I'm fine. Just waterlogged."

"Good." He nods and looks out at the others, silent in their rafts. "Link back together, now. Professor Douglas will take us back to Moon Isle."

"Are you sure you're okay?" Lee is kneeling in front of me.

I manage to smile at him. "I'm sure."

He breathes out a long, shaky sigh. "I thought you'd . . ." His voice fades. He's so pale he looks gray. His hands tremble as he rubs my arms and he's blinking quickly, though his eyes are slick with unshed tears.

I catch his hands in mine. "I didn't leave you. I'll never leave you." I'm in his arms again, resting my cheek on his chest as I listen to his strong heartbeat.

The boat jerks, lifting and falling in newly made waves, and I tense, pull back from Lee, and ready myself for another horror show—but sigh in relief as I realize we're just bobbing in the sea as a raft is connected to the speedboat. I look around and note that one of the rubber boats is missing.

"Jenny? Did she make it?"

"Yes," Rottingham says. "Though her raft did not."

I get a glimpse of Jenny, also blanketed in shiny silver, in the last raft with Paul and Michael. Behind the raft the ocean is turquoise and sparkling and completely cleared of oil.

"We really did it. The ocean is healed," I say softly, more to myself than Lee.

Lee sits beside me and puts his arm around me, holding me close. "The spill healed when Eliza shot up to the surface. It was wild. It was like a giant vacuum sucked it all up and then shot it down into the ocean floor. I don't know how a student could have had that much power. It should have taken a team of experienced healers to clean up that mess. Wren, what happened down there?"

I'm trying to sort through my thoughts—*where do I start?*—when Rottingham's voice interrupts.

"Yes, Wren, what *did* happen down there?"

I meet the dean's dark eyes and remember Celeste saying to him . . . *Stop acting so damn squeamish. You know what must happen. There can be only one.* Instead of answering, I reply with a question of my own. "Are you sure Eliza's okay? That Water Elemental's tentacle tore up her waist."

"I am positive she is perfectly fine, though she will be checked out by the school's healer. There was blood on her shirt so, of course, we examined her. Eliza not only healed the ocean; she healed herself." The dean's gaze never leaves mine. "What *did* happen down there?" he repeats.

I hit the dean with another question. "What did Eliza say happened?"

"Her memory is spotty, which is not unusual after such a trauma. She said the Elemental grabbed her and pulled both of you down with it. She remembers you mouthing words at her saying she should heal herself, which she somehow did—as well as healing the ocean from the oil slick. That's all she remembers."

"I saw her blood in the water. And I remember thinking that Eliza should heal herself—that maybe the Elemental would let her go if she used her magick. . . ." I pause and sigh. "I barely remember telling her to heal herself and then there was a big explosion and Eliza was gone. I couldn't figure out where the surface was and everything was going black, but then I saw the neon yellow from the Air Elemental and followed it up. That's about it. Everything else is pretty blurry."

Rottingham narrows his eyes. "Well, perhaps your memory—or Eliza's—will improve in time and then we will learn the rest of the story."

"Yeah," I say. "Perhaps." I scoot closer to Lee, put my head on his shoulder, close my eyes and my mouth—and do not speak for the rest of the return trip.

TWENTY-FOUR

Wren

Professor Douglas takes Eliza, Jenny, and me to the infirmary where the school healer checks me out and says that I'm fine but will probably be tired. Jenny is released, too, but they want to keep Eliza for observation. Apparently, she breathed in some seawater and must be watched closely for the next twenty-four hours. Professor Douglas informed me that Lee was with Dean Rottingham, observing firsthand how the council handles Trial accidents, so Jenny and I walk silently together back to Aquarius Hall. I'm surprised to see how late it is. The sun is a fading ember, drifting into the western horizon. *No wonder I'm tired.*

This day is never-ending. The Air Elemental is there, just outside the arched front doorway. I smile at it.

"Hi there. Long time no see," I say in a light, teasing tone—like talking to an Elemental is totally normal.

"*Wren*," it says in a whispery voice, and dips its cowled head, but not before I glimpse kind amber eyes.

Jenny and I step inside the hall and she turns to me. "It knows your name."

"Well, yeah. I introduced myself today when it pulled me out of the ocean."

"Why did you talk to it?"

I shrug and say, "I guess because it's the polite thing to do."

Jenny shudders. "It's not even human."

"Neither is my Frenchie, Grace Kelly, but I talk to her all the time," I say.

"That's totally different. Dogs are great. Elementals are disgusting. One of them, an *Air* Elemental like that one you just said hi to, killed that Leo moon on the Fourth, and now a Water Elemental almost drowned you, Eliza, and me. I don't want anything to do with them." Jenny's face is smooth and heart shaped, but as she speaks her lips twist like she's sucking a lemon, giving the soft lines of her cheeks a hard, mean edge.

"Jenny, today is the second time that Air Elemental, *our* Aquarius Hall Air Elemental, has pulled me out of a potentially fatal situation. It's not dangerous. It's protective."

Jenny's lip curls. "We're going to have to agree to disagree."

Without another word she heads up the stairway. I follow more slowly. My skin is scratchy from the dried saltwater and my hair is disgusting. I cannot wait to get my salt-stiff clothes off and stand under a hot shower for hours.

Which is exactly where I am when the sound of pounding pulls me out of my steam-filled bathroom. I wrap my hair in a towel and put on my softest sweatpants and an oversized T-shirt that has tiny Frenchies all over it and hurry to open the door. Sam rushes into my room, hurling herself at me so fast that we almost fall to the floor.

She hugs me tight and then steps back, holding me by my shoulders as she studies me. "Are you okay? I mean *really* okay?"

"Yeah, I'm fine, especially after a long shower. How'd you find out?" I ask as we sit on the end of my bed.

"I saw Lee as he was scurrying around after Rottingham. I was heading to meet up and practice with some other Taureans. He stopped long enough to tell me there'd been an accident during the Aquarius Trial, but that you're okay. I got here as fast as I could after I checked in so they didn't think I'd gone missing. They were already talking about your Trial; everyone is. They're saying Eliza, who barely made the top ten from the last Trial, pulled off a miraculous ocean healing." She lifted one brow. "What really happened?"

"We were pulled under the water by an Elemental. Eliza almost drowned. I almost drowned. I managed to get her to use a little of her magick before she passed out and I boosted it. It was so powerful it didn't seem real," I explain.

"So powerful that your boost healed the Pacific from a major oil spill. That's amazing. Rottingham was there, right?"

"Right. But that's not all. Eliza shot to the surface when

I boosted her magick and I was alone down there with the Water Elemental. Sam, it yelled, 'Fracturada!' into my face."

"Ohmygod, Wren. Fracturada, like Maya's fracturada?" Sam grabs her backpack from where she'd tossed it on the floor beside the bed and opens it, thumbing through the silver-covered pages. "In Spanish *fracturada* means 'fractured, or, broken.'"

"Sam, there's more."

Her eyes lift from the book. "*More?*" she squeaks.

"Yeah, the Air Elemental. You know, the one attached to this hall."

Sam nods quickly. "The one you always say hi to."

"Right. It showed up and got me out of the water. Sam, it whispered, '*There can be only one,*' to me."

"That's exactly what Celeste said to Rottingham!"

"I know! And it's freaking me out." My gaze drops to the open book on Sam's lap. The writing moves across the pages, indecipherable silver snakes. As I watch, the snakes slither together, wrapping around symbols and letters until suddenly one word forms in the center of the page. "Sam, look!"

Fracturada! blazes from the page, glistening like the moonlight from the rising full moon that's just begun slanting in through my open window.

Sam runs a hand through her hair and exhales a long, frustrated breath. "I just don't get it. The book has to be some kind of code, but I can't figure out the key to breaking it."

I take the book from Sam. I'm sitting closest to the window, perched on the edge of my bed. It's mesmerizing how glittery the silver writing is in the light of the moon. "We're going to figure it out. I can feel it. We're on the edge of discovering whatever it is that lets us read this stuff." I turn the page. At the top Maya's handwriting proclaims THIS! in all caps. Then my eyes take in the page below that one word and we gasp.

"You can read it, too?" I whisper the words, afraid to move or speak too loudly, afraid whatever has fallen into place to allow us to read the words will break.

"Yes," Sam says equally quietly. "But there's a glare from the moonlight and I can't see all of it."

"I don't want to move!"

"Don't," Sam says firmly. "Read it aloud. I'll use my Taurus magick to record it. Hurry."

I nod and start reading. Every time I finish a word it disappears. I don't freak out, though. I slow down, counting on Sam to store every bit. At first it's the same information Professor Scherer explained during the intro lecture Sam and I attended. A Spanish ship wrecked near the isle. The Elementals saved several of the passengers. Then the story changes and I have to fight to keep reading with no reaction.

"'The Elementals were intrigued by the humans, most especially three women—an elder named Catalina, a mother named Isabel whose infant drowned before the Elementals could reach them, and a young maiden named Selene.

"'The three women grew close to the Elementals. As they learned to communicate, the Elementals explained how difficult it was to be sentient but unstable, especially as humans were multiplying and spreading at such a vast rate that the Elementals were forced to retreat to the island for safety. They envied the physical stability of the women. In turn, the women were fascinated by the powerful magick the Elementals commanded.

"'The Elementals offered to make a deal with the women. They could not grant them power over elements, but they could petition the moon to gift the three women unique abilities ruled by their moon signs. If the moon agreed and gave the women power—and through them all humans—the women would in turn promise to use that power to stabilize the Elementals and to cloak their island and keep them safe from outsiders.'" I keep reading, though my palms feel slick with sweat and the words continue to disappear as soon as I speak them. "'The deal was made. The moon gifted power to humans through the three women who represented the three seasons of human lives—maiden, mother, and elder.'"

I turn the page and shift on my bed a little because I feel like I'm sliding off the edge, and the silver writing begins to unravel. "No, no, no, no, no!" I tilt the book so the moonlight catches it again and readable letters re-form near the bottom of the page, but the story has skipped confusingly ahead.

"'Because of Selene's actions the deal was broken. The magick fractured and limited. Since then, every generation the moon has been blessing one Mundane, creating her Moonstruck with conduit power so the three can be whole again and the sacred transfer of power complete. But she won't allow it. Each special Moonstruck has been murdered before she could join her magicks with the elder and the mother to complete the ritual.'"

I turn the page again and the silver writing swirls to form one sentence followed by one word.

"'She commands, *There can be only one.*

"'*Elegida.*'"

A cloud obscures the moonlight and I squint as I turn

another page. Nothing. Just more indecipherable gibberish. I turn another and another.

"Go back to the beginning of the book and see if you
can read more there," says Sam.

I turn to page 1—nothing. More gibberish, but I diligently
look at every page. I even switch on my bedside lamp so I
can see better, but the book is done giving us its secrets. With
a sigh, I close it and turn to Sam. "That's it. I can't read
anything else." But I don't need to read more to know I'm
in trouble. "Sam, I think the Elementals, especially my Air
Elemental, are trying to warn me. I think I'm in danger."

Sam nods. "I think you are, too."

I can't sit still. I get up and start pacing. "We definitely
can't go to Rottingham. I don't trust him or Celeste."

"Agreed. I would've said maybe we were being para-
noid before we overheard Rottingham and Celeste basically talking about getting rid of you. First that and now
the book. You're definitely in danger."

I continue to pace as a chill skitters through me. "The
book is talking about me. I'm the once-in-a-generation
Mundane created with special Moonstruck power."

"A conduit . . . 'creating her Moonstruck with conduit
power,'" Sam quotes. "That is an excellent way to describe
your gift. You're a conduit for moon power, so much so
that you boost the power of other Moonstruck."

"They'll kill me for it." I stare at Sam. "Ohmygod! Maya
found this book. She managed to read it. Or at least some
of it. We know she did because of the notes she made. What
if her death wasn't an accident?"

Sam's face pales. "Maya knew too much."

And now so do we. I can't speak the words aloud, but
Sam's stricken face says she's thinking them, too.

"Lee should know," Sam's saying. "So should his parents."

"No!" The word explodes from me. "I hate keeping anything from Lee, but we can't tell him about this. At least not yet. We don't know enough. There's a major gap in the story, and we have to fill it in before we say anything to anyone, especially Lee and his parents." I narrow my eyes at the book. "And he's Rottingham's apprentice, exactly like Maya was. It would put Lee in a terrible position, even a dangerous one, if he knew about all of this."

Sam draws a deep breath and then speaks quickly as her eyes plead with me to understand. "Wren, I only meant that Lee and his parents should've known about this—about the fact that Maya's death might not have been an accident. I didn't mean we should tell Lee or his parents or anyone else, even if we get more proof. I know you don't want to hear this, but you have to listen. Lee is highly driven. His ultimate goal is a seat on the Lunar Council. What he has accomplished here this summer is all about setting himself up to succeed. Everyone knows that. Rottingham knows that. And you can never forget it."

"Sam, Lee would not be part of anything that would hurt me."

"Not on purpose he wouldn't." Sam sighs and runs her hand through her hair. "But you're right. Lee loves you and he's a really good guy."

"Yeah, and he's smart. I'm surprised he hasn't figured out that I'm boosting power already."

"So am I. Actually, I'll bet he already suspects."

I finally stop pacing and plop down next to Sam on the end of my bed. "I can't keep from Lee that I can boost power, so I'm going to tell him before he figures it out, and when I do I'll ask him to promise not to tell anyone—not even Rottingham or Celeste—until I'm ready for them to know. That's reasonable, right?"

"Right. Lee will respect that. Good plan."

"And Lee would never break a promise to me."

"I agree. It's part of why he's such a good guy," says Sam.

"Okay, so Lee's going to know about my power, but that's it for now." I chew my lip, not liking that I have to keep everything else, including our suspicions about Maya's death, from him. It makes me feel disloyal.

"I need to do some major research into the origins of the Moonstruck—the true origins and not just the white-washed version everyone knows."

My stomach feels sick again. "Sam, you have to be careful. It looks like Maya was researching the Moonstruck origin story, too, and now she's dead."

Sam flutters her fingers, waving away my concern. "I will. Don't worry. You know what this means, right?" She doesn't wait for me to respond but continues with a smile filled with confidence. "I need to make a return trip to the restricted room."

"You mean *we* need to make a return trip."

Her smile widens to a grin. "We. Definitely."

The knock on the door makes both of us jump.

TWENTY-FIVE

Lee

I grip the bouquet of freshly cut sunflowers with a sweaty hand, my stomach somersaulting the same way it did back in fifth grade when I asked Daphne Prince to be my valentine. She'd said yes and for one glorious hour, I was in heaven. Then, we had recess with Justin Canfield, who gave her a necklace he'd stolen from his older sister, and suddenly I was tossed aside and he and Daphne were *sitting in a tree, k-i-s-s-i-n-g.*

I shake my head. There's no chance of being rejected by Wren, and Justin Canfield isn't even here.

"Get it together, Lee." I give myself a little pep talk, and hop up and down a few times as if I'm about to go out on

271

the court before charging the rest of the way down the hall to Wren's room.

I'm breathless when I reach her room partially from nerves and the other part from hopping around like a jack-rabbit. Voices come from inside, turned to dull mumbles by the thick wooden door, but I don't let that stop me from knocking. I'm doing this. I should have done it a long time ago.

Wren answers, the tips of her wet hair stained a deep maroon. The ends curl up slightly, and I want to brush my hands through her locks.

My throat is dry as I thrust the sunflowers at her. "I'm here to escort you to our first official date, milady."

Her cheeks flash bubblegum pink, and she takes the bouquet and presses it against her chest. "Lee, I . . . I don't know what to say."

"Say you'll join me."

"Of course she'll join you," Sam chirps, peeking out over Wren's shoulder.

Wren widens her eyes in an exaggerated way only she and Sam understand. "What about the—"

"You and Lee go have an *exquisite* time with your tea and tiny sandwiches or whatever you weirdos do when no one else is around," Sam says, pushing the door open the rest of the way. "I'll take care of our little research project." She brushes past us, clutching the thick leather book to her middle. "Bye!" She throws a wave over her shoulder and rushes down the massive staircase before either of us can stop her. Not that I want to. I've been waiting for this date for the past five years.

"I need to change." Wren frowns down at her outfit, and

it's only now that I realize she's wearing pajamas. "Hang on just a sec."

She closes the door, and I stand there only semi-awkwardly staring at the curving gold letters of her name.

She reappears in record time, bouquet in hand. She's changed into a cream-colored dress dotted with pink flowers, and she smells like mouthwatering strawberry lip gloss.

"I'm ready, milord."

I offer her my arm and relax a bit when she takes it while I refocus my thoughts. She's been through so much, and I just want to keep her safe and make her happy.

"Are you okay?" I ask as soon as we're out of Aquarius Hall and in between the pines standing like sentinels around campus.

She nods, her mouth working wordlessly.

"What happened out on the water, with that Elemental, it was—"

"I don't remember much of it." She pushes her hand through her damp hair and stares down at the sunflowers, their vibrance extinguished by the night. I can't help but feel the same about Wren.

"We don't have to talk about it. I mean, we can if you want to." I tuck her arm against my side and rub my thumb along the back of her hand. "I'm always here if you need me."

I guide her out from under the dense blanket of evergreens and into the glow of moonlight dousing Crossroads Courtyard. We walk in the familiar silence only she and I share, stopping just outside the dining hall's massive double doors.

She looks up at me, her eyes silver pools reflecting the full moon. "I'm always here for you, too, Lee."

Her words are satin soft and wrap around my heart and squeeze.

I tighten my hand into a fist, not wanting her to see that my nerves have me trembling, and knock. Luke throws the doors open, ushering us inside as the yellow glow of one hundred candles shudders in the breeze.

As the doors close behind her, Wren pauses. The sunflowers are by her side, her grip on them slack when she releases my arm to press her palm against her lips. "Lee . . ."

Unshed tears sparkle in her eyes while she takes in the bistro table and stools Luke and I carried over from Leo Hall, the white, lacy blanket I borrowed from Lily to use as a tablecloth, and the candles Luke and I confiscated from every hall and lecture room on campus.

He sets down the small boombox we borrowed from Poppy along with a CD she said was sure to *sweep your girlfriend off her feet*. It takes Luke a minute of pushing random buttons, but the music eventually starts. Stringed instruments fill the room, warm with one hundred flickering flames, before a breathy French voice pours from the speakers.

Her reaction is everything, but I can't keep myself from asking, "Do you like it?"

"I love it." She throws herself against me, and I bury my face in her hair. "I can't believe you did all this for me."

"There's more," I say, my heart skipping in my chest.

Luke reappears from the massive chef's kitchen situated off the buffet table, a white platter in hand. Unfortunately, neither of us can cook, but I grew up eating all the groceries the second my mother's assistant unloaded them, so I'm an excellent scrounger.

I escort Wren to the table and help her onto the tall stool before taking my seat across from her.

"For *ze couple*," Luke says, his French accent most likely offensive. To his credit, he *is* wearing all black like we planned. Even if it's a pair of claustrophobic-looking black jeans cut off above his ankles and an inside-out T-shirt with a logo that's now barely visible.

I lean over and whisper, "English, dude, not French."

His red brows knit together. "Damn, the music got me."

With a flourish, he sets down the platter. Wren squeals, clapping for the gravy boat piled high with chocolate, vanilla, and strawberry ice cream topped with half a can of whipped cream.

"It's not tea and finger sandwiches, but—"

"No cherries or nuts!" She beams and reaches across the table to take my hand. "Lee, it's perfect. *You're* perfect."

"I just want you to be happy."

"I am." But there's something in the way her smile dulls around the edges that tells me otherwise.

I clear my throat and pick up a spoon, hoping a change of topic will alleviate the tension. "I mean, who wants healthy stuff like fruit and nuts getting in the way of their ice cream?"

"Hey," she says, stabbing a vanilla mound with her spoon. "There's a banana under there somewhere."

Luke, who must have watched at least one episode of *Downton Abbey*, because he's doing a great job at disappearing into the background, returns with another platter. He continues to balance a carafe of hot chocolate as he sets down two mugs and a gold bowl overflowing with marshmallows. He pours the drinks and claps me on the shoulder before throwing up a peace sign. His footman duties are finished for the night.

Wren watches Luke leave and as soon as the double

doors close behind him she says, "This is really sweet and don't think I'm complaining at all, but it seems like you and Luke are actually friends. I don't get it. Luke is an ass. How are you friends with him?"

I shrug. "When I told him my vision, he offered to help."

"Okay . . ."

She's looking for more, so I take a deep breath and oblige. "You're right. Luke's an ass. He thinks he has to put on this senator's son front." I shake my head. "To be honest, if my parents hadn't stressed how important it was for me to be friends with him, I wouldn't have given him a chance. But I'm glad I did. He's pretty decent under all that immaturity."

"Well, okay then." Her grin twists, and for a moment, her expression is unreadable. "To you," she says, lifting her mug. Her smile returns, plumping her cheeks and creasing the corners of her eyes. "For setting up the best first date ever."

"To us." I pick up my own mug. "For today and all of our tomorrows." We clink them together, and marshmallows topple over both rims, falling to the table like bunny tails.

I take a drink and let the liquid chocolate wash down my throat. I know *what* I want to say next, but I'm not sure *how* to say it. But that's been the problem Wren and I have had our entire relationship. I lock my words behind my lips, spinning them around in my mind or transferring them onto a page meant only for me. I have to stop this. I have to say what I think, what I feel, with conviction.

I take a deep breath. "I haven't said anything yet; honestly, I was hoping you'd say something first, but I'm really proud of you."

"For?" she asks around a mouthful of whipped cream.

I lean forward and take her hands in mine. She doesn't need to look for a way out. She's with me. She's safe, and maybe I haven't done a good enough job showing her that. If I had, she wouldn't be keeping this secret. Whatever fears she has about letting me in end tonight. I'll prove to her that she can let down her walls.

"Wren, I know about your magick. I know you can boost the powers of other Moonstruck." She's staring at me with an expression that's even harder to read than before. I hold on to her, trying to send my support through our joined hands. "I felt it during our first Trial, but I didn't let myself believe it. I couldn't. What you do isn't supposed to be possible. But then there was the stadium and this morning . . . You saved Eliza's life. You cleaned up that whole oil spill in seconds." I lean back, shaking my head. The entirety of it is still too huge. "I cannot wait to see the look on Rottingham's and Celeste's faces when you tell them about your magick. It's . . . it's incredible."

"I'm not going to tell them. I'm not going to tell anyone." She pulls her hands from mine. "You and Sam are the only two who know, and I want it to stay that way."

"You can't be serious. You have to tell them." I'm not trying to be loud, but I feel like I'm yelling. I thought this would go down differently. In my mind, she was relieved. In my mind, we went to the dean and Celeste together. Instead, she's paper white, her eyes so big and round they could pull me in.

"I'm not comfortable telling Dean Rottingham or Celeste. Not yet," she says, looking down at the whipped cream sliding along the side of the gravy boat. "Each Trial and exercise teaches me about another piece of my magick. I want to discover as much as I can on my own, and I need time to figure that out. I'll tell them after the final Trial." Her gaze is back on mine, and it's so blue and endless that I can't help but think about the ocean. About how I almost lost her. "Lee, you have to promise me you won't tell them—not the Lunar Council, not Luke, not even Lily and Ruby. I won't feel safe, won't be able to really concentrate on figuring out exactly what I can do with my power, if anyone else knows. Promise me," she repeats.

I swallow and brush my palm along the back of my head. "You can't hide this. You shouldn't want to." I lean forward again as if it'll help her to see herself like I do. "You're special, Wren. I've known it since the day I met you. Everyone else should know it, too."

She sets her jaw and crosses her arms over her chest. "It's *my* magick, Lee. It should be my choice."

I open my mouth to counter, but there's nothing I can say to that.

"You're right." I smile at her, and she relaxes. "And you're amazing, so . . ."

"Guess I'm the complete package." A laugh lights her face, and she picks up her spoon and resumes her attack on the banana split.

I laugh, too, because she has no idea how right she is.

We continue like that, having the best night of our lives until the ice cream is gone and we're both drunk on sugar and high on each other. We leave behind the melted candles, and I guide her back out into the moonlight. I have another surprise for her, and the courtyard is the perfect place.

Before I can extend my arm in a gesture that will make me either the best boyfriend in the world or the most embarrassing, footsteps rush up behind me.

"I was totally going to leave you two alone," Sam blurts between breaths. "But then I saw you, and your date is over—"

I shake my head. "It's not. I—"

"Is everything okay?" Wren asks, head cocked, concern tightening her features.

"The standings are up, and both of you made it into the final!"

TWENTY-SIX

Wren

When we reach the standings board it's late enough that there aren't any other students hanging around, so we walk straight up to the short, typed list. I'm not surprised to see that Eliza's name tops the list. Lee is second, Luke is third, Ruby is fourth (yay for Ruby!), and I'm fifth.

"This is such BS," Sam mutters under her breath as she points at Eliza's name next to the big *#1* with one hand and clutches our mystery book to her chest with the other. "If it wasn't for—" Sam presses her lips together and gives me a wide-eyed look.

"Lee knows," I say.

Sam releases a burst of air before saying, "Well, then

Lee will totally understand. Eliza would have died if you hadn't boosted her power today, and the ocean would still be an oil slick. You should at least be number two on that board."

Lee clears his throat and shifts from one foot to the other. "To be fair, Dean Rottingham doesn't know Wren can boost power, because that's supposed to be impossible."

Sam rolls her eyes. "No. That's not being fair. Rottingham has been dean here for how long?"

Lee shrugs. "A while?"

"Decades!" Sam says. "And he can't figure out that wherever Wren is during a Trial or even an exercise like at the stadium, amazingly powerful things happen? *That* seems impossible. At the very least he should be seriously considering that Wren must be an Aquarius moon—and discussing that possibility with her."

"Why an Aquarius moon?" Lee asks.

Sam holds up a finger as she makes each point. "One, the tree *you two* healed during the first Trial. Two, the incredibly powerful way the stadium was soothed. And three, there's no way Eliza has enough magick on her own to heal herself and the ocean, but Wren was, *again*, present when massive power manifested. Rottingham should be able to make these connections unless he's completely inept at being the dean of this, or any other, academy. Sorry, Lee. I know you're his intern; no offense meant."

Lee shrugs. "None taken. I get what you're saying and I have to agree with you. Wren's special and Rottingham should see that."

I move closer to Lee and loop my arm through his. "Thank you for understanding and being on my side."

"Always," says Lee.

His support is important to me. I'm not super competitive, but this situation has me conflicted. Since arriving at the Academia de la Luna I've struggled to find my place, to fit in. At first I even wanted to be invisible. But I've changed. Fear has switched to anticipation. Hesitation has become confidence. *I feel powerful* and there's a big part of me that wants to shout it *and* get credit for it. I'm Moonstruck! Incredibly, impossibly Moonstruck in a way no one else is, but besides me only two people know about it.

As if she's reading my mind Sam continues angrily. "It's wrong Wren's not getting the credit she deserves. It's wrong and it's Rottingham's fault."

"Wait, Sam. I get that Wren's power is being overlooked, but how is that Rottingham's fault?" Lee puts his hand over mine where it rests on his forearm. "Wren hasn't told him, or anyone except us. And I understand why." He looks down at me; his kind eyes glimmer with warmth. "It makes total sense that you want to figure out your power at your own pace." Then his gaze returns to Sam. "But, again, that's not Rottingham's fault."

"Isn't it?" Sam snorts. "You seriously don't see anything weird going on here? One student died this summer. Four more almost died, including you two. The Elementals are out of control and neither Rottingham nor the leader of our council is doing anything about it. Celeste hasn't so much as shown her face since Wyatt's death. That doesn't seem strange to you? Add to that the fact that Rottingham is an experienced dean who knew Wren was different from day one. I mean, he went to her house to tell her she had to come to Moon Isle. He watches her. A lot. But he hasn't figured out *anything* about her power? I call total BS on that and total BS on Dean Rottingham!"

"Ahem."

The three of us startle and turn to see Dean Rottingham standing behind us. *Right behind us.*

Oh god, how long has he been there?

"Miss Hopp, is there a problem?" the dean asks.

I'm impressed that the only evidence of how freaked out Sam must be is the two pink splotches painting her cheeks. Rottingham's gaze flicks to our mystery book, which Sam still clutches to her chest, and my stomach churns. Immediately Sam shifts it down against her thigh so it's mostly hidden by her baggy boyfriend jeans. She nods and points at the list. "Yes. There is a problem. I don't think the standings are fair. If Eliza is number one, Wren should be number two."

"That's an interesting opinion," says the dean with a patronizing smile. "And not the first time a student has disagreed with the rankings."

"So this isn't the first time you've been unfair?" Sam's voice is cold and clipped.

Should I say something? Should I try to get Sam to be quiet?

As if I could. I know Sam Hopp. When she believes someone she loves has been wronged there is nothing that will shut her up. When Sam gets protective, she takes all that bubbly positivity she carries around with her and funnels it into righteous indignation that is especially effective because Sam Hopp is almost never wrong. So I stay silent, waiting for an opening so that I can distract Sam enough to give her time to cool off.

The smile slides from Rottingham's face. "Unfair? No. But, as I already said, this is far from the first time there has been a conflict with what a student wished the standings reflected and what they *actually* reflect." His sharp voice softens and the patronizing smile returns. "Samantha, I suppose you wish you'd made the top five. You should know you did make the top *twenty*-five, which is an admirable feat."

"Oh, please. Stop with the condescension. I'm totally fine with my rank. This isn't about me. It's about Wren not getting the recognition she deserves. You were out there with her today during the Trial, weren't you?"

Rottingham's jaw clenches and unclenches before he says, "Yes. I was there. Of course I was there."

"Great. Then you saw Eliza *and* Wren get away from that rogue Elemental and heal the ocean." Without turning away from Rottingham, Sam points over her shoulder at the list. "Logically, if you're going to rank Eliza number one, Wren should be ranked number two. Unless you have a reason not to follow logic. Do you?"

I hold my breath.

Rottingham's face is a thundercloud. His voice is flint. "Miss Hopp, someone with your intelligence should know better than to accuse the dean of your academy of being illogical. Perhaps you don't understand that I do not rank the students alone. The entire faculty vote, as well as the leader of our council, Celeste.

"Here is the hard truth that you seem to be missing." Suddenly Rottingham turns his gaze, bright with anger, on me. "Wren Nightingale, in the time you have been here at the Academia de la Luna, have you ever manifested any magick *alone*?"

I have to swallow before I can speak. "No."

Rottingham nods and his gaze shifts to Lee. "Mr. Young, is it logical to rank a student who has not manifested any individual power above those who have?"

I can't look at Lee. I stare at Sam instead as her eyes continue to skewer Rottingham.

"Well, Wren is ranked number five, which means she *is* ahead of a lot of students who have manifested powers," Lee prevaricates. Not that I blame him. He has promised not to tell Rottingham about my real power. What else could he say?

Rottingham claps his hands together. "There you have it! It can be argued that Wren has been ranked above students who have manifested considerably more magick than she ever has." The dean looks at me. "Don't you agree, Wren?"

I start to nod, but Sam interrupts.

"Bullshit!"

"That is enough!" Rottingham shouts. Then he straightens his tie as he draws in a deep breath and releases it slowly. "Lee, Samantha has worked herself up and is too upset to think rationally. I'm going to leave the two girls in your calm and capable hands. I'm quite sure that as soon as emotions aren't running so high you will be able to talk reason to them. Good night, all." Rottingham strides away, swallowed by the sapphire shadows filtering through the sentinel pines.

I watch him leave as I try to sort through what just happened and something catches my gaze. It's a person. Just a few yards from us someone is standing off the cobblestone path in a cluster of enormous pines ringed with mature ferns. Within the shadows all I can make out is a curvy silhouette. As they turn away, the moon breaks from the high clouds and I see a flash of their hair—something very light, almost white. Then they're gone, moving away in the same direction as the dean. I have a sudden urge to go after them. To see who just overheard everything we just said, but Sam's angry voice roots me in place.

"Do you see now?" Sam almost shouts at Lee. "There's something really off about him. Something off about all of this." She gestures around us to include the standings board and the entire campus.

"Sam, I get your point, and I agree that Wren should be ranked with Eliza, but what the dean said *is* logical." When Sam opens her mouth to protest, Lee's raised hand stops her. "Think about it. He doesn't know about Wren's ability to boost power, and whether he *should* be aware of it or not is a different subject, but keep this in mind—no one has ever had that ability before. So, *logically,* he's correct. They've actually ranked Wren higher than she should be."

Sam shakes her head. "Lee, I like you a lot. You're one of the good guys. But I'm not just talking about the Trial standings or whether Rottingham is inept. I'm talking about the entire academy. If you weren't such a rule follower and so determined to please Rottingham, you'd be able to see the whole picture."

My stomach wants to flip inside out. Even though I can't disagree with the truth in what she said, I hate that she said it. I look up at Lee. His face has lost all expression. "Sam, that's not being fair to Lee."

Sam deflates. Her shoulders lift up to her ears and her head bows. "I-I shouldn't have said that." She glances up. "I'm really sorry, Lee."

Through our joined arms I feel Lee's stiffness relax. "It's okay, Sam. I know you're only upset because of how much you care about Wren."

Sam nods. "I love Wren and I also care about our academy." Her gaze goes to me. "Sorry, Wreny. Not about anything I said to Rottingham. Sorry I hurt Lee's feelings."

"Hey, we both get it." I untangle my arm from Lee so I can hug her. "Thank you for loving me so fiercely."

Sam sniffs and wipes her eyes as I step back from her. "Hey, uh, I'm going to take off and stop interrupting your date. Sorry about that, too."

"Want us to walk you to Taurus Hall?" I ask.

"No, no. That's okay." She lifts the book. "I'm going to do some more research. Sorry again." She starts walking away but stops and looks back at us. "Lee, are we okay?"

Lee smiles and nods. "We're golden, Lady Hopp."

Sam's return smile looks ethereal under the moonlight. "I love you both, you gigantic weirdos. See you two tomorrow."

"Byeee," I call after her, and she lifts her hand to wave. I look up at Lee. "Are *we* okay?"

"Absolutely."

"I hate that our perfect date ended like this." I start to chew my bottom lip and then stop because *maybe our date can end better—like with-some-kissing better—and a chewed-up lip is not awesome for making out.*

Lee grins at me. "Oh no, milady. Our date is far from over."

TWENTY-SEVEN

Lee

The awkwardness has dissipated, and I continue with my plan, not giving it a chance to return. "Did you know, Lady Nightingale, there are DVDs in the library available for checkout?"

Wren's light brow arches with a smirk. "DVDs? Whatever could those be?"

"I daresay you have not spent nearly enough time minding your studies within the confines of the library."

Her laughter seems to glow pearlescent in the moonlight. "Is that so, Lord Young?"

I give a sharp, nineteenth century–esque nod. "If you

had, perhaps you would have discovered the special edition *Pride and Prejudice* boxed set circa the year of our Lord 1995."

"Colin Firth is my *favorite* Darcy!" She lifts onto her tiptoes, an excited squeal painting her cheeks primrose pink. "Did you know that Colin and the actress who plays Elizabeth dated in real life after filming? I mean, how could you not? He's amazing!"

"I look forward to every bit of *Pride and Prejudice* trivia once we're back at Aquarius Hall, but first . . ." With a bow, I extend my hand.

She takes it, her blush deepening. Her warm fingers send a shock of electricity through my arm, and I suppress a shudder as I pin my other arm behind my back and lead her away from the standings board.

"What are we doing?" Wren asks, a smile playing on her lips.

"Patience, Lady Nightingale." I spin her in front of me and hold her right hand in my left while placing my free hand on her lower back. "Now, if you'll excuse my momentary silence, I must concentrate."

I start with the gallop, the easiest nineteenth-century ballroom dance I found online months ago when I planned this aspect of our first date.

Step, close, step, close, step, close, hop. Step, close, step, close, step, close, hop.

There's no music, but that doesn't matter. Whenever I'm with Wren, it's easy to disappear into another world. As we bound around the cobblestones, her expression softens, her eyelids are heavy, and I know she's as absorbed as I am in this waking dream.

I slow my steps and pull her closer as I mentally repeat

the footwork for the dance that makes Wren sigh every time the lead characters begin—the waltz.

Three steps clockwise, three straight steps. Three steps counterclockwise, three straight steps . . .

Her eyes are still closed when she exhales a long breath, and there's never been a better sign of success. Her lids flutter open, and her irises are two shining moonstones, beckoning me close.

I bend down and press my mouth to hers. She lets out a startled gasp and relaxes as I cup her face in my hands. Her lips part, and my tongue sweeps inside. She is soft and delicious and all the things that make kissing someone irresistible. I've never had a physical connection like this. This is electric; it's magickal; it's right. Wren and I are supposed to be together.

I end the best kiss of my life and run my hands through her hair, pressing my forehead to hers.

"Thank you, Lee, for . . . for being you and for keeping your word even though I know it killed you to lie to Dean Rottingham."

"Sam was harsh, but she wasn't wrong," I say, feathering a kiss against her brow. "We all know I've changed my ways and am a rule follower now, but I would never do anything to break your trust." Our shadows dust the stones as we resume our waltz, and I lead us in a turn in front of the standings board. "Can I ask you a question?"

"Always." Her tongue glosses her lips, and heat swells in my middle. The question can wait. "Are you going to ask, or . . . ?"

"Oh yeah, sorry." I clear my throat, trance broken. Luckily, I've somehow managed to keep us spinning. "What's up with the book?"

"The book."

I wait for her to elaborate, but she doesn't. Instead, she chews her lip and stares over my shoulder.

"The ancient-looking leather one you and Sam are always lugging around. Sam literally had it with her tonight." I crane my neck, trying to meet her gaze, but she lifts her eyes to the full moon overhead.

"It *is* old. Like, *super* old. So old that vegan leather wasn't a thing back when it was written."

I stop dancing and release her. "What's going on?"

"What do you mean?" It's the middle of July, and the nights aren't cold, but she wraps her arms around her middle and shivers.

"We just did this back in the dining hall."

"Did what?"

"Wren, stop." I close the distance between us and brush her hair behind her ears. "It's me."

Her lips are pursed, and her eyes search mine. Whatever she's looking for, she finds, because the next words tumble out of her. "I think Sam is right about Rottingham. There's something wrong with this place."

My brow creases, and I glance over to the standings board. "Because you weren't ranked higher? Wren, they would have been well within their rights not to rank you at all."

"It's not about the rankings." She balls her hands and takes a deep breath. "It's the Elementals, things I've heard, Wyatt. . . . Have you even seen Celeste since he was killed?"

"What does that have to do with anything?" I ask, and I know I'm looking at her like she's spouting nonsense, but that's how it sounds.

"Nothing." She hikes her shoulders. "Everything. I don't know, but I don't trust it."

"Don't trust *it* or don't trust Celeste and Dean Rottingham?" I drag my hand down my cheek and temper my frustration. "Wren, they're the two most trustworthy people on the entire island. The two people who are here, making sure that after this summer we can all go out into the world, practice our magick, and stay safe while doing it."

"But what about while we're here? Wyatt is dead. Today Eliza almost died. *I* almost died." She shakes her head. "You just don't get it."

"I don't get it? My sister drowned in this ocean. More than anyone, I understand that accidents happen on Moon Isle. What I don't understand is where all this is coming from. I want to, but you're too busy keeping another secret to explain it."

"I don't want to talk about it!" she shouts. "Not right now. Today has been stressful enough."

"I know that, Wren; I do. When I thought I'd lost you—" A knot tightens in the back of my throat, and I take a deep inhale to clear it. "Maybe the problem isn't the dean and the head of the Lunar Council. Maybe it's the fact that this was all dropped on you at the last possible moment. You thought you'd be a Mundane and live in Fern Valley for the rest of your life, but now you're on Moon Isle surrounded by Moonstruck."

"That doesn't change the fact that something's going on here. Something's not right. I can feel it." Her eyes plead with me to believe her, but I don't see this place like she does. I've dedicated the past two years of my life to getting here and excelling when I did.

"This is your first time being around this many Moonstruck. You're uncomfortable and nervous. If anything, right now you should be relying on the dean and Celeste.

If your parents hadn't died, they would have prepared you for—"

"Don't talk about my parents!" Her voice ricochets off the cobblestones, and she pauses, her eyes filling with tears. "They have nothing to do with this."

"Wren, I only—"

"I don't throw your sister in your face whenever you're upset."

"I wasn't. I just want you to look at what's happened like I do." I step closer, and she shuffles back, tears streaming down her cheeks.

"I can't, Lee. Not tonight." Her voice breaks, and she swipes her eyes with the backs of her hands. "Thanks for the date and the dance. It was all really great." Wren turns and runs, her feet carrying her toward Aquarius Hall and away from me.

TWENTY-EIGHT

Wren

I hate that our date ended like this. My heart wants me to race back to Lee and tell him everything about the book and Maya's connection to it, about the things the Elementals have been whispering to me, about what Sam and I overheard outside the dean's office. *Everything!* But the rational part of me knows better. That part of me replays Lee's words, *They're the two most trustworthy people on the entire island.* That's probably what Maya thought, too, and look what happened to her!

"I can't tell him," I whisper brokenly as I hurry up the wide staircase. *Lee, please don't follow me. Please don't follow me. Please don't follow me.* The words are like a prayer echoing around and around in my mind. If he shows up at my room tonight I'm going to shatter into a million pieces right in front of him.

Are we going to break up now? Did we just break up?

No! I want to shout the word. Just thinking about losing Lee makes my chest hurt like I can already feel the jagged shards of my heart.

I reach my door and open it. "Lee and I are *not* breaking up," I tell my empty room as I close the door and go straight to my bed where I left my favorite pair of sweats and my soft, worn Frenchie tee. I'm out of my dress and wedges in a second, and wrap myself in the comfort of the familiar clothes. All I want to do is crawl into bed and pull the covers over my head, which I start to do but realize that my door isn't locked. In my imagination I see Lee opening the door and whispering my name and I know I can't face him. I'll tell him the truth, which could put him in danger as well as freak him out. I drag myself out of bed and turn the dead bolt on the door. I feel old, my body aching with the unknowns swirling through my thoughts.

Something crunches under my bare foot, and I look down at a folded piece of graph paper someone slipped under my door. I groan, almost unable to bend to pick it up. I flip it over, recognizing Sam's bold writing on the outside: *WREN.* I open it, reading once, twice, again and again, hoping the words will change.

AS SOON AS YOU'RE ALONE, MEET ME AT THE COURTYARD. I FIGURED OUT THE BOOK. IT'S WAY WORSE THAN WE THOUGHT.

Ice cream curdles in my stomach as I slip on my Vans and quietly open the door. I peek out just enough to be sure Lee's not in the hallway, and catch a flash of yellow when light from the chandelier glistens off his nameplate as his door closes.

Breathing out a sigh of relief I hurry down the stairs and out of Aquarius Hall. I look around for the Air Elemental, but the front of our hall is empty. I glance up at the full moon, which is a giant silver coin slipping down the sky, and realize how late it must be. *Do the Elementals sleep?*

My shoes make soft slapping sounds against the cobblestone sidewalk that leads from the hall to Crossroads Courtyard. The night smells like pine and jasmine. I breathe deeply, trying to calm my churning emotions. I've hurt Lee. Again. And this time I don't know how I'm going to make it right.

My body stops like I've run into an invisible wall. I *do* know how to make it right—the *only* way I can make it right. I have to decide to trust Lee completely and tell him everything, or we have to break up.

Well, I am not breaking up with Lee.

Yes, he'll be upset and distracted when he finds out about the book and Maya's connection to it. He may even be pissed off—at me for keeping it from him, at Rottingham for, well, being nefarious. Maybe at the world for being unfair. But Lee's not a child. I have to believe he can handle this. I also have to believe that I can trust him with anything, or else how is our relationship ever going to work?

I make myself move forward again and this time I walk with determination. Sam said she figured out the book and that it's worse than we thought. That means we'll have proof about whatever is really going on here at the Academia de la Luna.

With real proof I can tell Lee everything. He'll definitely want to help Sam and me deal with what's going on because it'll be the right thing to do and Lee always does the right thing.

The pain in my chest dissipates and the weight pressing down on me lifts. My steps are a lot lighter as I round the last curve in the sidewalk before it straightens to spill into the courtyard—and I almost run into Lily and Ruby. They have their arms around each other and are kissing. *Kissing!*

They break the kiss and turn to look at me.

"Oops, sorry, you two!" I say. "Carry on and don't mind me."

Ruby's arm is around Lily's curvy waist. Lily snakes her hand across Ruby's shoulders before she grins at me. "Hey there, Wren." Her face is flushed and extra beautiful. Lily is several inches taller and a lot more voluptuous than lean, athletic Ruby, but she looks delicate in their embrace. "How was your big special date with Lee?"

"How do you know about that?" My stomach is back to feeling sick.

"I heard Luke talking about it. Lee's been planning it for days," says Lily.

Ruby's eyes are extra bright as their hand caresses Lily's hip. "How was his dancing?"

"How do *you* know about *that*?" I ask.

Ruby shrugs. "Lee tells me stuff. A lot of stuff, actually, because he talks too much, but he says we're friends and friends listen to each other."

"That's really nice of you, babe," says Lily.

"I know," they say. "So, the dancing. It was bad?"

"No," I say quickly. "It was really sweet."

"Then why are you all puffy and red like you've been crying?" Lily asks.

I sigh. "It's complicated."

Ruby nods sagely. "Relationships are difficult." Their gaze lifts to Lily. "But worth it."

Lily bends and kisses them softly before her attention returns to me. "Is that why you're out here so late? Because of your complicated date? Do you want to talk about it?"

"No, actually, I have to go. I'm meeting Sam at Crossroads. She's, uh, tutoring me."

"Wren," Lily says. "You've been to practically every lecture. Maybe you should relax a little. This summer isn't all about studying. It's also about forming relationships and moving toward our futures."

"All work and no play is unbalanced," adds Ruby.

I open my mouth to agree with them, but a scream pierces the night. "What the—"

But Ruby is already moving. "It's coming from Crossroads. You two stay behind me." They sprint down the cobblestone path so fast that Lily and I struggle to keep up.

As Crossroads Courtyard comes into view I can't figure out what's going on. There are several students gathered around the center of the circle. Lily and I slow, and as we do my eyes scan the group, looking for Sam.

"Oh god! Someone get help!" says a guy I recognize as a Taurus moon whose room is a couple of doors down from Sam's.

The girl beside him turns away from whatever the rest of them are looking down at. Her face is streaked with tears. "She just fell from the sky. She just fell."

"It's the Elementals again. It has to be," says another guy as he staggers away to puke.

We've caught up to Ruby and we're right behind them as they push through the wall of students.

At first I don't understand what I'm seeing. She doesn't look like a person. She looks like a broken doll. She's lying in the middle of something liquid and dark, like the oil that slicked the surface of the ocean. Then the metallic scent hits me. It's blood and the pool of it is expanding.

"Lily, get the healer. I'm going for Lee." I hear Ruby's voice like they're far away, but they're suddenly right in front of me, touching my shoulder. "Wren, stay here. Stay with her. Comfort her. Lee will be here soon." As Ruby races away toward Aquarius Hall and Lily, sobbing, runs toward Moon Hall, the doll opens her eyes and looks at me.

It's Sam.

"No!" I lurch forward and fall to my knees beside her. The warm blood soaks my sweatpants. "No, no, no, no, no, no." I'm panting the word, over and over. I touch Sam's face. Her head is tilted toward me. Tears stream from her eyes, sliding into what is now an ocean of blood.

"Wreny." Her voice is barely a whisper.

"Don't talk." I brush a strand of hair from her cheek. "Just breathe. It's going to be okay. Everything is going to be okay. Lily's getting the healer."

Sam's body twitches as she lifts one finger to point at something several feet from her head. I don't look at what she's pointing to. All I can do is stare at Sam's body. It's flattened. Broken. Her legs are all wrong. So is her neck and with a wave of dread I realize she *shouldn't* be able to look at me because her head *shouldn't* be turned in my direction.

"It's okay. It's okay," I repeat. "Don't move."

"The book . . ."

Her finger twitches again and I follow it to see the big leather book lying a couple of feet away. A piece of graph paper, like the one Sam wrote the note on, sticks out from it, flapping in the night breeze like the wing of a dying bird.

"I'll get it. It's going to be okay." I repeat the empty words as panic builds within me, making me so cold I clench my teeth to keep them from chattering.

"Now." Her finger twitches again.

I grab the book with one hand and take Sam's in another. Her fingers are as cold as mine and slick with blood. "Okay, I got it. See? Nothing to worry about, just—"

She squeezes my hand. "Must . . . listen."

I lean closer. "I'm here. I'm not leaving you."

Her gaze captures mine. "*Listen!*" She whispers the word and then coughs. Foamy blood leaks from the corner of her mouth to mix with her tears.

"Okay! I'm listening!"

I bend down, her lips are almost touching my ear. The words come haltingly. She takes breaks between them to draw breath, which rattles as more blood leaks from her mouth. *"Book . . . in full moonlight . . . read it . . . map . . . she'll kill you if she can . . . find the other . . . finish ritual."*

Then there are no more words. I lift my head so I can look into her eyes. "I understand. Don't worry. Don't worry about anything. I'll take care of it. I love you," I tell her. "Always and forever, Sam Hopp."

Her bloody lips lift into a smile. From that smile a long, rattling breath escapes and then Sam's eyes are no longer focused on me. She doesn't draw another breath. Her fingers go limp in mine. I can feel her soul leave. It's a wave of sizzling energy that lifts from her destroyed body. For just a moment it wraps around me like a cocoon of love, and then it's gone. She's gone.

Sam is dead.

"Wren! You must move so I can help her!"

I realize the healer is trying to push me away from Sam. I look up at her wide, concerned eyes and shake my head. "No. No, you can't." I release my best friend's hand, smooth her hair back again, kiss her forehead, and then I'm standing there, clutching the book as more and more people rush to the courtyard.

I'm jostled, pushed away from Sam.

But it's not Sam. Not anymore. Sam is gone.

I think the words but can't feel them. Not yet. I can't feel anything except the book pressed against my chest.

"Where is the dean? Someone get Rottingham!" the healer shouts.

Dean Rottingham. No. No, I can't be here with him. No.

Like my legs are more machine than human, they move and I'm sprinting away from Crossroads Courtyard and the empty shell of my best friend. As I run, Sam's last words play over and over in my mind. *Book . . . in full moonlight . . . read it . . . map . . . she'll kill you if she can . . . find the other . . . finish ritual . . .* I let the words hook me. Let them pull me forward. They're important. They're what Sam said with her last breath.

In full moonlight . . . read it . . .

Sam wants me to read the book in the light of the full moon.

Whatever Sam wants I'm going to do.

Wanted. Past tense. Sam is dead.

I shake the thought away. *No. Don't go there. Take it one step at a time. Do what Sam wants you to do.*

I'm so cold that when the book begins to warm I almost drop it. My legs stop moving. I've run to the rear of Moon Hall where there is another courtyard. It has a fountain in the center of it and it's smaller than Crossroads, situated just off the back of the hall, close enough to the big building that it isn't completely shaded by pines. Instead, it's washed in the light of the full moon, silver and bright—so bright that the marble bench beside the little fountain casts a sapphire shadow. Woodenly, I walk to the bench and sit. Somewhere in my mind I know that the dark spots of wetness on my knees are Sam's blood.

Don't think about that. Just do what Sam wants you to do.

I nod and relax my grip on the book, resting it on my lap. I open it, allowing it to fall to the page Sam had bookmarked with the graph paper. I ignore the blood on my hand and focus on the paper. It has pencil marks on it—a mixture of a blueprint and a map, labeled MOON HALL. Part of it is circled. Then my gaze is pulled from it to the open book. The light of the full moon bathes the pages, calling forth letters that form words, and words that form paragraphs. All of it is legible.

I begin to read.

TWENTY-NINE

Lee

I'm pacing, and I swear I'm going to wear a trench in the fluffy rug that's matting beneath my feet. I thought I did everything right. There was ice cream and a footman, embarrassing old dancing, our first kiss, and there would have been more, but it all fell apart.

I grip the back of my neck, squeezing the tension that's quickly morphing into a headache. I don't know what I did wrong, and that's what kills me. If I understood, I would fix it, but there's no point in going to Wren's room to ask more questions she'll refuse to answer.

Three swift pounds on my door save the rug from annihilation. I rush to open it, blowing out a quick calming breath. Wren will be on the other side, and if she doesn't apologize, she'll at least explain. We can move forward. All we need is to communicate.

I open the door, and Ruby's red sweatshirt is like a wound where I thought for sure my girlfriend would be. "Wren needs you."

There's a twinge in the hollow of my heart. An ache in my chest I haven't felt since that night—since the dean came and my mother's wails split the paint from the walls and the doors from their hinges. It's death, and I will gladly offer myself to its scythe if Wren Nightingale is gone.

I don't think, I just act, sprinting after Ruby and out the front doors of Aquarius Hall. My classmates are there, too, a tide being pulled but toward what?

I can't ask. I can't speak. My lungs are hot coals screaming that they'll burst into flame if I don't stop, but so be it. Consume me from the inside out as long as I'm alive long enough to keep Wren safe.

We're nearing the crowd, and it parts as if Death is granting access just for me. I don't know when I stopped running, but my body is as heavy as stone while I stand at the edge of a lake of blood. It encases Sam like a mat in a frame, her twisted body on display.

There's something wrong with this place.

Wren's words are all I hear, drowning out the cries and curses of the growing crowd. I'm consumed by the warning she issued. The warning I didn't understand. The warning I still don't understand but know is real. As real as Sam's bloodied, broken body.

Who will tell her parents?

A hand claps onto my shoulder, but it's not Ruby's or

Lily's or Luke's. It's the same tight grasp that kept me from diving into the oily Pacific.

"Lee, find Luke. I'll need both of you to assist with the other students." He's talking to me like there isn't a corpse on the ground. Like I couldn't reach out and touch my friend's body. Like her blood isn't sticky and warm beneath my shoes.

I stumble backward, shaking my head. "I have to help Wren."

But where is she? *Ruby will know. Find Ruby.*

I search for their scarlet sweatshirt, but my eyes keep landing on the pool of blood winking in the moonlight.

Dean Rottingham steps in front of me, blocking my view of Sam, becoming my entire world. And maybe I should let him. It would be easier, wouldn't it? To let him make the rules and follow them instead of doing it on my own. But isn't that how we all got here?

There's something wrong with this place.

"Lee, focus. You get Luke and connect with Professor Douglas. *I* will locate Wren."

"What about Celeste?" I shout, and Rottingham tenses. "Shouldn't we *connect* with her?" My gaze narrows at the dean, his jaw clenched, gray-flecked temples pulsing. "Or is another dead student not a big enough deal for her to make an appearance?"

I don't wait for a response. I tear away from him, jogging around a group of huddled students and smack into Ruby. Lily is in their arms. Her red hair masks her face but can't hide the anguished howls erupting from her quaking chest.

"Lily saw her heading back behind Moon Hall," Ruby says.

I appreciate that I don't have to ask. I appreciate that Ruby understands me without words. I appreciate their strength. But, most of all, I appreciate the fact that running away from them now without a second glance or word of thanks is not a strike against me or a declaration of ungratefulness. Like they said, Wren needs me. And it's the only thing that matters.

I skid to a stop in the lesser-trafficked courtyard now swollen with light from the full moon and drop to my knees in front of Wren. She doesn't look up from the closed book on her lap, her mouth moving as she traces the leather cover.

"Wren . . ." My throat tightens with emotion, and I'm ashamed to acknowledge that some of it's relief. She's not the one with the vacant stare and broken body in the middle of Crossroads.

"Celeste, she and I—" Wren buries her face in her palms and screams.

I place my hands around her wrists and focus on my magick. With Wren's power surging through my veins, my heartbeat is wild, a caged thing frantic to break free.

"Don't!" She pushes me away, and I catch myself before I fall back.

With her magick, I'll have more than enough power to heal her. I can take this pain away if only she would let me. Two years ago, I'd wished I could do the same for my mother. I couldn't, but I can soothe Wren now. Perhaps that's why she wants to keep her distance.

"I can help you," I say.

"I don't need that kind of help." She sniffles, swiping at the tear tracks glistening on her cheeks. "I need to do what Sam wants me to do. I need to finish what we started. I need to—" She pitches forward, arms wrapped around her middle as a sob tears from her throat.

I swear the ground shifts beneath me. This spot will never be the same.

I wrap my arms around her and pull her close, her knees and the leather-bound book digging into my chest.

"Stop!" she shrieks, surging to her feet and shoving me so hard I crash onto the ground as the book skids along the cobblestones. "Everything is broken and wrong."

"We can fix it together," I say, brushing moss from my pants as I get to my feet. "But you have to tell me what's going on."

"Sam is dead!" Another shout as tears stream down her face.

"I know." My eyes burn, and I want to comfort her, but that's not what Wren needs right now.

"Sam's dead because of me. Because *she'll* only allow there to be one. Sam figured it out. She knew how much was at stake, and they killed her." Her chin quivers, and she inhales a shaky breath. "Next, they'll come for me."

"Who?" I ask, resisting the urge to reach out to her. "The Elementals?"

"Celeste and Rottingham!" The names echo between us, and I take a step back. "I'm not only an amplifier. I'm a source of the power. A conduit. The *elegida*. Celeste and I both are. That's why they want me dead. Celeste will only allow there to be one!" She turns back to the bench and swipes a crumpled, blood-smeared piece of paper from the stone before holding it out in front of her. "I'm going here. To the attic. To Celeste. And I will make her pay for what she's done."

I lunge forward, grabbing her hand as she turns to charge

toward Moon Hall. I've stored my magick. I won't heal her if she doesn't want me to, but I will make her listen. "This is not the way. If Celeste and Rottingham actually killed someone you can't go storming in there. We have to go to the rest of the Lunar Council, the professors, my parents. You can't do this alone."

"There is no one else, Lee. Don't you get it?"

My gaze searches hers for something to hold on to, but all I see are anguish and fury.

"Look at the book." She motions to the heavy tome, cast aside and shining in the light of the full moon. "Read it. You'll see. Maya did, and they killed her, too."

I release her hand and hurry to the book she and Sam spent weeks protecting. My sister's handwriting litters the margins, and ink slides across the pages like mercury, forming silver letters as I squat down.

Because of Selene's actions the deal was broken. The magick fractured and limited. Since then, every generation the moon has been blessing one Mundane, creating her Moonstruck with conduit power so the three can be whole again and the sacred transfer of power complete. But she won't allow it. Each special Moonstruck has been murdered before she could join her magicks with the elder and the mother to complete the ritual.

I pick up the book, my breath leaching from my lungs. "This doesn't make sense. This can't be right. Who is Selene? Why is Maya's writing all over this book? Wren—"

I turn to her, but she's gone, the heavy doors to Moon Hall closing behind her.

THIRTY

Wren

The door closes behind me and I pause only long enough to glance at Sam's map. She's highlighted a stairwell that goes up to a third story Moon Hall is not supposed to have. It's that third floor Sam has circled. Within the circle are two words written in highlighter: *CONDUIT CHAMBER*. I look to my left. There it is, an industrial fire door that's tucked into a shadowy corner. I sprint to it, push it open, and dart inside. Gone are the ornate wood paneling and the opulent chandeliers. I've stepped into a vertical tunnel with an iron staircase wrapping around the inside. Sconces protrude from the smooth stone walls, throwing shadows all around me that flicker like ghosts.

I have to hurry! I can't let Lee catch me! I can't let anyone catch me.

This is about vengeance for Sam. This is about making Celeste and Rottingham pay, and I'm starting with Celeste.

I clutch the map in my fist as I pound up the iron stairwell, my feet hammering quick echoes as I run.

I hear the door open when I've made it to the second-floor landing.

"Wren!"

Lee's shout is a goad that has me moving so fast my lungs are on fire. I make it to the third-floor landing before he can catch me.

But there's no door! No opening at all. The stairs dead-end at a stone wall. I hear Lee's feet on the steps behind me, getting closer and closer.

"Wren!"

"No, this can't be right." My hands tremble as I open the map again. I've followed Sam's yellow highlighter path, though it doesn't dead-end at the wall but instead leads to a room. It's hidden, but it's there.

Hidden . . .

Just like the restricted room in the library.

The metal beneath my feet vibrates as Lee bursts onto the landing with me and skids to a halt. I look over my shoulder at him. He has the book under one arm. His other hand is raised, palm out.

"Wren, it's okay. Just stop a minute. I think you're right. There is something going on. Let's talk about this."

I shove the map into my pocket and press both of my hands against the wall.

ELEGIDA glows in bright gold letters just above my head

as the wall clicks and then slides open silently and I step into a living nightmare.

"What the hell?" Lee says from behind me as he enters the room.

"It's the Conduit Chamber," I whisper through numb lips.

The room is enormous. It must run the entire length and width of Moon Hall, but its shape is impossible. It's a huge circle and not the giant square that makes up the building below us. And then I realize the room isn't actually circular. It just appears to be because the enormous beveled-glass skylight in the ceiling is circular and through it cascades the silver-white light of the full moon. I squint up at it, holding one hand above my eyes to shield them from the brightness of the moonlight intensified by mirrors that hang from the skylight like a bizarre version of a child's mobile. Rays of moonlight are captured in the different-shaped and -sized glossy surfaces, and it's so bright that I can't make out what else is up there. I blink several times, focusing not on the mirrors and light but on the inky darkness of the rest of the ceiling and the strange shapes hovering there like human-sized bats. My vision finally adjusts and shock jolts me as the shapes take form. They are cloaked Elementals—silent and utterly still except for their eyes, which blaze neon yellow and red, blue, and green as they stare down at the circle of light illuminating the floor and one person. Celeste.

The moment my gaze goes to the leader of the Lunar Council I feel it, the blossom of heat beneath my ribs. My body is so cold that the warmth is a shock. I gasp as the heat expands and becomes a rope that pulls me forward toward the pool of moonlight and the woman hovering in the center of it.

"Wren, wait. This isn't safe." Lee reaches out and grabs my wrist. "Ouch!" he gasps, and releases me, shaking his hand like my skin scorched him.

But I can't think about that now. I can't think about anything except Celeste.

I step within the circle of light, and the Elementals immediately react. The chamber is filled with the susurrus of waves kissing a shore, wind riffling through tall grass, fire feeding on wood, leaves caressing one another as the Elementals swoop down from the ceiling to form a circle around us, creating a pocket of privacy with Celeste and me at its center. And in the seething mass of beings made of air, fire, water, and earth my gaze catches on a pair of familiar amber eyes within a churning fog of neon yellow.

It's my Elemental.

"Wren!"

Lee's voice jars me. I glance over my shoulder at him. He's standing just outside the pool of moonlight semi-obscured by the circling wall of Elementals.

I want to reach out to him, but the tug in my chest is too insistent.

"I'm sorry" is all I can manage as I stagger forward.

The leader of the Lunar Council hovers just above the wooden floor, held by delicate silver wire that glistens in the focused moonlight. I *need* to move closer to her and as I do I realize that it's not wires holding her off the floor; it's moonlight made tangible. The gossamer moonbeam threads wrap around Celeste like a chrysalis.

Celeste's eyes are closed. She appears to be sleeping. I have time to study her. She's wearing her incredible cloak that lifts around her like wings. Her long hair floats with the cloak. Its color has changed. The slim white blaze has expanded.

I take the final step to her and her dark eyes open and focus on me. She doesn't seem surprised. Her lips lift into the beginnings of a smile. Gracefully, like she's a prima ballerina, she reaches down toward me, her hand open and beckoning.

I cannot stop myself. I don't want to stop myself. This is where I'm supposed to be. What I'm supposed to do. This is my destiny.

I slip my hand into hers.

Celeste's fingers close around mine like a vise. A sunburst of light blooms between us. An almost-unbearable pulse of heat sizzles through me. I have never felt such incredible power. I'm blinking my vision clear as silver threads of moonlight begin to form around me, caressing my skin, live electric lines feeding me energy.

I can do anything!

Celeste's smile widens to show her teeth. She leans forward. Our silver threads weave together and for a moment I think she's going to embrace me, but instead her other hand clamps around my throat.

"There can be only one!" she hisses.

I try to lurch back, away from her, but her grip on my throat is unmovable. "What are you doing? We need to join. We have to try and complete the ritual. It's what the moon and the Elementals want!"

Her eyes narrow and her lip lifts in a sneer. "So the book found you. You read it and think you're all-knowing. Ignorant, arrogant child. You aren't completing anything. You're ruining a balance I've maintained for centuries!"

Shock shivers through me as I finally understand. "You're not her descendant. You are Selene. The original maiden."

"Perhaps you're not so naive after all." Celeste's voice is calm, like we're chatting over tea in a garden instead of hovering in the middle of a bizarre room surrounded by flying Elementals as a more-than-two-centuries-old wild woman is on the verge of choking me to death. It's completely surreal. "You make guesses and string together clues as you play the hero, but you actually know nothing. Let me impart some final wisdom to you. You're not a hero. You're a child who has gotten in the way. I will not allow you to destroy all that I've worked so long to hold. Rottingham may have lost his nerve, but I have not. What was your little friend's name? Something charmingly simple. Sam, that's it. Oafish, but curious. Far too curious."

I want to throw up. "You killed Sam!" I shriek. Grief and rage course through my body, paralyzing me. Even were Celeste not choking me, I wouldn't be able to breathe.

Celeste's grip tightens on my neck. My gaze is graying and tunneling, but still focused on the original maiden. Her hair is now streaked with white. Her face is different, too. Older. She'll never again be mistaken for a student.

Celeste leans forward, her face close to mine. Her smile is perfectly beautiful, perfectly cold, perfectly deadly. "This is why none of you ever win. You don't care about what's best for everyone. You care only about what's best for yourself." She laughs, low and menacing, and I know beyond any doubt that the leader of the Lunar Council is going to kill me.

Then a single phrase whispers from my memory: *The strength of the maiden.*

I am not powerless.

"You don't get to tell me what I should care about!" I hurl the words at her as I lift my hand, and like it's a blade I chop it down on Celeste's wrist.

With a cry of pain, she releases my throat, though she still has my other hand trapped within hers. Her dark eyes widen and her lips form a sneer.

"Good. I prefer a fight to a surrender." Celeste's free hand reaches into the threads that surround us. Her fingers form shapes so quickly they blur as she speaks one word, "*Cuchillo!*"

The silver moonlight threads swirl, rushing together to form a razor-edged knife. The blade glistens as Celeste grabs its hilt and slashes down. This time, when I jerk back, I know my power and use it. I break her hold on my hand as her feet touch the floor. She's grinning as she circles me.

I try to scramble away, but the Elementals have created an impenetrable wall. I'm trapped within the pool of moonlight.

Celeste lunges at me. I spin away, though not quite fast enough. A slender line of pain slashes across my back. Adrenaline makes my senses sharp and focused. I'm powerful, but I'm no match for her. If I don't get away, she *will* kill me. I need Lee. I need to escape, but if he's still out there, I can't see him.

No! My panic calms, and I clench my hands into fists. I will not let Sam's death be for nothing. Celeste will not win.

We continue to circle. She's fast, but not as fast as me. Now that she's middle-aged, my reflexes are quicker, and I use that one small advantage and keep dodging, turning, and retreating. Her jabs barely miss me as I search the whirling neon rainbow of Elementals until I find the glowing amber. I raise one hand, palm up, beckoning as I speak the words I embody, "The power of the maiden!"

The Air Elemental, *my Air Elemental,* explodes from the others and takes my hand. The roar of a great gust of wind lifts me away from Celeste and I cling to the Elemental's arm, balancing on whirling currents of air as we join the mirrored shapes dangling from silver threads high above the floor.

There are a dozen, two dozen Wrens—all looking back at me—a pale girl dressed in blood-soaked clothes with wide blue eyes who is gripping the arm of a cloaked being as we hover midair. I'm mesmerized by my reflection. It's me, but not me.

My face is different, less round. My cheekbones are more prominent. My neck is longer; the curves of it and my collarbones are graceful and strong. The biggest shock is my hair. The fuchsia tips are the same, but they look as neon as the Elementals against the rest of it, which is as black as a new moon night. Slowly, I touch my hair and then my face. Nothing remains of my childhood. Instead, a young adult stares back at me. I reach out to the closest mirror, wanting to touch the maiden within its surface.

"No!" Celeste's shriek echoes from below.

I don't even glance at her. I'm trying to find Lee, but the other Elementals are no longer whirling around the circle of light. They've become statue-like again, hulking shadows and confusing figures, a forest of shapes splashed with the glittering reflection of the full moon. I blink at the dots of light dancing in my vision. *Did Lee leave? Go for help?*

"Lee!" I shout. "Where are you?"

"Wren!"

Moonlight pours over him. He's on his knees in the middle of the circle of light beside Celeste. She's crumpled on the floor, eyes closed, the dagger she'd materialized sticking out of her shoulder.

Lee tilts his head back. His tortured gaze is filled with tears. "Oh god, Wren! What happened? What did you do?"

What did *I do*?

I can't look at him. I turn to my Elemental and bury my face in its cloaked shoulder. "Get me out of here."

"*Doncella,*" the Elemental whispers. With a flick of its powerful arm, it covers me with its cloak before it soars up, shattering through the glass skylight.

I look down in time to see Lee cover Celeste with his body as slivers of glass rain from the ceiling. Then there is nothing but the night and the wind and the Elemental who carries me up. But I'm not looking up. I'm staring at Lee. Glass falls from him, shards of glittering light, as he straightens. He doesn't even glance up. He's completely focused on Celeste. Lee lifts her in his strong arms, cradling her like she's a delicate child. As he moves toward the door Celeste puts her head on his shoulder. She looks up then. Straight at me. Just before Lee steps out of the circle of moonlight, she smiles a flash of white teeth.

A sob begins in my chest and rips through my body. I've lost Lee. I've lost Sam. I've changed into someone I don't recognize. Tears wash down my hot cheeks. I try to think through my grief.

"I have nothing left." The words wrench from me. I feel like my heart has shattered with the glass and fallen, unnoticed and unwanted, all around Lee.

My Elemental's hand slowly touches my face, wiping away the tears. And then we turn to face the full moon.

Her light bathes me. Her power fills me. *I have Her. I don't know what comes next, but the one thing I do know is that I'm Moonstruck, the chosen one, the maiden, and from this day on my life and my world will never be the same.*

THIRTY-ONE

Lee

Celeste is unconscious in my arms, a dagger hilt deep in her shoulder. But her chest still rises and falls. Her pulse still flutters with life against her neck. She's alive.

I stare up at the gaping hole in the ceiling, jagged spikes of glass rimming the circle like the deadly teeth of a bear trap.

"Wren—" I choke out past the knot in my throat. She's not vicious, not a killer, but I'm only left with what remains within this room no one knew existed.

There's an explanation, I tell myself. *One beyond revenge. One that involves Maya and that book and—*

My heartbeat roars between my ears as I weave around

the Elementals who kept me from Wren. Beneath their cloaks, they pulse like the lighthouse Mundanes see when too close to our shores.

I burst through the open doorway, my footsteps like jackhammer strikes against the stairs as I reposition Celeste and charge down to the first floor of Moon Hall. I am a mess of emotions, of fears, of confusion. I can't focus my intent or my magick. I can only push my body forward.

I wish I could rewrite history and go back to that night all those days ago when the ferry brought us to this place. I wish it were just Wren and me and the sunrise in the apple orchard.

Celeste stirs, her dazed eyes locking onto mine. "Thank you, Lee." She looks older now, and I wonder if Wren had anything to do with that. There's more to her magick, but every time I think I have an answer, I'm left with more questions.

"My sister," I pant. "Maya Young. Did you know her? Do you know about the book? Do you know where the Elemental took Wren?"

My questions are as unfocused as my thoughts, and I know I should wait until Celeste is healed, but the explanations, the truth, are in there.

"Save me. Please, save me."

Celeste's eyes roll back, and I'm running faster now, nearly jumping down the steps. "It'll be okay," I say, my voice as firm as the dean's, as my father's. "Everything will be okay."

I yank open the fire door and race through the main floor of Moon Hall, exploding out the double doors and into the courtyard where I learned my sister's secret and watched Wren piece together a puzzle I'm still unable to figure out.

I sprint back to Crossroads, back to Dean Rottingham, back to Sam and where it all went wrong, and I realize I wouldn't return to the night Wren and I arrived. I'd go back further, to the night that started it all. I'd go back to Maya's eighteenth birthday, and I'd tell her not to leave, to ignore our parents and our magick and everything that built the Youngs. If I could rewrite history, I would grow up long before now. I would turn my back on magick, stay with Wren, stay in Fern Valley, use my hands to shelve books, and let my magick drip from my cells until I was as close to Mundane as Bradley and Joel.

Instead, I am here, two people's blood sticky on my skin, another piece of my heart missing.

ACKNOWLEDGMENTS

Thank you to Daddy Bean for being The Best!

We appreciate our wonderful agents, Rebecca Scherer and Steven Salpeter.

Thank you to Emily Suvada for saving us from a lot of stress.

We love working with our new editor, Tiffany Shelton. We know this is just the beginning!

Kristin and I want to specially thank our production team. This book is so beautiful! Thank you: Kerri Resnick, jacket designer; Kelly Chong, jacket artist; Jonathan Bennett, interior designer; Eric Meyer, managing editor; Melanie Sanders, production editor; Diane Dilluvio, production manager; Barbara Wild, copy editor; Michelle Cashman, marketer; Zoe Miller, publicist; Maria Snelling, audio marketer; Steve Wagner, audio producer; and Drew Kilman, audio publicist. It takes a village!

Our biggest thank-you is, as always, to our readers. We appreciate your enthusiasm and support so very much.